The Sureness
of Horses

Kevin Arnold

Manzanita Writers Press
Angels Camp, California

ISBN 978-0-9968858-3-6
LIB of Congress Control # 2018941613

Manzanita Writers Press
manzapress.com
manzanitawp@gmail.com

The author and editors would love to hear from you. Please direct
questions or comments to TheSurenessofHorses@gmail.com.

Cover photo: John Corcoran
Biography photo: Scotty Arnold
Layout design: Joyce Dedini

For Carol Tague Arnold

Acknowledgements

Thanks to the magazines, websites, and collections where some of the poems and quotations that are blended into the text of this novel have been previously published. They're listed in the order they're included in the novel.

—"The Love of Aged Horses." Jane Hirshfield kindly allowed the inclusion of her poem, from which the novel's title is taken. She was recently awarded a Guggenheim Fellowship for Creative Arts. The poem was initially published in *The Atlantic* in 1994.

—"Teddy Bear," by the late Jim Standish, was included with the poet's permission. It was initially published in *Fresh Hot Bread* by Waverley Writers.

—"Invitation to the Opera" was initially published in the *Dallas Opera News*. The poem was also featured on *YourDailyPoem.com*, and in *Nineteen Poems around a Divorce*.

—The horseback-riding quote at the beginning of Part II, by Pulitzer-prizewinning novelist Jane Smiley, is included with her gracious permission. It's taken from her essay, "Everything I Need to Know I Learned from a Horse."

—"Riding Lessons" was initially published in *Manzanita* as "At Webb Ranch." The poem was included in *Nineteen Poems around a Divorce* as "At Jasper Ridge Ranch."

—"Japanese Graveyard on Kauai" was published in the 25th anniversary issue of *caesura* magazine, in *Nineteen Poems around a Divorce* and in *Fresh Hot Bread* from Waverley Writers.

—"The Sick Rose," by William Blake, was first published in 1794, when it was included in his collection titled *Songs of Experience* as the 39th plate. The oft-quoted incipit of the poem is "O Rose thou art sick." It is in the public domain.

—"The Thaw," by Edward Thomas, considered a master of the short poem, was written in 1914 or 1915, shortly before he died during World War I. It is often paired with a poem of the same title written about twenty years earlier by Henry David Thoreau. It is in the public domain.

Part I

It is not enough for a horseman to know how to ride;
he must know how to fall.

—*Mexican Proverb*

1

Wade's eyes snapped open when something heavy slammed into his shoulder. *So, this is First Class?* Why had he let the ticket agent talk him into an upgrade?

Rubbing his shoulder, he glanced up to see an attractive woman in a fitted silk blouse, her hand balancing the package that had hit him. "I'm so sorry," she said, standing in the aisle. Her voice had enough of a drawl that Wade guessed she might be a local Dallas woman.

The large, bubble-wrapped package looked too big for her small frame. "You must have had quite a time getting it here," he said.

"A gentleman helped me—he's seated in back. I thought I could balance it on the arm until a flight attendant came by, but it somehow slipped. Could you?" Wade found himself staring at her hazel eyes, which were focused on the bin above their heads. "Possibly?" she asked.

It was all Wade could do to hoist the package up and jam it into the overhead bin.

"It's my jumping saddle—with trophies, stirrup sets, and a few other things I didn't trust to the movers."

Wade hoped she was assigned to sit next to him. He smiled at the thought of this alluring female in one of those stretchy riding outfits he'd seen in movies. She didn't have that ribbon and bows, half-girl, half-woman look you see in Texas. Her diamond stud earrings weren't ostentatious, but close. Lone Star State or not, she belonged up in the front cabin. He was in luck, he thought as she squeezed past him to get to the window seat. She brushed against his knees. When the attendant came through, he found the courage to offer to buy his new seatmate a drink.

Her eyes shone. "You're kidding, right? They don't usually charge up front here."

Oh, damn, got that wrong. Mark Twain had it right—better to keep your mouth shut and let people think you are a fool than to open it and remove all doubt. She asked for water, making Wade feel even sillier.

After he'd screwed up, what could he say? Everyone at work said Wade had the gift of gab, but something about this woman left him tongue-tied. He wondered how he appeared to her, his salt-and-pepper messy hair, bags under sagging blue eyes evident. Perhaps Wade could reopen a conversation by telling her about his poetry professor who had moved to Dallas to teach at SMU—if indeed she was a local as he suspected. Yes, he'd try it.

His conversational gambit worked. This captivating woman, who Wade guessed was his age or a few years younger, had heard of his teacher and seemed to relax. "I grew up in Dallas," she said.

"Why does that not surprise me," he said, a little too sure of himself. "I mean the accent. It's charming, but it places you."

"Well I'm a Texan, but I'm moving—*moved*—to California, down on the Peninsula. Palo Alto. When that saddle gets to the barn out there, I'll be a Palo Altan."

Wade was happily surprised she was willing to reveal so much. Could she be as curious about him as he was of her? "Now there's a coincidence," he said. "I've lived in Palo Alto almost twenty years. The town's changing, though."

She took a sip of water. "How do you mean?"

"Nothing left of the sleepy college town," he said. "Silicon Valley has changed that forever."

He had to stop staring at her eyes. A birthmark showed above her left eye, a shade lighter than her skin tone. Wade thought of the medieval cathedral builders who purposely built in one flaw, so as not to compete with God.

A noise came from a pet carrier she had squeezed under the seat in front of her. No doubt in Wade's mind—the muffled mew of a cat. "Micah's been sick," she said to him. "There you go, Micah," she said. "You get better now." As she extended a finger into the cage, he saw a wedding ring. *Damn.*

She pulled a book from her bag. Wade read the title, *Equestrian Confidence over Big Jumps* and saw the cover image of a horse jumping over a tall hedge.

"How could you get a horse to do that?" he asked. "Incredible."

She handed Wade the book. "It's a challenge, for sure. My trainer thinks that if you ask a horse to jump above three feet, it can no longer think about the rider. It takes everything the horse has just to clear the jump. You have to prepare the horse with confidence, and once the jump starts, take care of yourself."

He imagined how she'd look in those sexy clothes riders wear. He thumbed through the pages of pictures, stunned at a horse jumping over a small car. "You actually do this?" he asked, and immediately wished he hadn't sounded quite so naive.

"It's fun," she said. "I mean, I've never jumped a car, just standard rails. And oxers, where they put two rails a few feet apart, so the horse has to stretch."

After he gave the book back, he said, "If you want my honest opinion, it looks terrifying. I'm Wade Middleton, by the way," and held out his hand.

She took his hand warmly. "Diana Buchanan," she said, emphasizing her last name as if he might know it. "And by the way, I always appreciate honesty." She re-opened her book. Taking her cue, Wade retrieved a poetry book from his briefcase. He kept thinking about her, but he didn't talk, not wanting to seem pushy.

Somewhere in the middle of the trip, over Arizona or Utah, he figured, she folded her tray table and stood up.

"I'll take a stretch, too," he said. As they were getting up, the plane lurched and she stumbled against him, and his arms instinctively embraced her taut body.

"Oh, sorry," she said, and pulled away, laughing, her hazel eyes flashing. Later, when he leaned toward her to resume the conversation, he discovered that she was asleep. His questions would have to wait.

∞

On the three-hour flight, as the plane lumbered on toward California, he watched Diana, a seemingly perfect stranger from a different world, sleeping peacefully beside him. Even in sleep, she had good posture. He thought of how she'd held her glass when she drank the water—like a fine wine—and her smile when she heard him say that they lived in the same town.

Wade thought about his ex-wife, Liz, and how they had drifted apart. She was with another man now, on the East Coast, which seemed to be the other side of the world.

Dating as he was turning forty-four hadn't been part of Wade's life plan, but here he was, staring at the beautiful woman beside him, wondering if there was any chance they'd get on. His hunch—or was it just hope?—was they just might.

∞

Diana awoke when the Captain gave his prepare-to-land speech. As the plane taxied to the gate in San Francisco, he gave her a long look. There was something so evocative about her eyes. He wanted to extend their stay together. He had to think quickly, though. They were both going to Palo Alto—perhaps share a ride? "Are you headed south?" he asked. "My car is in the airport garage. Could I give you a lift?"

"Thank you, but I'll just get a cab." She motioned toward the overhead bin. "But you might give me a little more help with that package."

He wrestled the parcel down from the overhead bin. It seemed even heavier than he'd remembered, and the bubble wrap made it awkward to grip. As they moved up the aisle, Wade rested the package on seat backs, which worked fine until he left the plane. Stepping carefully up the ramp, he awkwardly hugged the saddle to his chest as his briefcase hung from one shoulder, his overnight bag from the other.

Inside the airport Diana walked briskly. Her purse dangled from her shoulder as she held the pet carrier. Trying to keep up with her, he asked, "Have you checked anything?"

"No, all I have is what I'm carrying and the saddle—thank you so much for helping me, by the way. A true gentleman."

Wade tried to lift the heavy package up onto his shoulder, but he felt something in his back snap. He could no longer hold the saddle; all he could do was try to manage its fall. He followed it with his hands, dropping to his knees. Plastic bubbles popped as it hit the floor. "Sorry. I'm so sorry." He tried to stand up, but a shooting pain in his back made him collapse into a crouch.

"Are you all right?" Diana set her cat carrier down and lightly touched his shoulder. "Here, let me get a cart."

He struggled to help her wrangle the saddle and their bags onto the cart, then leaned on its handle as if it were a walker. *Pathetic.* He forced a smile.

"This is all my fault." Lines deepened on her forehead. "How can you possibly drive?"

"I'll be fine once I'm headed down the freeway." He reached around and rubbed his throbbing back.

"I don't think so." She shook her head as she studied how he was standing. "Look at you. You'll have to leave your car here. Why don't you ride along in my cab?"

"Thanks, Diana, but I need my car. I have to pick up my dog from the vet. Thanks for the offer, though. A few years ago, my back snapped like this—the doc called it a muscle spasm. A couple of days and I'll be good as new." Wade no longer wanted to extend their conversation. This was not only painful, it was embarrassing. All he wanted now was to get out of the situation.

After a pause, Diana said, "I caused this. I should help. We could take your car, I guess. I'll drive. How does that sound?"

Wade was in too much pain to argue. In the parking lot, he was relieved to spot his small Audi wagon and guided the cart that way. Together, they dumped the saddle in back. Diana loaded her pet carrier and his bag, then opened the passenger door and adjusted the passenger seat so it was almost flat. "That should be good."

When she started to pay at the exit booth, Wade tried to pull his wallet out, but a shooting pain stopped him. He tried to be positive, thanking her and promising he'd pay her back.

As Diana drove onto the 101 Freeway, cool sea air from the window she'd cracked open took his mind off the pain. Orange and purple sunset clouds spilled over the amber hilltops. Fingers of fog filled the valleys.

"I had a convertible in my twenties," he said. "A Corvair with over a hundred thousand miles. It was fun. This would be a great time for a ragtop, just cool enough to put the heater on."

"I had a convertible back then, too—a white Porsche with red leather seats," she said. "My husband, Rob, had it waiting for me in the driveway for my birthday with a big ribbon around it. I remember riding in it was tough on my hair. Between that and the helmet hair from riding horses, I spent half my time in the shower."

"So you kept riding horses but stopped putting the top down?"

"Riding's different." She smiled. "Helmet hair is something you earn."

Who was this woman, and why was Wade so attracted to her? And who was Rob? Must be her husband. It was strange to see a woman he hardly knew sitting in the driver's seat of his car, the same woman he'd watched, entranced, as she slept on the plane.

He asked what she thought of Palo Alto.

"It's different from Dallas. I've lived in Texas all my life. Horse people are pretty much the same everywhere, though, but there are more English saddles out here in in the Bay Area, the world of hunters and jumpers. Western—you know barrel racing and roping—not so much on the West Coast," she laughed. He loved that laugh.

"The pace is quicker than in Texas," she added. "My travel agent says Silicon Valley's becoming an international destination." She pointed at the cars in the oncoming lane, completely stopped now. "The traffic looks brutal—is it always like that?" When he nodded, she ventured, "But the weather sure is easy to get used to."

"It seems every company has to open an office here," Wade said. "In some ways, it's a bizarre place to live. At any rate, the schools are good. That's a big part of why we pay so much to live here." He remembered from the plane conversation that she said she had children. He foolishly thought his back was better, so he slowly raised his seat back to upright. He did it to seem less pitiful, but his back didn't appreciate the adjustment and a spasm twitched his back. "How do we get *you* home?" he asked, trying to ignore the pain. "Do you want to phone your . . . husband?"

"I think Rob's in Chicago. Or headed to Los Angeles. I forget." With one hand, she fumbled in her purse. Wade did not miss the fact that she sounded uncertain of her husband's whereabouts. She pulled a phone out, handed it to him and said, "Could you call me a cab?"

Wade made the call, which produced a taxi just as they pulled into his driveway. "Perfect timing," he said.

Still in severe pain as he worked his way out of the passenger seat, Wade struggled to stand and leaned against the car door for support.

Diana put her arm around his waist and helped him into the house. "You can hardly stand up."

He hobbled to the couch. "I'm fine."

"I hate to leave you like this," she said softly.

He would have liked her to stay longer, but he didn't know how to persuade her, especially with a taxi waiting. "You've done more than enough, Diana."

"You might give me your vet's number," she said. "To look at Micah and let the office know you won't be coming in to get your dog tonight."

Wade reached for his wallet, trying to ignore the pain that shot down his leg. He managed to open his billfold and pull out money for his parking and her cab, along with one of his business cards. He wrote down the vet's information and his home number on the back of the card. "In case there's a problem."

"Thanks, but I insist," she said as she returned the money to the coffee table. She studied his card. "It says you're a sound engineer. Rob tells me there are hundreds of engineers out here—he says that half the lawyers he meets are Stanford engineers as well."

"They call me an engineer, but I was an English major, and I didn't go to Stanford." Saying it that way made Wade wonder if he didn't measure up. "Like I told you on the plane, maybe while you were dozing, I traveled from the Midwest to the University of Washington, up by Seattle. My company makes sound systems, mainly for movie theaters."

"That's interesting," her voice trailed away. "I've always thought working with customers would be fun." She looked out at the taxi. "I'd better check on Micah and deal with the cab."

Through the front window he watched Diana help the driver load the saddle into the taxi. Even with her help, the young cabbie almost dropped the bundle as he lifted it into the trunk.

Then Diana moved her pet carrier into the cab and brought Wade's carry-on bag into the house. "Sure you'll be all right?"

"Thanks to you, I will be." He had given her his number but couldn't think of an excuse to ask for hers. At the door, he didn't know whether he should hug her goodbye until she moved forward and shook his hand like a businesswoman.

After she left, he took three ibuprofens. His only voicemail was from his daughter Amelia, in college back East, asking, "What do you want for your birthday?" To not turn forty-four was what he wanted. He'd get back to Amelia later.

He remembered the touch of her hand on his shoulder. He pictured her as she had driven him home—her confident manner.

He also had never met anyone who didn't like convertibles, which made him smile.

Wade woke up his laptop and searched "Diana Buchanan Horses." A dozen images were displayed, many of them photos of her accepting ribbons and trophies from men and women in suits, probably the ones who put on the horse shows. One article from two years earlier showed her age as forty, so she must be forty-two now, two years younger than he was—though he would have easily believed it if the article had said she was thirty-five. In a few photos, Diana was jumping high fences, holding her reins far up the horse's dark brown neck, up by the head, her body almost totally horizontal, a real athlete.

The pills kicked in. He felt drowsy and fell into bed. He'd never had much to do with horses, nor had he any interest other than routine trail rides in Half Moon Bay until now. Horses were another world entirely, so why did he even think about this realm she inhabited?

Still, now that he'd met Diana, he fell asleep pondering ways to contact her.

∞

The next morning, Wade awoke to a repeated noise. He opened his eyes; light streamed in around the drapes on the sliding glass door of his bedroom. He squinted to bring the clock into focus.

Eight twenty . . . the doorbell . . . this early, on a Saturday? His back complained when he stood up and pulled on his robe and shuffled through the living room to open the front door.

He greeted the lean, tall man in his doorway. "Jorge! Good to see you, guy. I thought you were in San Antonio. Are Marita and Eva okay?" Jorge and Marita were practically family. Wade was godfather to Eva, their five-year-old daughter.

Jorge smiled as he entered, but his broad shoulders were stooped, his usual assurance missing. "I'm glad you're back, buddy."

Wade went into the kitchen to make coffee, but was so sore that he stopped. He leaned against a stool and motioned for Jorge to take over the coffee-making duties. "Sorry, Jorge, I threw my back out coming home from Dallas."

"I guess we both have problems," Jorge said as he poured water into the coffee maker. "I was supposed to be in San Antonio with Marita and Eva. Marita misses her old friends. But Lydia canceled my trip." Jorge gave him a nervous glance.

This wasn't good. Lydia was Jorge's boss. Wade moved slowly into the living room and sat on the sofa, watching Jorge in the kitchen. It had been almost a year since he had turned Jorge's personnel file over to Lydia. Wade had been promoted to sales, reporting to the company's owner, but he was hesitant to have his people work for Lydia. When Wade reluctantly handed the files to her, she had barely thanked him—she didn't ask him one thing about any of his employees.

Jorge sat down across from Wade. "To start with, I'm out over two hundred bucks in ticket change fees, and Lydia's not the only one who seems to be freezing me out. Nobody lets me in on things, especially the managers. It's not like when you were in my corner. Being in the dark sucks. Could you talk to her?"

Jorge had never asked Wade to do anything like this for him, so he hated to say no, but he had to. "I'm out of management now, Jorge. There's nothing I can do."

His friend slumped, almost as if he'd been hit, and straightened enough to pour two cups of coffee.

Five years earlier, Wade had helped persuade Jorge to leave El Paso and come to California when he recruited him. Now he stared at his friend's stooped shoulders and, on the spot, changed his mind. He would help. "Okay," he said, "I'll go see Lydia on Monday. Just don't expect miracles."

Jorge straightened up. "Well, you *were* kicked upstairs."

"I'm just 'Ray's sales guy' now—not part of management." He looked at his friend, who probably thought Wade could fix any of his problems. But Wade knew he didn't have that kind of clout with Ray

Snyderman, the company owner. He took a deep breath, inhaling the coffee aroma.

Jorge's cell phone rang. "It's Marita," he said, stepping away to take the call. He sounded relieved when he told Marita, "Wade is going to help me."

As Jorge talked on the phone, Wade thought about his friend's wife, Marita. When he first met the woman, she had been in full bloom, pregnant with Eva. Born in Cuba, she was smart and ambitious, full of energy. With that flowing black hair and intensity of expression, Marita could have been an actress.

Last spring, when Jorge's car was in the shop and Wade arrived to pick him up for work, he couldn't help but remember the way Marita had put her hands on the door where he had lowered his window and said, "I think of you often." As she leaned down, her robe had fallen open. "I'd love to thank you for all you've done for Jorge." Marita had followed Wade's eyes and brought her hand slowly to her breast, and he felt guilty. Marita had a little smirk on her face that might have showed she didn't mind. Wade tried to put her out of his thoughts. She was, after all, Jorge's wife and mother to his goddaughter.

Jorge put his phone in his pocket and returned to the table. "Marita thanks you for helping." He paused. "Rest that back. I'll see you Monday."

Enough daydreaming about Marita. Wade had to work out how to broach Jorge's situation with Lydia. His friend could demonstrate sound systems like no one else, but Lydia never warmed to him. From the way Jorge told the story, Wade guessed Jorge didn't understand what he'd done wrong. What could he say to defend his friend if he didn't know what had put him in the doghouse in the first place?

Wade needed to find out what was going on to protect Jorge's family. He didn't know exactly what was expected of him as godfather to Eva, but working to keep the child's father employed was something he *must* do. Wade had enough fear of God that the word godfather reminded him that this was one responsibility he shouldn't screw up.

2

Wade stretched his legs in different ways, testing his back. Every move hurt, some more than others. No way could he drive. How could he get his beagle Keats home from the vet? Saturday was the day he normally caught up on chores—exchanging his bachelor bundle at the neighborhood laundry. Groceries. Oil change. Not one of those tasks could be done without driving.

He thought again about Diana. Nothing online gave him any hint of how to contact her—was looking for her a lost cause? When he checked his voicemail, no message from Diana.

He had one voicemail, from his boss Ray Snyderman, with a message directed to the entire SnyderSound Company. "My fellow employees," Ray began, without his usual executive energy. He showed an uncharacteristic hesitancy in announcing an all-hands offsite meeting. Wade tried to imagine what lurked behind Ray's voice and remembered Jorge's Saturday morning visit—could they be related?

He could only get comfortable sitting or lying down, so he settled in his living room on the couch, surrounded by pillows, with his Mac laptop and the phone. He started in on the mail, paying a couple of bills. He picked up the poetry anthology on the coffee table and read one of his old favorites, "The Love of Aged Horses," by a poet he respected, Jane Hirshfield. He wanted to show the poem to Diana. *But you can't. You can't even text or phone her. Remember, she has your number, but you never got hers.*

Back to the Mac. An email from Ray detailed the specifics of the offsite meeting—they'd convene next week in the elegant, spacious Stanford Theater in downtown Palo Alto, which seemed like overkill. The entire company had fewer than two hundred and fifty employees. He remembered that Ray had recently quizzed Wade more closely than usual on the company's sales prospects. Something strange was going on.

Midmorning, the phone rang. It was Diana. "I have a surprise. Would you mind if I stopped by? Perhaps in an hour?"

"Mind?" Wade asked. "I'd love to see you."

Diana was coming over. He showered, then quickly dressed, donning his favorite shirt and pressed slacks. His excitement faded when he looked at his living room as if through Diana's eyes. She'd already seen it, but that was at night when all he could think of was getting to bed. Wade realized it hadn't changed much since the divorce. Full-length windows blocked by too much furniture, including an assortment of tall, canvas director chairs, what they used to call butterfly chairs. Even a wrought-iron purple denim ottoman that didn't match any of the other furniture. Still, he remembered being happy, his legs stretched out on the denim, a poem on his lap. The ottoman had to go, but one thing he'd keep was the brown leather recliner he'd bought at a garage sale, the one he wrote poems in.

The picture on the piano of his ex-wife Liz was so prominent that it looked like a shrine. He thought of her on that farm in Massachusetts, where she'd settled five years earlier. Although he still felt pain from the divorce, over time he had lost his anger. He should have taken her picture down long ago—it had been there when they were still married, and he occasionally turned it face down onto the piano, but he'd never removed it. Once the center of Wade's life, she was now Amelia's-mother-on-the-other-coast. Wade swapped her picture for one of Amelia clowning around in front of her artwork.

His daughter looked small next to her large black-and-white triptychs of her photography installation. He stood back to see how

Amelia looked in the silver frame on the piano. Better than the picture of Liz, for sure.

He had wanted to return Amelia's phone call to find out what was going on in her life but not to discuss his upcoming birthday. With so little going on in his own life, he hated to think he was moving so quickly through his forties. He put off returning her phone call. Being careful with his back, he dragged two stained chairs and the ottoman to where he kept the trash bins outside the garage.

Wade's back throbbed, but still he filled a bag with fading photographs and mementos brought back from trips—a starfish from Florida, a hand-painted pink elephant from Thailand—and took them to the garage.

The bookcase also needed attention. When he went to a reading, he liked to buy the author's work, so books were crammed everywhere. He weeded out the shelves and with growing discomfort, carried three more shopping bags to the garage for donations.

That was about all the cleaning up he could do before Diana appeared at the front door with her surprise—Wade's beagle Keats ran in, tail wagging wildly. The dog went a little nuts, leaping up in the air in front of his master. Wade had trained him not to jump on people; even at his wildest, Keats controlled himself.

Diana looked relaxed in jeans, a dark blue LaCosta golf shirt and cordovan loafers with gold horse-bits. The red of her hair gleamed brightly in the sun. He wanted to touch her. "The vet let me take him. I showed them your card and left my cat—that was enough." She laughed. "Keats, what a name for a beagle."

"Named after one of my favorite poets. His howling's not the least poetic, that's for sure. You should hear him when I leave."

"I got a preview already," she said.

He watched Diana as she looked around. He imagined she lived in a pricier part of town. His was a simple three-bedroom ranch house in South Palo Alto that he'd bought years back but could never have afforded had he tried to buy it today. What would she think of South

Palo Alto, all these single-story postwar houses on streets named after the contractor's kids? *I can't feel embarrassed by where I live.*

"I like the openness," she said cheerily.

"It's an Eichler home," Wade said. "He was the builder—Joseph Eichler. The idea in the fifties was to make stylish houses for the masses. They probably weren't meant to last as long as they have." He watched her survey the beamed ceilings and the indoor-outdoor patio through the sliding glass door. "California Casual, to take advantage of this weather. I've always loved it."

"I'm beginning to love it, too." Her eyes stopped at the framed photo on the piano. She looked over at him and raised her eyebrows.

"My daughter, off at Bard," he said.

"Back East, *that* Bard?"

"Yeah, it's hard to think Amelia is three thousand miles away. She's a photography major and loves it. I never see her anymore, but there's a chance I'll take her to Mexico over her spring break." Wade stole a glance at Diana to see her reaction.

"She looks like she's having fun," Diana said, and picked up a poetry book he had left out on the coffee table. She thumbed through it, then set it back down. "So you do like poetry."

"I go to readings and workshops, and I write some," Wade said. "I think of it as my hobby."

"Rob hates poetry. He makes jokes about poets and calls them losers."

That stung. Wade wondered if Rob would think of him as a loser. He changed the subject. "How'd it go with your cat?"

"Micah's not in good shape. I may lose her. She's seventeen." Diana was quiet for a minute, looking away. "If I have to put her down, it'll be hard."

"What about your kids?" he asked.

"We had the two of them after Micah came into our lives. The cat was our trial child."

"Sorry about your cat. I remember when Amelia's iguana died,"

Wade said. "We buried him under a tree, which is probably where a lot of suburban iguanas end up." He coughed. "Your kids must be younger than my daughter Amelia. She was a junior in high school about that time."

Diana looked away again, and then said, "And my kids are younger. Robbie is starting seventh grade, and Beth will be a freshman at Palo Alto High School."

"*Paly*, they call it. That's where Amelia went," he said.

She picked up the anthology again, and asked, "Do you have a poem in this book?" Her eyes met his.

"Not yet."

"Can I see one of your poems?"

"How about I show you one at dinner next week?" Wade asked.

She pursed her lips and stood up, brushing off what he thought was dog fur. "I don't date. I'm sorry." He must have shown a crestfallen expression, so she said, "It's not you, Wade. My husband and I are separated, but we have an agreement. It's a long story."

He got up and followed her to the door. "So you *are* still married. I noticed the ring."

"Well, not really *married*." She drew into herself, tightening her lips, which made her seem like a different person. "We live apart now."

"But . . . you don't date?" Wade surrendered to the pain in his back and leaned on a chair.

"I tried dating in Dallas. I wasn't ready, and it upset the kids, so I told everyone I wasn't interested." She walked over to the piano and picked up Amelia's picture, regarded it closely, and set it back down. Her face relaxed, and she asked, "Would having a cup of coffee be considered a date?"

"Absolutely not," he responded.

"That might be the right answer," she said. "So, let's think about coffee. It'd have to be after the kids start school. But that's next Tuesday. I'll text you so you'll have my number."

Wade raised his eyebrows. "It's not a date," he smiled.

∞

When Wade saw Lydia in the lobby the next day, he told her he'd like to talk to her about Jorge. Later that day, she came to his office, her ash-blonde hair pulled away from her face. She came in, sat down, and as she leaned forward, she flipped the date page back and forth on Wade's desk calendar. Was she checking his appointment schedule or just asserting herself?

He considered the two of them equals since they both reported to Sherry Snyderman, the marketing director and Ray's wife. Wade was senior to Lydia, since he'd preceded her, and his real boss, Ray, was the president of the company. Lydia obviously didn't see him as her senior. For someone just out of Wharton business school, Wade thought she was pretty nervy. Wade hoped he'd eventually be named sales manager but didn't bring that up.

"Let's get down to business," she said. "You wanted to talk to me. About Calderon, I'm sure. I hope you don't ask me to do anything special for him."

Not wanting to tip his hand, Wade shrugged.

She sat back. "If this is about the trip, about him wanting to see his family, forget it. Trips get canceled all the time. We're running a business, and we needed him in Denver. Jorge's the one who bought nonrefundable tickets. He creates more problems than he solves."

"I never experienced that with him," Wade said.

"Well, that was when you were managing him—maybe *you* were better at it." She laughed, but the muscles around her jaw looked taut. "You're strictly sales now. I manage the techies. I'm committed to support your sales efforts, but seriously, don't get mixed up in this. It's inappropriate."

He worked to keep a poker face. "What's he done?"

She ignored his question and shot back, "All right, I know you're tight with the owners—Ray and Sherry." She stared at him. "I may call them Mr. and Mrs. Snyderman, but *I* am Calderon's manager. He reports to *me*."

"I brought him in. He's the best customer tech at SnyderSound," he said. "He can make systems sound better than they really are, you know that."

"There's more to the job than making the equipment run." She rose and walked to the door. Over her shoulder she added, "Don't get involved."

Watching her disappear around the corner, Wade turned her words over in his mind. Isn't getting involved what life is all about? Isn't that what he was seeking, more involvement—with Jorge, with Ray, even with Diana? Hearing the words, "Don't get involved," felt like death. But how could he not help the only guy he could talk to when he was in the throes of his divorce from Liz?

∞

Diana and Wade met for coffee at Peet's, across the street from the high school where her daughter had just started. Most of the people in line for coffee were dressed for work, but a fit young mother wearing a red Stanford jogging suit pushed a Swedish baby buggy while chatting on her cell phone about a real estate open house—the lawn had to be trimmed *just right,* she said. She seemed like such a negative stereotype that Wade said to Diana, "All of Palo Alto's not like her." They neared the counter.

"She's fine," Diana said. "Relax."

He winced.

"How's your back?"

"It's pretty much healed," Wade lied. He straightened up, making it hurt more.

They chose a table outside, where they could see kids coming and going. "So where does your interest in verse come from?" she asked. "Why do you write poems?"

Wade shrugged. But her sincere interest intrigued him. "The world doesn't especially want poets. I'm not talking about Plato. He wanted to banish them. I'm talking about here and now. Poetry makes people nervous. Sometimes it's not taught well in school—

makes people uncomfortable. I've come to grips with the fact that poetry is just something I do. Doesn't make much sense. I'm doing fine making a living, helping Amelia through Bard. Poetry isn't about money, for sure. I always think of those two apocryphal twins, poetry and poverty."

Diana frowned. "Not all poets are poor, are they?"

"Even famous poets like Keats and Poe—two of my favorites— were up against it financially. I went to Keats's house on the Spanish Steps in Rome. His final letters, written when he was twenty-five, named which debtors should be paid upon his death, and in what order. He knew there wouldn't be enough compensation for all of them. So early on I decided never to depend on poetry for money." When he finished, he fell silent. Something about Diana's put-together appearance—her perfect haircut, pressed shirt, the way her earrings matched her circle pin—made him uncomfortable.

"Poetry must be a big part of your life," she said.

Wade stirred his coffee. He wasn't at all sure she'd like his writing and wished she would stop talking about it. At the very least, he wanted to get to know her better before sharing it with her. "How are your kids doing?"

She wasn't put off. "Okay, come clean." She looked right at him. "Did you bring one of your poems?"

He smiled. "As I remember, that proposition involved dinner."

She raised her eyebrows. "I give up, we'll talk about kids then." She sat back and crossed her arms.

"Well, actually, I did bring you something, and it is a poem—just not one of mine. It's from an old magazine. It's by Jane Hirshfield, a poet who lives up in Marin County." He opened up to a page in the *Atlantic* and, after mentioning the title, "The Love of Aged Horses," began reading—

Because I know tomorrow
his faithful gelding heart will be broken
when the spotted mare is trailered and driven away,
I come today to take him for a gallop on Diaz Ridge.

Returning, he will whinny for his love.
Ancient, spavined,
her white parts red with hill-dust,
her red parts whitened with the same, she never answers.

But today, when I turn him loose at the hill-gate
with the taste of chewed oat on his tongue
and the saddle-sweat rinsed off with water,
I know he will canter, however tired,
whinnying wildly up the ridge's near side,
and I know he will find her.

He will be filled with the sureness of horses
whose bellies are grain-filled,
whose long-ribbed loneliness
can be scratched into no-longer-lonely.

His long teeth on her withers,
her rough-coated spots will grow damp and wild.
Her long teeth on his withers,
his oiled-teakwood smoothness will grow damp and wild.
Their shadows' chiasmus will fleck and fill with flies,
the eight marks of their fortune stamp and then cancel the earth.
From ear-flick to tail-switch, they stand in one body.
No luck is as boundless as theirs.

"I like that line about the sureness of horses," Diana sighed. "If you have their attention, their skittishness disappears. I enjoyed poetry in high school and in one college class, but I don't read much of it anymore. The poem's wonderful, but why did you save it for me?"

"Horses," Wade said. "I thought of you."

"That poem is about a lot more than horses," Diana said. "It's about love." As soon as she said that she turned away to watch a large group of high school students cross the street and fan out into different shops.

"It seems that at almost any time of the school day, a quarter of the Paly kids are here at this shopping center," Wade said. "In the Midwest, we went to school in the morning and stayed all day."

"Same here. Your daughter—Amelia, is it? You told me she enjoyed Palo Alto High School, though."

"It was good for her."

"You know, the loneliness in that poem makes me think of Beth," Diana said. "She's out of her element. My daughter has always gone to schools where everyone knows everybody else. She even talked to her grandmother about missing Dallas. I hope she's not wanting to go back."

He took a sip of coffee. "Is that even a possibility?"

"I suppose she could stay with my parents. She's just unhappy all the time."

"That bad, huh?"

"She stares out into space, which she's never done before. It's hard to start a new school without knowing anyone."

Wade nodded.

Diana looked over at the high school buildings. "She was in tears this morning. She spent hours on the phone talking to her old friends in Dallas until late last night. The one kid she brought home from *Paly*, as you call it, seemed to be a druggie, but I could be misreading just because she had tattoos, and, Beth says, hidden piercings. Beth's so down on herself that I don't know what to think. She thinks her clothes are 'too Texas,' and the other day, somebody made fun of her drawl. I never thought of her as having a drawl."

"Maybe it's just typical high school stuff," Wade said. "When Amelia was Beth's age, she looked down at her shoes and asked me what Adidas stood for. She couldn't have been more than thirteen. I told her I didn't know. 'Well, I do,' she said. 'All Day I Dream About Sex.'"

Diana laughed with more hearty spirit than Wade expected. "What in the world could you say to that?"

"Nothing. They test us, they do." He stirred his coffee. "I'm surprised you moved out here. It took courage."

"I don't know about courage," she said. "A lot was circumstance. After Rob and I split up, his firm opened a new branch out here, off Sand Hill Road, and his father asked Rob to run it. *Buchanan, Snow, and Tyler.* They have eighty lawyers out here now and hundreds more in Dallas and, well, all over the world. After a while, I agreed, for Beth and Robbie's sake, to come to California too. My friends thought I was crazy, but if I stayed in Dallas, the kids would always be on planes. Holidays would have been impossible." She looked at her hands before she continued. "Last spring Rob bought a large house in Woodside—an estate, I guess. He put my horse's name— Gray Cloud—on a corral there, but I refused to move the horse. Rob's not happy about it, but I'm more comfortable at Jasper Ridge Ranch where I can ride with my friend Jolene, who owns a wonderful horse named Artemis."

Wade hesitated. "Why would he want your horse to have a home with him? Does that mean he wants you to come back to him?"

"At times he still begs me to rethink it, but since that one time, in anger, when he told me, 'Good riddance,' that was the end for me. He's complicated, so sometimes he wants me back, and he truly loves the kids. But we both know it's over." She raised her cup to her lips and took a sip. "Everything's supposed to be as close to *the way it was* as possible. That's the agreement, for the kids' sake." She shrugged. "He's been generous financially, at least so far—no problems there." She played with her earring and looked away.

Wade drank his coffee, noticing that the half and half was not enough to overcome the brew's bitterness.

"I guess I shouldn't even be having coffee with anyone." She glanced at the storefronts in the shopping center and back over at the high school. "Well, maybe California isn't as bad as I thought—just a bit foreign. In Texas, everybody knew his or her place. I don't like to think of myself as sheltered, but maybe I have been. You're from the Midwest, too, right? There's a part of California that seems on the edge, unsettled. You know—how everybody keeps re-inventing themselves, You know, where an engineer with an MBA starts a real estate project or a health application for PCs or a trendy new restaurant—?"

"The rise of Internet companies has made Palo Alto more the center of things. Calling Harvard *The Stanford of the East* was a big joke when I moved out here, but I just read that Stanford passed Harvard as the number one business school in a poll. This area's coming into its own."

More kids crossed the street. A few joined them in Peet's, but most went into places down the way, an early lunch crowd. "I'm sure I'll adjust," Diana said. "The scenery around here, just the way things look, is beautiful, and I don't miss the humidity back home one bit," Diana said. "Rob is grudgingly impressed with the people, too."

Wade nodded, trying to understand what she meant by that comment. "Well, I'm certainly glad you moved out here." In the bright sunlight, the green of her hazel eyes overwhelmed the brown. "I don't totally understand this no-dating idea. I'd like to get to know you better, that's for sure." His forwardness shocked him. But something about Diana made him comfortable saying what he felt. "Maybe I can be kind of a town host for you. A tour guide." He paused. "Would you like to see where Steve Jobs lived? It's not marked but people drive by it slowly. I guess it's like a shrine, now." He drove her the eight blocks to the English cottage-style house on Waverley.

"Inconspicuous. Tasteful," she said.

Her words put Wade at ease. Even though she seemed very comfortable financially, she didn't appear to like ostentation. He pointed out the modest house next door to Jobs's old place, a two-story white saltbox with a picket fence, not even slightly pretentious. "That was Steve Young's place when he was the San Francisco Forty-Niner quarterback."

She seemed surprised, almost shocked. "Tony Romo's house wouldn't squeeze into that entire lot, even if you added the lot next door."

Wade struggled to remember who Tony Romo was—right, the Dallas quarterback. Romo played a while after Steve Young, but that must be who Diana was thinking of.

She smiled and said, "The last word I thought I'd use to describe California was quaint. Palo Alto is going to take some getting used to."

3

A few weeks later, more than two hundred SnyderSound employees gathered in the lobby of the Stanford Theater, a historic building that had been restored to its original golden-age-of-movie-houses glory. Ray Snyderman, looking gaunt in a SnyderSound polo shirt and a sport coat, mingled with others in the lobby, his balding head shining under the fluorescent lights. His smile seemed even more pasted-on than usual. Dark circles ringed his eyes.

As the SnyderSound employees filed into the theater, Jorge, looking a bit too casual in jeans and a t-shirt, joined Wade. They sat together toward the front. Jorge said, "Think he's going to announce the holiday party?"

Wade chuckled lightly, as did the woman next to him.

Jorge continued. "Maybe he's planning to give everyone in the front row a hundred bucks to get the crowd going." Wade's second response to Jorge's gallows humor was more subdued. The woman, too, looked away.

Ray took the stage, which was set with a stool and small desk with a plastic water bottle, but no podium. He thanked them all for their hard work. "Times are tough. Even with such a robust technology economy, our little industry is troubled. People aren't going to the movies as much as they did five years ago or even last year. Maybe it's DVDs, or Netflix, or the Internet, who knows, but the problem starts with the fact that people aren't filling the seats." To illustrate the decline, he described five sales situations Wade was working on all of them and was pleased Ray had his facts right. Except for an old customer in Portland, who was pressing on with a twelve-theater remodel, each one was postponing or canceling orders.

"For the first time in our history," Ray read from note cards, "we're going to have to let some people go. After we get back to the office, I'd like you to meet with your manager. They've all reserved the rest of the morning to talk to you about who will be affected."

After he read from the cards, he paused and looked up. "As many of you know, my dad founded SnyderSound as a storefront radio shop in Redwood City. He never laid anyone off, and I never intended to." Ray's voice quavered. "But our business simply can't support our current structure." He paused again and took a sip of water. "Management will shrink, too. I wish I had something better to say, but that's the situation. I wanted to tell you all in person."

Jorge leaned over to Wade and whispered, "So what do you think—Lydia's history?"

Jorge managed a laugh, but they both knew he was whistling past the graveyard and that his situation was grim. For starters, Jorge had to meet with Lydia, while Wade would meet with Sherry, who had always been friendly to him. He told himself to stop worrying about Jorge and concentrate on his own situation. Checks to Bard College and to Amelia had almost wiped out what he had in the bank from the refinance of the house after the divorce. If the paychecks stopped, he'd have to tap his 401K or start drawing on the second mortgage the bankers had set up. He would have to look for another position somewhere in a related field, maybe take a huge cut in pay.

Wade left Jorge on his own and headed to Sherry Snyderman's spacious office. She looked up from her desk and motioned him to sit in the seat across from her. In a dark green turtleneck with a couple of splatter spots, she looked more like a soccer mom than a marketing director. After the pleasantries, she said, "I'll get right down to business, Wade. One of us is out of a job. The good news is, it isn't you. Ray and I decided that I would step down, at least until things pick up."

Wade drew a deep breath. "I'm sorry to hear that, Sherry."

"It's okay. I was already taking some afternoons off to be with the kids. Ray and I thought I should either start putting in sixty-hour weeks or . . . leave. You know I love this company."

"I'll miss you. We all will."

"I enjoyed working with you and the customers, and I hope to attend some dinners, but as Ray's wife—no longer as marketing director. This is the right decision, I'm quite confident."

"You seem relaxed about stepping down."

"I've had a few weeks to get used to the idea. I'll enjoy having more time for the kids. I only had you and Lydia as direct reports, so that level of management will disappear. Everyone's into flat organizations now."

Wade stiffened in his chair. "Lydia and I have been having words."

"About Jorge, right? I know all about that, more than you imagine." Sherry took a long breath. He wondered what was coming. "After working with you for six years, I have no idea about your politics."

He didn't know where she was going with that. "Are you asking me now?"

"No. I *shouldn't* know. Ray and I have gone over this a lot lately. You're involved in sales. Leave your politics in the parking lot." She looked away, then back at him. "You've never met the Andersons from Las Vegas, have you?"

"Ray's mentioned them. They'd planned five new theaters, right? I heard they're postponing."

Sherry glanced out the window to a well-tended lawn and garden, a lush view Wade knew was available from only a few offices. "Yes. We hope to get that business next year." She looked back at him. "The Andersons are rock-ribbed Republicans."

Wade sensed where this was going. "I know Jorge can come off as a little arrogant sometimes."

"Yes, he can. He kind of stepped on his tie in Las Vegas." She laughed nervously. "I was just using a phrase, but part of the story is that Jorge wore an American flag tie that day, red white and blue. After a demo, thinking he was among friends, Anderson asked Jorge how he voted."

"Oh, my," Wade said.

"I guess Jorge told Anderson something obscene about where the Republicans could put their program. It didn't go over *at all*. Now Anderson rides Ray about keeping a radical on the payroll, and it doesn't look good for Jorge."

Wade took a deep breath. "Knocking Republicans wouldn't cause a stir around here, but as you describe the Andersons, I get it. So Lydia's not acting on her own, huh?"

"There are wheels within wheels, Wade, you know that."

On the lawn outside, Wade watched a gardener brandish a weed-whacker. "Jorge was the best tech I ever hired. Even Lydia admits he has strong skills. I agree we should listen to our customers, but not on something like this. If you let him go, are you sure it would be a good business decision?"

"He was a good hire. Nobody's questioning your judgment about that. And I like Jorge, too, Wade, but Ray said, and this is a direct quote: 'Calderon is history.' He wanted to make sure I told you."

"This doesn't sound like Ray to me. I'd like to talk to him."

"I don't think that's a good idea. Ray's making a lot of changes quickly, and Calderon is one of them. It would be best if you stayed out of it. Really."

"We don't have many Hispanics on the payroll," Wade said. "Couldn't there be a legal problem in firing him?"

"Ray worried about that too. An employment lawyer convinced him to deal with Jorge gradually. That's why Ray read from note cards this morning—one wrong word and you've got a lawsuit on your hands. To dot all the i's and cross all the t's, Ray is giving Jorge a short probation period."

Wade hesitated, stunned. "Not good," he said. "And my new manager will be, let me guess, Lydia?"

Sherry nodded. "Temporarily, yes. Ray keeps his direct reports to a minimum, so he wants you to report to Lydia until we can afford to replace me with an experienced marketing director."

Something twisted in his chest. "All this is a hundred percent decided?"

"Ray needs you in sales. You know how to work with people—he says it's your gift. He said to let Lydia do the admin work."

"This is hard, Sherry." Wade stood up.

"Don't spend too much time worrying about Jorge. This is all for the good of the company."

The paranoid part of him was relieved his job wasn't on the line, so he could keep writing those checks to Bard and stay on the escalator of house prices going up in Palo Alto and maybe get to know Diana better without worrying where his next paycheck was coming from. But he felt responsible about Jorge, because he'd helped convince him to move out here, and then there was Marita, of course, not to mention Eva, Wade's goddaughter. He had to get out of the room.

Lydia was waiting outside Sherry's office, looking uneasy. "Next," he said, and gave her thumbs up, but she just stared warily at him.

At the bottom of the stairs, Wade spotted Jorge down a long hallway before Jorge saw him. Wade stepped back into the dark stairwell. Now that he knew what was going on, there was nothing he could say to his friend that could help him.

∞

Diana and Wade talked on the phone two or three times a week, but he sensed that she was keeping him at a distance. She was always friendly with him, but he wanted something more. Even though she had made it clear she wasn't interested in dating, Wade hoped that maybe she would come around. Many of their conversations involved Diana's concern about her daughter and the details of Amelia's high school experience. Safe talk. They scheduled another coffee date, this one at the Palo Alto Café on Middlefield on Saturday morning.

The café was a comfortable neighborhood corner storefront with a coffee roaster the size of a small car. Even its sofas and tables seemed to emanate a deep coffee smell. The loose shirt Diana wore over her riding pants reminded him of the adage, "You can't hide a good figure." A guy in line in a business suit didn't keep his eyes off her as she took a seat at a table while Wade stood in line. When Wade joined her, hot drinks in hand, he asked about her kids.

"Beth and Robbie are with their dad until dinnertime. The little guy's doing fine, that's the good news." She knocked on the rickety oak table for luck. "I don't know about Beth. One minute she claims she's happy, and the next she's babbling on like she's eight years old again. She's still on the phone to her old friends in Dallas every day."

"Outside interests help get kids cope. Amelia had her photography, even back then. I imagine Beth rides horses?"

Diana took a sip of coffee. "Beth might have been the only teenaged girl in Texas with no interest in horses. I wonder if it wasn't to spite me. Believe me, I did everything but take her over jumps myself." Her voice trailed off as she looked thoughtfully at him. "You seem down."

Wade was surprised that Diana picked up on his mood so quickly. "It looks like a good friend of mine at work is about to lose his job. Actually, he is more than a good friend, more like my best friend. Like a brother. I've been told by my boss to stand by and do nothing."

"That must be awful." She frowned. "Watching something unfold, yet being powerless to change it. That seems familiar."

Wade put his hand on her wrist. "Really? Powerless doesn't sound like you."

"Since I separated from Rob, I've tried to hold what's left of the old life together for the kids. Maybe that's kept me from moving forward. If it weren't for the horses and my faith, I don't know what I'd do."

He was pleased she turned her hand to accept his. "I've been through a divorce, too. Maybe I understand better than you think."

"How did things end?" she asked.

When Wade said, "She left me," Diana's eyes locked onto his. "Have you ever ridden horses?"

"I've always wanted to," Wade said. Maybe she found out something he didn't know about himself. Or was he just saying what he thought she wanted to hear?

"How's your back?" she asked.

"Healed. A muscle pull. All better." It hadn't hurt much lately, so what he said was close to the truth.

"I'm headed to Jasper Ridge Ranch. Would you like to join me?"

"Sure, I'd love to. I can show you a shortcut, a way to cut across the Stanford campus." The errands he'd planned would have to wait. "Follow me."

Every time they met, it seemed, they were getting easier with each other; she talked about horses and her kids, and he talked about work and Palo Alto. He'd been so relieved when she didn't pull away when he touched her. He led her white SUV across the Stanford campus. As much as he would love to get close to Diana, he wasn't positive about riding horses and wondered again why he had told her he'd always wanted to. Well, it wouldn't happen that day—he wasn't properly dressed.

Some of the campus roads were torn up, and even where there wasn't construction, traffic was bumper-to-bumper. He'd forgotten there was a football game and zigzagged around to avoid traffic. On the far side of the campus, the landscape took on a rural look. As they turned onto Alpine Road, he waved Diana on ahead. She led him through a gate onto a private farm road.

Harvested corn stalks stood in the field to the left of the road, haphazard skeletons, yellow and brown. Like the corn stalks, the gnarled branches of a raspberry patch had been abandoned until spring. Silicon Valley seemed far away. A line of silver and white horse trailers stood at the ready next to a meandering stream. The wide spaces between the trailers and the empty fields conveyed a luxury of space unusual on the mid-Peninsula. Rail-fenced riding rings and ramshackle stalls suggested a simpler time. In the distance a green ridge punctuated with spreading oaks, but no houses, made an irregular outline against the sky.

As they passed the new-mown fields, he lowered his window to breathe in that fresh earthy smell. The paved road ended, and their two-vehicle caravan slowed to a crawl. A sign indicated, WHOA—5 MPH PLEASE—SPEED SPOOKS HORSES, and Diana's SUV slowed to a crawl. They passed a woman who was leading three unsaddled horses back to the stables, then another row of parked horse trailers. Two women rode by, their saddles small, more like you'd see under jockeys Wade had seen at the racetrack than the saddles he'd seen in movies. Although he enjoyed the solitude of his own car, he also wished she were there with him—there was so much he wanted to ask her. The smiling twenty-something brunette driver of a station wagon leaving the ranch waved to Diana and then to Wade, as if they were all in this horsey world together. He waved back.

They each parked near one of the buildings. Diana got out, carrots in hand, and went into an open barn with Dutch-doored stables on both sides. Wade joined her as she approached a tall light-gray horse in the first stall. The horse made a friendly sound through its nostrils—a loud cat purr. "Great nicker, Gray Cloud." She fed her horse a carrot, then backed off and handed the other to Wade. "Hold this. I'll get Artemis from the next barn. You two should get to know each other."

She came back with a cinnamon-colored horse, tying it to a post near Gray Cloud. "Artemis belongs to my friend Jolene. I think I mentioned her to you before. Her husband works with Rob." She motioned for him to feed the horse the carrot.

Wade held onto the thick end. When the horse bit down, exposing her huge teeth, he flinched, and the carrot hit the floor.

"Relax, Artemis would be mortified if she bit someone. She's a lady." Diana picked up the carrot and handed it back to Wade. "Hold it by the thin end. When she takes it in her teeth, snap it off."

This time when the horse chomped down, he held onto the stub and wrenched the carrot sideways.

Diana patted the horse's broad flank. "Now," she said, turning to Wade, "Give her what's left with a flat hand."

He held his hand so flat that his palm stuck up higher than his fingers. Artemis brought her lips forward at the last minute and deftly pulled the carrot point into her mouth. Her soft, dry lips barely grazed his hand. The horse's eyes were larger than his knuckles and seemed intelligent, soulful. The intimacy of gazing into a huge animal's eyes surprised him. And she smelled good, too, a sweet smell. Or was that the hay? Wade had ridden horses a few times on trail rides, but he had never felt this kind of intimate connection with a large mysterious animal.

"Here, I'll show you a little about grooming," Diana said. Looking small next to the horse, she grabbed one of the horse's back legs, easily flexing it up into her hand. "Keep your eye out for rocks," she said, cleaning his hooves with a metal pick. "A pebble can hobble a horse."

She handed Wade the pick. "I wouldn't allow you to clean her hooves if Artemis weren't such a gentle lady." She nodded toward Artemis and turned to work on her saddle, which was draped across a fence. She sponged it off carefully.

"Is that the saddle I dropped at the airport?" Wade asked.

She nodded. "Nice to have it back." Diana looked over her shoulder at him. "Bring your hand along her back tendon."

At first, he faced the same direction as the horse. As Wade tried to mimic Diana, he realized he was standing the wrong way. After a sheepish glance toward her, he turned around and touched the back of Artemis's leg. The horse lifted her leg and held it up as Wade dug out a clod of dirt.

"See, nothing to it," Diana rubbed an oily cloth across the saddle.

As he cleaned the other hooves, a small pickup drove up and parked by the barn, right next to them. A wiry, silver-haired man in a weathered flight jacket waved from inside.

"Hey, Cliff," Diana called to him. "This is my friend Wade. Thanks for taking Artemis out yesterday. She needs work."

Cliff gave a mock salute from the truck. "Good to see you, Diana. I've got to scoot. But I've got something for you—that book I promised." He pulled out two thin spiral-bound books. Photos of Jasper Ridge Ranch and its people showed through the clear plastic covers. He handed them copies. "The ranch ordered 200 of these. I can afford to give two away."

Wade thumbed through it quickly, reading a couple of the captions underneath the photos. It drew him in, but he couldn't read it in detail as Diana returned Artemis to her barn and asked Wade to help her move a painting from her horse trailer to her car. "This is the last thing I couldn't trust the movers with. I packed it under the haymow."

They folded down the seats of her SUV and drove to her trailer.

She opened a side door, where a large canvas was covered with a sheet. "It's not heavy," she reassured him, "just bulky."

"May I see the painting?"

She hesitated before she pulled back the sheet. Wade studied a younger Diana in a dark coat and yellow vest. Looking like a magazine model, she was holding Gray Cloud's reins while accepting a silver tray from a man in a red coat. She looked exquisitely beautiful, a picture of controlled energy.

"Was this long ago?" Wade asked. "It somehow seems like a scene out of another era."

"About a year ago. You're probably fooled by what everybody's wearing. That's what we do in the hunt—even in California. In honor of the sport."

"What's a hunt?"

"Kind of a riding club. I often ride with them. As I said, there's one out here, too. You've seen it in the movies, haven't you, where everybody dresses up in tall boots and coats, like in the picture, and rides behind the hounds? They gave this to me as my going-away present."

Wade had to admit he was intrigued, drawn in mainly by Diana but also the uniqueness of what they were doing. A club with traditions, a physical activity in touch with the past. After another glance at the painting, he said, "A champion!" Diana looked more carefree in the portrait than she seemed now. The more-open smile, frozen in time, made him realize this last year had rocked her world.

"Not exactly a champion. That was just one event—a steeplechase." Seeing Wade's baffled expression, she added, "It's a full-tilt race with jumps. A lucky day, that's all."

Following Diana as she drove out toward Alpine Road, Wade felt as if he'd experienced a breath of fresh air in Silicon Valley. The painting brought him into a whole new world, and feeding Artemis had been inexplicably moving. Artemis' eyes! And Diana, so attractive in every way, and so at home out here. As he was leaving, a teenage girl rode confidently by on a huge brown horse, completely in control. Despite his reservations, he pictured himself becoming a serious horseback rider. If these kids could do it, how hard could it be?

He pulled out into traffic, ready to leave horses behind and get back to his usual life. This weekend—errands. Next week, plane trips and sales calls in Santa Barbara and Salt Lake City. He hoped he wouldn't run into Jorge. The thought of seeing him brought him right back to his friend's grim reality. At least Wade still had a job.

∞

Wade wanted to tell Jorge outright that he was history, to quote Ray, but he couldn't. As well as he got on with Ray, his boss would have written Wade off in a heartbeat if he thought he'd betrayed a trust. "Not much is more important than loyalty—nothing, really," Ray had said repeatedly. Wade had seen him turn on people dramatically if he thought they'd been disloyal.

He kept asking himself how he could warn Jorge without exposing that Wade knew his situation was hopeless. He thought he might have an opportunity when Jorge came into the lunchroom one morning. As Wade was reading the *San Francisco Chronicle* before joining a conference call, Jorge walked over to him, and Wade stood up. There wasn't much time, so Wade came right to the point. "Are you getting your résumé out to places?"

"I'm going to tough it out here." Jorge was adamant. "I don't think Ray's announcement applies to me."

Wade shook his head. "The Valley's hot. If I were you, I'd be looking. I found some leads for you. Here's a list."

Jorge looked it over. "No, I've decided to try to hang in here. I'll get through this probation thing and ride it out. Lydia was much nicer yesterday."

Wade put his arm around the shoulder of his friend. "I'm late for my conference call, but as a friend, I tell you it's time for you to start a gonzo job search. You've got great skills. The response you'll get from these people will make you feel better, even if you stick around here."

Jorge shrugged.

Wade suspected that Jorge wasn't going to do one thing for himself until SnyderSound walked him out the door, and that worried him.

∞

At home that night after dinner, Wade read the book Cliff had given him at the ranch. The book began centuries earlier with the story of the native Costanoans, before the land was broken up into ranches. The creek that ran through the ranch had been wilder then, providing not only steelhead trout, which still swam there, but salmon, too. Now, except when it flooded, nobody thought much about the San Francisquito Creek running through Jasper Ridge Ranch.

Wade liked the way Cliff had detailed how the ranch had changed hands, ending up in the estate of Leland Stanford. The University owned it now—rumor had it that Senator Stanford continued purchasing property even as he was facing death. Another interesting detail—the ranch had been used for artillery practice during both world wars.

Skimming through the book made Wade think about Diana and her intriguing life. What if Wade just called her up, instead of waiting for her move—why not? What did he have to lose? He dialed her number. When she picked up, he asked, "How was your day?"

She hesitated long enough that Wade thought she might be surprised to hear from him. Then she said, "Rob took the kids to the beach, someplace called Half Moon Bay, so I've been alone since noon."

"I've been reading Cliff's book," Wade said. "He has an engaging style. Who would think anyone could make Jasper Ridge Ranch seem so interesting."

"I love the trail along the stream. That's one thing that's better than Texas by a long shot—we don't have many green trails like that. I'm on my way to the ranch right now to check on the horses."

"How about some company?" Wade asked.

"I'll only be there for a few minutes. Rob's bringing the kids back tonight. I doubt it's worth your time. But if you're interested . . ."

"I am. I'd like to see the ranch at night. Can I pick you up?"

She hesitated. "No, thanks. But how about I meet you there in fifteen minutes?" While Wade wished they were going together, he understood that Diana probably intended going slow, not jumping into a relationship. He tried not to take it personally—convinced himself it was her nature to be careful.

When Wade drove onto the ranch property, the moon hung low over the far hills behind Jasper Ridge itself. Because of the oaks, the hill's outline against the sky was blurry, making it unclear where the hill ended and the sky began.

The ranch had none of its midday busyness. Except for a light in a distant barn, it seemed they were alone. The first stars had come out. The moon was close to full, and Wade could see quite clearly without lights. He took a deep breath, trying to let the ranch fill him up.

Diana had already led Gray Cloud out of his paddock and tied him to a rail inside the lighted barn. "I let Cliff ride him today, so I want to make sure he's okay."

"You just like to spend time out here," Wade said.

Diana laughed. "You're starting to understand me." She put a halter on Artemis and tied her next to Gray Cloud. She pulled back Gray Cloud's upper lip under a light, pointing out purple numbers inside to Wade. "See that tattoo? Every thoroughbred has one, to mark horses for the track."

"So they know for certain which horse won the race?"

"Right." Diana hesitated before she said, "You've got it." She carried her saddle from the tack room and threw it over Grey Cloud's Dutch door.

"Why do you use such small saddles?"

"For jumping," said Diana. "Western saddles are like easy chairs, but too bulky to jump in. You can't move with the horse."

She started oiling her saddle. Wade hoped she wasn't tiring of his questions. "I rode one time, with Amelia," he said. "In the middle of a long train of slow horses. They had saddle horns, so I guess they were Western. I'd hate to come over a jump and land on that horn."

She didn't look up. He wondered how to ask her if he could ride and chanced one more question. "If I were to give these little saddles a try, what special equipment would I need?"

"Are you really interested? If you are, you wouldn't need much. A boot with a heel."

Wade looked down at his loafers. "I have a pair of cowboy boots at home—Wellingtons. That's all I need?" This was getting real, making him a little nervous.

Diana seemed to take her time thinking it over. Finally, she said, "I have an extra saddle and a spare helmet. I could scare up a western saddle—they *are* safer."

"No, if I were to do it with you, I'd try one of those little ones— it's not *too* dangerous, is it?"

"Maybe you could ride Artemis. *She* wouldn't throw you. If she trips on a front foot, though, you could come off."

"How likely is that?"

"At a walk—as fast as I'd start you out—not at all."

Wade hesitated. "Maybe I could ride her on that trail by the creek?"

She laughed. "Not the first day!"

As she carried her shiny-clean saddle to the tack room, she looked like she owned the barn, the ranch, the whole county. When she walked back over to Wade, it was all he could do not to reach out and kiss her.

4

That night Wade dreamed he was naked, walking, leading Artemis up above Jasper Ridge Ranch. A bear appeared in a field and began chasing him. Artemis ran off on her own. Bears can move fast, but Wade had a head start and somehow knew that if he could get to the water, he would be safe. He dashed downhill with the bear gaining on him. He made the creek and jumped in. It was a hot summer day, and the cool water felt good. The bear entered downstream, his attention now on fishing, making him less ominous. Wade tried to catch salmon in his hands before they got to the bear, but they slipped away. He held one briefly, but it was slimy in his hands and escaped. The bear devoured it in a few bites. He gave up and lay back in the cool water. Let the bear have his fish. Artemis came over next to him and drank from the stream.

Once awake, he rolled over in his bed, trying to glean any sense from his dream. It had seemed so real.

∞

Diana and Wade still didn't go out at night, but they spent time on the phone and had an occasional cup of coffee together. Sometimes he asked her, and twice she asked him. When they got together, usually at the Palo Alto Café, they grilled each other about their histories as if they were studying for exams.

One afternoon Diana told him Rob's Dallas law firm, with its new branch up on Sand Hill Road, was one of the biggest in the country.

"My life seems uninteresting in comparison, I'm afraid."

"Not really." She leaned forward. "You have more going on than those guys Rob used to bring home, I assure you." When Wade rolled his eyes, she laughed. "Tell me more about your job—I don't know anything about Silicon Valley."

He explained how he had been involved in sales from the technical end and was now working with customers full time, directly with the CEO. After a while he told her about Jorge's probation. "Theoretically he can get himself out of the dog house," he said, "but Sherry—the owner's wife—indicated it's just a required step on his way out."

"Ouch." Diana looked away. "If you told your friend he was being let go—Jorge, right?—you could lose your own job. So, you *are* stuck in the middle."

He sighed. "You got it. I go to the office determined to tell him as much as I can without telling him outright. I even called people who could help him—two managers in other companies and a headhunter. When I told him, he just glanced at the paper and stuffed it into his pocket. I don't think he's called anyone."

"You talk about him like he's your brother. But you don't have much in common on the surface level. He must be good at his job."

"He is. I hired Jorge, and I remember how impressed I was when I interviewed him. He'd just finished his associate's degree in electronics. Eventually we became very close. I was honored when he and his wife asked me to become their daughter's godfather. It's a role I take seriously. I helped him and his wife move out here from El Paso, and I feel responsible for him in some way."

"It's an interesting situation. What does the godfather role entail?"

"Eva's only five, so I haven't done much yet," Wade said. "I show up at her birthday parties loaded down with presents. I've set up an account and put aside a little money to help with her college. I don't know what else is involved."

She stirred her coffee and nodded slowly. "Does he have problems with customers very often?"

"Almost never. Most customers love Jorge. He can set up a killer sound system in an hour and fix most problems over the phone. You'd like him if you met him, Diana."

"Is he a poet, too?"

Wade laughed. "Jorge? No. He's an engineer without the degree. He has a real knack for systems. I think he's not looking around because he thinks a miracle will happen, and he'll keep his job. When I was in management, I learned that sometimes you have to be blunt. I have no idea what Lydia's telling him. And by the way, even Jorge has no idea I write poetry. Nobody at work does. I want them to think of me as a good business guy, a pro. Imagine a tight situation comes up. Would you send out your poet?"

Diana laughed. "That sounds a little negative, but I guess I understand. Still, I want to see more of your poetry. I want to *know* you."

Wade took a moment to respond. The person he showed in his poetry felt different from his public self. Yet she wanted to get to know him, and he loved that. But sometimes his poetry was so raw he didn't want her to know. What to do? After a huge sigh, he decided to go along. "Okay—you can laugh with me at my latest *accomplishment*—a rejection slip from *Poetry* magazine. I just got it in the mail and threw it in my briefcase, proud that it was initialed by an editor, with a scrawled word—*Sorry*."

"May I see it?"

"This is probably a mistake," Wade said, finding the poem, with its paper-clipped rejection slip, "but I'll read it to you." He folded back the rejection, cleared his throat, and began . . .

Invitation to the Opera

They say to handle each paper once,
but I can never do that with the opera invites,
for I am someone who would like to like opera.
So when one comes, along with the bills,
college reunion and credit-card offerings to my ex-wife,
fundraising letters from my daughter's expensive college,
small magazines that published my work
(magazines I keep renewing but never find time to read),
it's the opera offer I can't throw away.

It would be so good for the kids if I could get them to go.
I wonder whether to subscribe or just pick one or two.
Perhaps start with a familiar name.
La Traviata, Madame Butterfly, Aida, or *Carmen.*
Or how about these colorful ads for the new ones:
The Death of Klinghoffer or *Nixon in China*—
any program that puts the stars in tails and flowing gowns.
Some Wednesday, Friday, or Saturday, maybe next season
I'll be there, part of the daringly-dressed audience
as the lights dim. Imagine me in that heart-stopping
quiet just before the songs echo into the night.

"That's fun," Diana said. "We always went to the opera openings in Dallas."

There was that *we* again, he thought. She must have seen some emotion on his face, because she said, "Sorry, old habits die hard. Say, I have a girlfriend back in Dallas who lives for the opera. Can I have a copy for her?"

"Sure, take this one." He removed the rejection slip and handed her the poem.

"I'll send this to Sally, if you don't mind. How many times did you rewrite it?"

"A bunch—it's embarrassing. Sixty times at least, probably, not including little one-word changes."

"Sounds like that guy who kept rolling the rock up the hill. Sisyphus, right? Do you want to be like him?"

"It's kind of who I am, Diana. I get a poem going, you know, and just work on it. I'm not sure where the words come from or why. Once I start, the poems seem to nag at me, wanting me to change a word or a line break or something."

She moved closer to Wade and reread the poem silently, her hands delicately holding the paper. "I see what keeps you coming back." She was so close he could put his arm around her, but reading his poem through her eyes made him so nervous that he didn't.

"There's a local reading Friday. Maybe you could come."

After another long look at the poem, still sitting on the table, she smiled. "It wouldn't be a *date*, right?"

"Of course not," Wade said, feeling his face grow hot, because he wished it *were* a date. But she'd be with him. "No date, but how does a *shared cultural event* sound?" he asked.

∞

The night of the poetry reading Diana was as insistent on driving herself in her own car as Wade was intent on picking her up. They compromised by meeting at the café, which was only a few blocks from the reading. Wade got there early and went over the opera poem in his car while he waited. When he saw her drive into the parking lot in her large white SUV, the kind you see in motorcades, he was glad they were meeting at the café first, and that he could drive. He didn't know if his reservation came from an environmental concern or some class issue, but some of the poets were just scraping by in expensive Palo Alto, and he'd be much more comfortable pulling up alongside the other poets in his little Audi wagon than he would have in her land-yacht with its Texas plates.

As he thought this, he questioned why he was uptight about what kind of car he showed up in. Something about class—could he possibly craft a poem on that subject? Then he remembered trying to write about the concept of class differences in an essay on *The Great Gatsby* for sophomore English and the problems he ran into—was Gatsby pursuing Daisy because of class, even though he had more money?

Class was hard to pin down except as something people cared about but shouldn't. Wade felt a little twinge of a headache and realized he hated thinking about class. He'd eventually given up on the essay and instead wrote about the novel's symbols, starting with the obvious ones—the green light at the end of Daisy's dock and the eyes of Doctor T. J. Eckleburg.

Diana walked to his car with her usual fast pace, which he associated with decisiveness. He was attracted to her bold, assertive manner. Indeed, he thought as she climbed in, he liked everything about her—her reddish dark hair, her eyes set off by just a hint of makeup, the way she dressed, tonight a matching sweater and skirt with a scarf—seemed both tasteful and appealing. *And, let's face it, sexy*. He'd recently begun to have dreams about Diana, of kissing her. Looking over at her seated in his car this time, he decided that, if all went well, he'd try to get closer to her sometime that night.

He drove through the few blocks in the "South of Oregon" half of Palo Alto, Wade's home turf. "This area had been orchards and a dairy farm until the fifties, when it was divided into lots and sprinkled with a couple of strip malls and fifteen or twenty churches," he told Diana. "The reading is in a Quaker meeting house." He drummed his fingers on the steering wheel, glad to be joining his friends but not sure how Diana would like them.

They walked into the entryway of the simple one-story structure, already buzzing with poets. He steered Diana toward an earnest-looking Spanish professor who'd taken up poetry in midlife and had already won an award. After he introduced them, the two found things to talk about. His worry about whether Diana would be comfortable here dissipated as he watched them chatting comfortably.

As they stood in line for Wade to sign up to read, Jim, a regular, cut in front of them. Jim was well over six feet, with thinning hair escaping from a bandanna—a hill of a man, almost a mountain. Diana stepped back. Wade knew that Jim wasn't the kind of poet who would appeal to her—and not just because he lived in a trailer in a friend's driveway.

Out of Jim's earshot, Wade whispered to Diana, "He can be a little overwhelming, but Jim is a founder of this group and writes good, strong stuff. Years ago he wrote a poem about Whitman that I still love. You'll see—he's reading before the break. I don't read until after."

They walked into the carpeted meeting hall where chairs faced one another in an oval. The podium was at one end of the oval, in front of a fireplace.

"There must be sixty people," said Diana. "Will they all read?"

"No. Less than half, I'd guess." A few poets brought props. One read a poem that picked up the rhythm of a Conga drum he played. Another read a poem about her sister and passed around a faded snapshot of the two of them as children. But most of them, often shyly, unfolded their wrinkled piece of paper to read their poem.

The Spanish professor began with a short poem, first in English, then in Spanish. The English version, with so many short one-syllable Anglo-Saxon diphthongs—Wade heard one line as "I bent down to touch my toes"—made Wade wonder if anyone could make it sound as lyrical as the smooth Spanish.

The poems that followed were as diverse as the people. Some had a political slant, some were a bit angry. Even more were humorous. The funniest moment came when an older woman read a poem about a frog-licking contest. Wade stole glances at Diana, who smiled and nodded through most of them.

Jim, in his tie-dyed bandanna, played a kazoo before he started his poem about a stuffed teddy bear with a headband like Jim's that his lover, now departed, had given him. Not too long into the poem it became obvious that Jim had been using the teddy bear to masturbate.

Diana said, "Oh, no. *No.*" Her face was taut. She whispered, "It's just *awful.*"

Wade said, "Shhh, it takes courage to read a poem like that. Let him finish, at least."

Jim modulated his voice down for the ending.

"... it's starting
to stink. When it gets too bad
I'll leave it outside her kitchen door, hanging
by its little headband."

Diana wrinkled her brow and kept moving in her seat, leaning forward and then back, crossing and uncrossing her legs. She leaned over and whispered, "That was just plain sick."

"There's misogyny, I'll admit that, but in there somewhere is a plea of loneliness."

"I can't believe nobody walked out."

"Diana, relax. Look, a few people are clapping."

She looked Wade up and down. "I'm sorry, but I'm leaving."

Wade felt she'd stabbed him. "But I'm reading after the break."

"No one would put up with that garbage in Dallas, I assure you. I don't belong here. These are things not to be brought up, period." She shook her head. "I bent the rules to come out tonight, a mistake I won't make again." She stood to leave. "Take me to my car."

When Wade hesitated, she said, "If you can't give me a ride, I'll have to walk."

He put his head down and followed her. People moved their knees aside to let them pass. When they got out the door, Wade didn't look back, but he knew people were staring.

They got into his car and drove toward hers, silent the entire way.

When he parked in the café parking lot, she hopped out without a word and climbed up into her SUV. Wade walked up to her window. She lowered it and said, "Thanks for inviting me. I wish it had worked out differently." She started her engine and drove off.

Wade took deep breaths of the cool air as he watched her taillights brighten at the stop sign and dim, and then disappear.

"*Goodbye, Diana,*" Wade whispered, as he drove back to the Friends Meeting House to read his poem. He didn't want to share his sadness and managed to read without incident. A couple of people he hadn't met, who identified themselves as opera fans, even came up to him afterwards and thanked him for his poem. He wished Diana had seen how much people seemed to like his work.

Diana—gone. Would they even get a chance to say a real goodbye? What about that kiss he had fantasized about. Oh, what difference did that make? She was gone.

∞

Later, falling asleep, Wade pictured his freighter and her cruise ship on opposite courses a mile apart, two ships passing in the night.

Early the next morning, in bed, Wade was dreamily back in the lonely days of his divorce. One of the best things about being married, he used to assume, was that you get to relax. With the romantic side of your life settled, you can concentrate on other things like work and poetry. He cringed as he remembered how wrong he was. Taking Liz for granted had been the worst mistake of his life. He was blind and got blindsided. One night he was sitting at his own dining room table across from this guy Liz had known since high school, this lanky fellow, "Brad." Wade's third eye knew Brad was a problem even then, but he was just finishing a poem that night, so Wade ignored his instincts. He worried not a whit about Brad and his family's farm in Western Massachusetts. That was a bad decision, and before he knew it, Brad was taking Liz to that farm. The fact that Wade's parents had stuck together through thick and thin hadn't prepared him for her resolve.

When Liz said she was leaving, Wade gave up and focused on their daughter Amelia. He didn't want her to go through having her mom on one coast and Wade on the other. And his resentment entered in, too. He was so angry that whatever chance he had of holding on to Liz was destroyed by his unforgiving surliness.

∞

Saturday, as he was waking up, again he dreamed he was back in the lonely days of his divorce. In his restless dream, Diana replaced Liz, and then she, too, left Wade. He turned over and tried to get control of his thoughts. How could he have been so wrong about Diana?

He would miss her—seeing her at the café in that riding outfit, yes. He'd certainly miss the hope of having a woman in his life who was secure enough that he could count on her. He'd miss horses, too. It was hard to believe that all that would suddenly disappear. Maybe he would take riding lessons on his own. Without Diana. At any rate, the relationship had been nipped in the bud.

What could he have done better? He and Diana had just started out, so the situation was completely unlike the one with Liz, whom he had lived with for eighteen years, but the pain felt familiar. It must be the poetry. But Diana hadn't even waited to hear any of his work at the reading. Had her interest in his writing been a lie? Wade had instinctively defended the poet that she railed against. Did he make a mistake, shushing Diana? Instead, should he have given credence to her concerns? One way or another, it was over. Perhaps his biggest mistake had been bringing Diana so deeply into his poetry life when they'd only just met.

On that sour thought, Wade got out of bed. After coffee, he whipped up an instant breakfast mixed with blueberries in the blender and started in on his day, beginning with the routine of caring for his dog. He ordinarily bathed Keats in the shower, but he decided on using the kitchen sink instead. Turned out that the basin wasn't big enough for a full-grown beagle. Water splashed all over the kitchen as he sudsed him down and rinsed him off. He grabbed two fluffy towels, one for each side of the dog.

The phone rang, and he put the towels down to hear Diana's slightly amplified voice on the answering machine. "Wade, are you there? I'd like to talk to you. I'm sorry about last night."

Keats shook wildly, soaking Wade's pants. Diana's voice on the machine churned up some pain—how easily she could turn him into a Prufrock, the creation of the poet T. S. Eliot when he was young . . . *decisions and revisions that a minute will reverse.* He picked up the phone. "Oh?"

"I don't want to talk about that other guy's poem, as it really bothered me. Still does," she started. "But would you mind answering one question about *your* poem, the opera one? The one I didn't stay to hear you read aloud last night?"

What was she thinking? "Sure," he said.

"I read your poem to Sally over the phone, you know, my friend in Dallas, and she asked me to fax it to her. She's a free spirit, but she may be just the person I needed to talk to. At any rate, she completely turned me around about last night's meeting. I was wrong. But, still, I have a question. The guy in your poem has never been to the opera. My question is—have you?"

"That's easy enough. A handful of times, yes."

"I guessed that. Even though the guy in the poem supposedly hasn't been to the opera, I gathered that you must have. And I guessed you like the art form."

"Yes," Wade said, uneasy about shading the truth in his work.

"Sally says they call those poems *confessional* poems. Is that right?"

He wished they could stop talking about his poem. Still, he was overwhelmingly relieved that she'd called and, moreover, she'd apologized. But he had to answer her question. "I prefer the phrase self-referential, but, yes, confessional is the popular term."

"Aren't you supposed to say what actually happened?" she asked. "That's where I'm confused. I mean, you've been to the opera, but the guy in your poem hasn't."

"It's a gray area," Wade said, impressed by the sincerity of her interest. "A self-referential poem has to be true, but in its own way. There are layers of truth."

"Well, at any rate, that's not why I called. What I hope you're telling me is there's some chance that the guy with the bandanna never even touched a Teddy bear."

Wade laughed into the phone louder than he intended. "Sorry." He'd had no idea that this was where she was leading. When he settled down, he said, "For the sake of Teddy bears everywhere, I wish that could be true, Diana. But . . . I doubt it. We'll never know for sure, of course. I guess I could ask Jim."

"Anyway, I'm not pleased with how I acted." She hesitated. "But I deserved it, I was interrupting a poem. And poems mean more to you than they do to me. Some of those poets seemed so negative. I like positive people who get out and do things."

"Like what?" he asked.

"I don't know, just about anything—you know, throw dinner parties, ride horses, go skiing, *things*."

"The world you talk about, dinner parties and horses, is pretty distant from mine."

"You sound like you've written me off."

"With what you said last night, *yes*, I thought you'd written me off. You seem different today," he said.

"Wade . . . how about lunch tomorrow?"

No wonder Shakespeare compared women to the ever-changing moon. Wade hesitated, then said, "I guess we could meet downtown— *Il Fornaio* or *Evvia*, even *Maddelena's*."

"Oh, I was hoping you'd come over here. I wanted you to see how I fixed my place up."

"Sure." What a turnaround. Not just to see where she lived, but to be invited in.

Before he hung up, she gave him her address. It was at one of those new luxury downtown condos. These three- or four-million-dollar apartments were part of a new America. Wade's opinions about this luxury growth ran the gamut of how wonderful it was for Palo Alto, to resentment that he could never afford them, and a little provincial, "I'm here—pull up the drawbridges" thrown in.

5

Wade had stayed away from his office to avoid Jorge, whom he feared might show up at any time. He'd fallen behind in finishing the sales report Ray expected of him every Monday, but Diana's invitation gave him new energy. He decided to pop into work and get the report out of the way on Saturday, when there was little chance of seeing Jorge.

For the report, Wade needed to update fifteen customer situations. He sent a few emails to customers, so he could update it on Monday. Noon in California, when he'd report, would be afternoon on the East coast, so he could include a few last-minute responses.

He was consolidating what data he had when Jorge appeared and plopped himself down in his guest chair. "You should have protected me, you sonofabitch."

"Oh, Jorge, what's going on?"

"You see the CEO every day, Wade. The *owner*. You couldn't do anything?"

Wade turned toward him, face to face. "I did all I could, Jorge, really. The company is in a lot of trouble. Tell me exactly what Lydia has done."

"She put me on probation, the bitch."

Wade tried to seem surprised, but wasn't sure Jorge bought it. So he took a different tack, a somber tone. "We kind of saw that coming, didn't we?"

Jorge stood up by Wade's window, which overlooked the parking lot. "We? You really couldn't keep this from happening?"

Wade shook his head as he watched the few people coming in to work on a Saturday. He sighed deeply. The roach coach made its noisy entrance, staccato notes playing on its musical horn. Wade remembered the food truck had started coming in on Saturdays since the reduced staff worked more overtime.

"Well, you could at least buy me a cup of coffee," Jorge said.

"Sure." As they walked downstairs, he asked Jorge if he'd called those prospective managers. "You know, that list I gave you. At least call that guy at H.P. Larry used to be a neighbor, the nicest guy and he seems interested. He's expecting you to call him."

"That may not be necessary," Jorge said. "I'm doing a lot better. Lydia's been civil, almost nice, ever since I started this probation thing. She even smiled at me yesterday. Besides, I have *you* in my corner. I still do, right?"

At the food truck Wade turned directly to his friend. "Of course I'm in your corner, Jorge, but you know I'm out of management, so I've kind of lost my vote. Technically I work for Lydia now, too. By the way, you'd better watch it around her when she smiles. I mean that."

Jorge shook his head and changed the subject. "So are you and this Diana, you know?" He gyrated his hips forward.

"No, we're not," Wade said, rolling his eyes and awkwardly mimicking Jorge's hip motion. "But I'm hoping we'll still ride horses. And she's invited me to lunch."

"Horses? Man, you're going to get yourself killed." He gave Wade a little hit on his shoulder. After ordering his coffee in Spanish, he turned and said, "This Diana must be some woman."

"Yeah, she's got my number," he said. "I'm kind of hooked."

∞

Once they walked back upstairs, Wade stood outside his office and tried to get Jorge to leave, saying, "Meanwhile, call those numbers. Start with Larry and mention my name."

"Ever since you interviewed me on campus down in El Paso, Wade, I've trusted you. You're a big part of the reason I took this job. Face it, Marita and I wouldn't be in California if it weren't for you. And Eva. We're so proud you're her godfather."

Wade inhaled deeply and held him by both shoulders. "Jorge, I couldn't help you last month, and I can't now. But in that job search world, you've got to network. They're all expecting to hear from you. At least I know for sure that Larry is. Call him, okay?"

Jorge nodded as he left, but Wade doubted he'd call anyone.

∞

Only one week earlier, when Diana walked out of the poetry reading, Wade had been convinced things were over with her forever. He still found her appealing—more than appealing—and he liked the way he felt when she was around. Like he'd told Jorge, she had his number. She had made a pretty deep impression on him, but still, their worlds were too far apart.

When she had invited him to her condominium, his joy was tinged with confusion. Well, today should tell the tale, he thought as he drove to the posh condominium area of Palo Alto near downtown, found her address, and parked on the street.

In the lobby, he pushed a button on the keypad next to her name. When she picked up, Wade said, "Hi honey, I'm home."

She laughed. "Oh, you *are* silly, Wade. Come on up." She buzzed him into a small elevator. The door opened at the top floor onto an outdoor alcove. A teak loveseat and an impressive half-size brass statue of a horse flanked the front door. When she opened it, she gave him a quick hug. "It's good to see you again."

In the kitchen, a table in the corner had been colorfully prepared for two. When he realized she'd set it for them, complete with cut flowers, it gave Wade an unexpected warm feeling and a tad of hope.

"Let me show you around," she said. The living room decor, designed for entertainment, with English foxhunting scenes interspersed among more modern artwork on the walls, caught Wade's attention. One of the horses reminded him of Artemis. The table in the dining room could seat twelve or fourteen people easily. Wade imagined she hosted great dinner parties. His dining room could never accommodate more than eight for a dinner party.

Diana showed him the kids' bedrooms and the guest room where her cat lay sprawled in a sun patch on the bed.

She led him to the intimacy of her bedroom, complete with a fireplace and balcony, more like a suite, her bed topped with a small mountain of pillows. Several crosses were affixed to the wall across from the fireplace. One was at least a foot tall, almost square, with four red and white arrowhead tips coming off the wings of the cross. "Isn't this a Maltese cross?" he asked.

She nodded. "Yes, I got that in Valletta. I used to bring a cross home from every trip." She pointed to an ebony one. "I like this one from Kenya."

"So you're religious?"

She laughed. "I know Californians dismiss Texas as being a part of the Bible belt, but that's where I'm from. If it weren't for my faith, I could not have survived the last eighteen months."

He was thankful she had told him that—it helped him understand her. He hoped she wouldn't ask him about his religious beliefs, which were strong but difficult to explain. He believed in God, but her display of all these crosses made him nervous.

The pictures scattered around the room included horses and dogs. Diana was jumping horses in several of them, sometimes big jumps—the rails she was clearing were shoulder high. Her mastery overwhelmed him. Who said *do one thing well?* Wade thought it might be a Zen saying—better not bring that up.

She pointed to a picture of herself with a frizzy-haired blonde woman about her age, with red-framed glasses and a big smile. "That's Sally, my friend from Dallas. She's the one who loves poetry and opera. Since I sent her your opera poem, she's now a fan of yours and not at all happy that I walked out of the poetry reading—she said

I was being *rude*." Diana took a deep breath. "I don't like to think of myself that way, but perhaps she's right."

"I'd like to meet her sometime and thank her." Now that he had learned how Diana thought, he could begin to see the whole incident from her perspective. He scanned the other photographs. "No pictures of Rob?"

She laughed, shaking her head. "All his photos seem to have gone missing since the trip out here."

Wade nodded approvingly. He could make out the Great Wall of China in one shot, and the Pyramids of Giza in the background of another. "You obviously travel a lot."

"Rob and I were always taking trips. I've finally come around to thinking travel might be a fool's paradise after all. I haven't been out of the country since we separated except once, to Merida—you know, the Yucatan. Rob thought we could patch things up in a foreign place. It didn't work, of course, although I did like that part of Mexico." Wade liked that little "of course" she threw in.

In the kitchen, he took a seat at the counter while Diana made lunch. She glanced over at him as she whipped up a sauce, folding in spices. She toasted bread and basted some whitefish under the broiler. "We can start with this salad. Sorry, the tomato's a bit too firm. I don't usually drink wine at lunch, but I left out the bottle in case you wanted some. If it looks good, open it."

Wade hesitated. He didn't often drink wine at lunch, but maybe today . . . "Okay, I'll do the honors," he said as he twisted the corkscrew and pulled the cork. Through the window he could see a hint of the University's red roofs and the hills beyond. "Quite the view," he said.

"I liked the idea of being near shopping and restaurants. I walk a lot." She moved over to him at the counter. "Wade, I've been working up the courage to tell you how Rob and I hit the rocks. We met at a sophomore mixer at SMU and were together our last three years of college. It went by effortlessly. We got married the summer before he started law school. It was all kind of a dream. Then Beth and Robbie came along, and the dream grew. Eleven years. Then . . . " She dabbed her eye with the corner of a linen napkin and pulled away from the counter.

Wade reached out and touched her arm. "You've got my full attention, but I know it's hard."

"This might be a good time to serve lunch." She fumbled with the silverware.

After preparing and serving plates, she picked at her food as she continued. "One day, out of the blue, I got a call from a woman across town. She said Rob was involved with her daughter, an Aggie student with a summer job at the firm." She turned away. Her eyes glistened. "A second-year intern. Such a cliché."

He shook his head. "I'm sorry."

She used her napkin to dry her eyes again. "When he first told me, I was determined to hold the marriage together. He said the affair was over, but he was still looking at other women. Before then I guess I'd always glanced the other way. I spent hours in the gym to stay slim, and one day I bought six hundred dollars' worth of lingerie at Neiman-Marcus."

Wade tried to envision such delights. "That's a lot of skivvies."

Diana smiled and said, "Oh, these were a lot more than underwear. But push-up bras and lace panties aren't probably something I'm supposed to talk about with a man. I have to admit, one of the reasons I'm not dating is that it's so foreign to me. My experience pretty much started and ended with Rob." She squeezed a lemon onto her fish, juice squirting her eye, and she laughed.

Wade guessed that she hadn't dated much. He loved being with her this way, with her opening up to him. He nodded as he ate the tender fish, which broke apart with a touch of his fork.

"This subject makes me sweat." She wiped her forehead with a napkin. "At any rate, a few months later at a party, I got jealous of a woman I thought Rob was paying too much attention to. Maybe that last flirtation was innocent—I'm not sure—but one way or the other, I stopped caring right then. I could tell you the exact moment." She left the rest of her fish on the plate, put her fork down, and patted her mouth with the napkin. "No trust, no glue."

When they finished, she cleared the dishes. "It's been three years now since I left that big house in Dallas. It had seven bedrooms and a second kitchen out by the pool. I've kind of been standing on one foot."

Wade shook his head. "For standing on one foot, you seem awfully stable." He took her hand. She squeezed his fingers, and her touch warmed him. "You're going slowly. That seems to be your style. You've put your kids first. You'll never be sorry for that. And Rob's law firm definitely seems to be," he looked around, "cushioning life's blows."

She shrugged. "The firm's grown fast. It's still Rob's father's, but Rob's office out here is getting to be as important as his Dallas location, now. The Enersystems account, you know, the account Jolene's husband, Billy Tyler, heads up? The company has energy projects all over the world now. It's become the biggest account in the firm."

They made small talk as if they were old friends with nothing left to decide when, really, nothing at all had been decided. As they finished, Wade noticed the music Diana had playing softly in the background, James Taylor singing, "You've Got a Friend." She seemed so much kinder today, so much softer. He sang along with the phrase, "and ain't it good to know?" before he looked at her and asked, "May I have this dance?"

She looked up and moved toward him. Her body was familiar in his arms, as if it were not the first time. It took all his control to refrain from kissing her.

On leaving, passing through her front door, he brushed against her. Impulsively, he leaned over and tried to kiss her. When she backed off, he took her hand. She guided him over to the loveseat placed outside the front door.

Rather than embrace, Diana pulled away from him and looked at her watch. "I worry that Rob will come back." Then she shrugged. "Of course, he has to phone me to get in. Since he's paying the rent through his firm, he thought he deserved a key, but I said no. He didn't like that one bit."

When Wade said, "Let's go back inside," he cleared his throat.

She took his hand and held it gently, but shook her head. She wrapped her arms around his neck for a kiss, and said, "I'm not sure I'd trust myself." They were soon as breathless as teenagers. "We'd better take it easy," she said.

Wade froze, but Diana smiled up at him. "Don't stop, though."

They held each other and kissed some more. Her lips felt so soft and responsive. He pressed against her. "You'd better go now." But she didn't make any sudden move to get up, and he pressed harder. They were about to lose themselves to each other.

∞

Diana loosened up the reins on the no-date rule. Wade still didn't come over on the nights she had Beth and Robbie, but they spent most of the other evenings together. She made wonderful dinners, after which they'd snuggle and tease each other.

She told him she was not sure if their relationship should become intimate, but Wade resigned himself to waiting. He hoped she was bridling at the bit as much as he was.

∞

If there was any consolation, at least Wade's horseback riding picked up. He rode Artemis twice a week, while Diana schooled him on horsemanship—everything from how to control Artemis while he slipped the bridle over her head, to the subtle messages, like pressing his thighs against her sides and whispering encouraging words in her ear, that he gave her as he rode. Diana gave Wade most of his instruction until an incident occurred when he was learning to trot, one that scared them both.

She was riding Gray Cloud, and he was mounted on Artemis

next to Diana on the oval track surrounding the polo field at Jasper Ridge Ranch, feeling pretty good about how he'd been improving his technique. As Artemis trotted, churning both legs on one side, then the other, Wade concentrated on how her back rose up and down with each step. He worked on the knack of moving with her. As he concentrated on his position in the saddle, he was inadvertently loosening his reins.

Just then the wind blew a gate open across the field and Gray Cloud shied. Wade spun around in his saddle. Diana stayed up on Gray Cloud, but in reaction Artemis shied too—a sudden sharp twist to the left—and Wade fell off on her right. The wood-chip track was softer than he'd expected. He lay there for a moment, not sure what had happened. More embarrassed than hurt, Wade noticed the fear on Diana's face as she knelt beside him. And he saw that she was close to crying, her face twisted in what Wade thought was an attempt to hold herself together.

Wade groaned and sat up.

"This is my fault. We're going to have to get you lessons from a real trainer. I'll find someone here at the ranch. Edward doesn't like to teach *up downs*, as he calls beginner lessons, but maybe he'll make an exception. We've got you way beyond the basics, so maybe he'll do it." She helped him stand. "Your back is healed, right? You didn't hurt it, I hope."

"Yes, it's healed. One hundred percent, and I'm okay. The only thing that hurts is my pride." He dusted off his shirt and his pride.

∞

Soon Wade was taking lessons from Edward and a couple of other trainers at the ranch. Diana and he still rode regularly, too, side by side in the training rings and occasional trail rides off the ranch. Wade also noticed Diana seemed more relaxed now that she did not have to teach him everything. She'd quiz him on what he'd learned, but she seemed happy to have handed his tutelage over to those who taught riding all day long.

∞

For Wade's birthday, Diana offered to take him out on the town. "It'll be a real date, but I insist on treating you." She kept the dining location a secret. He was pleasantly surprised that she wanted a real date with him, and even more impressed when they drove into the valeted parking lot of the Village Pub in Woodside—a place he always wanted to go but, except a couple of times Ray had hosted a lunch for customers, Wade never frequented because of cost. It had a reputation as one of the best restaurants in the San Francisco Bay Area, and it lived up to its promise.

They started the evening early because Rob was returning the kids at eight-thirty. Wade and Diana were among the first dinner guests at the Pub, so the waiters were extremely attentive, almost hovering. They ordered the signature salmon with a butternut squash sauce, which they both loved. A chardonnay, a flourless cake, a dark roast coffee, and the evening was nearly complete.

Back at her condo, she gave him his presents, and he opened two packages to find Jodhpur boots and half-chaps, the leathers that riders use to protect their calves.

He wanted to stay with her, to thank her in ways other than words for the evening but once he tried on the chaps, the clock ran down, and the children's arrival was imminent. It was time to leave.

∞

Long before Thanksgiving, the two talked about Christmas plans. They both expressed a desire to be together for the holiday, but she felt duty-bound to return to her family in Texas. "Tradition can provide security in a time of change," she said on the phone one night.

Wade was disappointed. But he had no comeback to Diana's logic, so he accepted that she would spend Christmas in Dallas. He would miss her, but at least he'd have Amelia, who would be coming home for a visit.

He thought about trying to persuade Diana how comforting it would be for everyone if Beth and Amelia could spend time together.

He wanted Beth to see how Amelia had made Paly work for her, but he had to admit to himself that he still hadn't met Diana's kids—he'd talk with Diana about them for hours, but always *in absentia*, so he never brought Beth and Robbie up to Amelia.

In the end, Wade would spend Christmas without Diana, and, though she said she didn't care about Rob—"Really," she had said, "There's zero chance we'll get back together. Please don't be jealous of him." Still, Wade didn't like to think of her spending all that time with the man. He was, after all, still her husband. But Wade wanted to trust what she said was true—that she had no interest in Rob, that her one motivation was to have her kids with their grandparents for the holidays. Since he agreed with that goal, there was nothing he could say. Besides, he rationalized, with Amelia coming, it would give him a chance to think about who he and Diana were together.

6

The Wednesday before Thanksgiving, Jorge showed up in Wade's office around nine-thirty in the morning. "I thought you were working from home today," Jorge said, but he seemed glad to see Wade.

"I wanted to, but Ray's up in San Francisco with his banker buddies, and I have this report due Monday. You look sick or something. What's up, buddy?"

"When I tried to sign on to the computer, I got one of those unauthorized user messages."

It could be an error, but Wade doubted it. "That could be anything," he said, trying to cheer Jorge up. He put his sales reports away in a drawer.

Jorge seemed nervous. "That's not all. There was a post-it note from Lydia on my computer screen when I came in. She wants me to see her in her office at ten."

Wade looked at his watch. Lydia would see Jorge in twenty-five minutes. "The computer message could be a glitch," he told him. "Why don't I call down there for you?"

"Thanks." He sat down.

Wade tried to sound nonchalant with the help desk. "Jorge Calderon is working with one of my customers and there seems to be a problem. He can't log on."

"Sure, Mr. Middleton, I'll check and call you back."

When the phone rang, it wasn't the help desk. It was Günter, the personnel chief. *Not a good sign at all.* Wade spun his chair around, turning his back to Jorge.

"Wade, my good man," Günter said, "I understand Jorge Calderon is working with one of your customers. You might want to get on top of that. I'll come by your office this afternoon, okay? I can take you through all this." Wade knew that Günter's words were management jargon for 'Jorge's out of here, so you'd better adjust.' They signaled the end of Jorge's stint with the company, and a sense of futility set in, but he didn't want Jorge to pick up on it.

He agreed, ended the call, and turned back to Jorge. "It's fifteen minutes before you go in to see Lydia, right? Maybe it'd be good to take a walk around the parking lot, settle your thoughts."

"What did the help desk say?"

Wade had to face it head on. "It was Günter. You may be right—they may plan to walk you out the door. If they do, leave with your self-respect. The Valley's booming—you'll get another job."

"You knew this was coming, didn't you?"

"I *feared* it," Wade said, hearing his defensiveness as he said it.

"I thought you had pull. You let me down, Wade." Jorge's eyes squinted, glittered.

"I tried to help, I really did, Jorge. What *did* you do out in Las Vegas to piss the guy off? And why didn't you even hint to me what had happened? That Anderson guy might have called Ray."

"I started to tell you what happened, but I didn't understand it, and I was embarrassed," Jorge said. "Anderson is weird, a right-wing nutcase with the greasiest smile. I said some things to him I shouldn't have. I'd take them back if I could. It shouldn't cost me my job."

"Those are the types you have to be careful around."

"What can I do?" Jorge sounded desperate. "I need this job."

"It might be too late. Maybe too late for a long time."

After a long silence, Jorge said, "Okay, just tell me how to get through this meeting with Lydia."

"If you can stand a little humor, I'll tell you what my crazy uncle said. 'If you're going to get fired, sew some mistletoe to the back flap of your sport coat, hold your head high, and walk proudly out the door.'"

"You're not helping, Wade."

"Sorry. I understand. Be civil. Remember, no matter what their opinion is, you're a valuable person. You know that, and I do, too. Sorry for the cliché, but don't burn your bridges. There's always the delicate issue of recommendations. If you go too crazy, you could lose not only this job, but your next one too. Just be yourself, you'll do fine. Call me when you get out of the meeting. I'll take you for a drink or something."

∞

Wade had just hung up with a potential customer in Santa Barbara when Jorge called. "Yeah, they canned me. Günter sat in the office across from Lydia's as she fired me. I figured he was there to protect her if I threatened her or something. Can you imagine?"

"Jorge, how are you holding up? Tough deal. I hope we can get a drink later. Regarding Günter, you're probably right. It's probably standard procedure these days. Where are you now?"

"At my goddamned desk. Günter is coming back in ten minutes to escort me out. I put Eva's picture into a cardboard box, and I guess I'll take a few papers. They can keep their fucking service award."

Wade remembered fighting to get that award, which came along with $500, for his friend. But Jorge was right—it seemed like a worthless piece of paper now. "Like I said, maybe later I can take you out for a drink. Make sure you take your contact list—you never know when you'll want to phone an old customer or friend. Tell me exactly what went down in Lydia's office."

"Her desk didn't have a paper on it—completely bare, no calendar, no nothing. She waved her hand for me to sit in a small chair in front of her desk. The blinds were open behind her, so I couldn't see her face, just the outline. She started right in—I think I remember exactly what she said, 'I'm sorry we have to let you go. We're giving you two weeks' severance, plus I see you have six vacation days coming. We'll pay you for those too.' When I asked about the probation period, she said I'd improved, but 'not enough to keep you on. Things are very tight.'"

"Give me a break," Wade said.

Jorge continued, "I think I clenched my hands then, because her voice softened a bit. I might have started to get watery eyes or something because when she looked at me, she changed her tone. She said the company appreciated how hard I'd tried. Then she shrugged and said, 'There's some paperwork I'll need you to sign. And we need your badge.'" Jorge spoke in a monotone, almost as if this had happened to someone else.

"I pulled the lanyard with my badge from around my neck," he continued with a little laugh, "and handed it to her like a gold crown."

Wade sighed, and closed his eyes, as if that could shut out what Jorge was going through.

"Gotta go, Günter's here," Jorge said.

"Call me from your car."

Wade dashed to a window where he could see the lobby door. Jorge came out, walking ahead of Günter, carrying his box with the picture of Eva inside and little else. The scene played like a sad movie. He hoped this was the end of a sad story but had to admit it was just as likely to be the beginning of an even worse one.

∞

Two hours later Jorge called Wade back. "I couldn't go home. How can I tell Marita?" He was rambling, his words slurred. "I drive around—can't find Steve Jobs' house—he got fired from the company he founded, so it helps to think of him today—bosses are such idiots. Steve Jobs—can't believe he's gone, man. Dead—just like that. Which street is it on again?"

"Have you been drinking?"

"I stopped for a beer. Jobs was fired, right?"

"Close to it," Wade said. It was an event he'd studied. "Banished to another building, forced out. His house is at the corner of Waverley and Santa Rita. It's charming, has one of those roofs that wrap around into the eaves, like in Carmel."

"I've driven up one street and down another. These homes aren't very big, but you can tell they're expensive," Jorge said. "Teslas are like Chevys here. There's a Maserati." Wade could hear Jorge breathing into the phone. "Wait. Yep. There's where he lived. I'll park in front of it, underneath this big oak. Gardeners are tossing a lawnmower and a backpack blower into their truck bed. Until now, I felt way ahead of guys who come across the border to do any job at all." Jorge's voice quavered. "Hey, I have a job like a gringo, I wanted to tell them." Wade heard a bitter laugh. "Now I'm jealous of their outdoor lives. So carefree. My job paid more in a week than they make in a month. But today, I envy them."

7

Christmas crept up on Wade. He reconciled himself with Diana's visit home to Dallas, but that was before Amelia called and canceled *her* trip, a visit they had planned for months. She told him she had fallen behind and needed to stay at Bard through Christmas Eve to make up an exam and didn't have enough time to come to California. He remembered falling behind in college himself, so he couldn't get too mad at her, although deadlines were harsher in his day. He trusted Amelia enough that he didn't doubt what sounded like an excuse. He didn't remember anyone being able to make up an exam in his day. Times change.

At any rate, there was nothing Wade could do. He bundled up the presents he had purchased for her and air-expressed them to her at Liz's farm in Massachusetts and tried to move on to other things.

He tried to write a few poems, but nothing was flowing. Then he tried to at least send some old ones out, but he was too churned up even to do that. He ended up watching a late-night political comedian on TV.

He decided to take a page out of Diana's book and *do things* to get through the holiday week, recalling her voice the day she first invited him to her condo. "I like positive people who get out and *do things.*" He knew from her tone she wasn't putting him down, or even denigrating poets. That was her authentic voice. Wade was convinced they could learn from each other. Perhaps he could find a way to put her slightly more in touch with her heart while she coaxed him out of himself.

He started his Christmas at his old church on Tuesday night. He hadn't been there in three years, and it felt good to be back for the Christmas Eve service. He realized that churchgoing wasn't as much about religion, as it was being involved in a community. No wonder he hadn't been around lately, he didn't know anybody there.

∞

The next morning, Wade headed up to San Francisco for breakfast near Union Square, bringing his laptop. In bed that morning, he'd started a poem in his head and hoped that he could start work on it.

An ocean fog bank enveloped San Francisco, so the city streets were cloud-like and almost empty. Union Square without the press of people seemed strangely freeing. After a walk around the square, he followed the trolley tracks up to Sears Fine Foods, so popular with tourists that a line often formed out the door. Not today. The few patrons seemed to be families from out of town. A waiter—judging by his accent, Russian—invited Wade to sit at a table for two in the front window. Their signature silver-dollar pancakes were worth the trip. A young woman in a Harvard sweatshirt with the family at a nearby table reminded him of Amelia, so he turned away from her and looked out on the deserted, overcast street. The phrase "lonely Christmas" popped into his mind.

After the waiter cleared his plate and mused aloud about having to work on Christmas Day, Wade entered the lines he'd been working on into the computer. He only came up with two stanzas:

Fragment, Christmas Morning

On the Peninsula, in the fuzzy clarity of first light
    I vow to be easier on myself yet
    work harder for the things I care about.
        Life seemed so simple before I left home!

In the city, the only other soul in Union Square
avoids my eye. He is blanket-wrapped,
pushing a shopping cart. When he looks up
we regard each other as in a holy place.

He couldn't let himself get down like this. Perhaps a drive would cheer him up. He headed toward his car. Before long he was in his Audi, headed toward the ocean, passing scores of homeless people in Golden Gate Park. The homeless reminded him of the man with the blanket from earlier that morning. Wade was relatively lucky, he thought, but the thought didn't cheer him up.

The city ended at a three-story tourist mecca overlooking the Pacific called Cliff House. He parked and poked his head into the coffee shop. Should he have a latte? Most of the customers were grouped in families, too. He turned around and walked along a path overlooking the beach. Couples huddled under blankets. Couples, couples, couples. Would he be with Diana next year? He couldn't answer that question, he thought as he walked back to his car. Instead of taking the freeway home, he decided to follow Highway One, along the Pacific. Yes, that would be good, an unexpected way home.

Heading south, he drove thru the blustery beach town of Pacifica and passed the Devil's Slide area, with its new tunnel. How quickly the landscape became rural—fifteen minutes from the city he saw horses grazing. Farther south, Highway 1 once again ran close alongside the shoreline. At Half Moon Bay, he passed a wooden sign on a run-down horse stable that advertised OCEAN HORSEBACK RIDES. He vaguely remembered taking Amelia once to this stable a few years earlier. After the owner had convinced Wade that Amelia would be safe, he stayed back and worked on his computer in his car while he waited for her.

Now alone on the highway on this quiet Christmas Day, Wade pulled a U-turn and parked in front of a makeshift office where a small man wearing a large-brimmed white cowboy hat greeted him. Wade asked him if he could ride in tennis shoes.

"Sure," he said, "Our stirrups have a toe in 'em, not like them fancy English things. You'll be fine, sonny. Hop on that paint, we're about to head out." Wade hated to admit how much he liked being called Sonny as he neared the ripe old age of 44.

The poorly-groomed nags made Wade sharply aware of the quality of horses he was used to with Diana. He was assigned a dappled Appaloosa gelding named Painterly. He sank into his Western saddle— compared to an English saddle, it *did* feel like an easy chair—and joined a chain of somnambulant horses walking down to the beach. There was no detouring from the path—nose to tail all the way.

He couldn't stop thinking about Diana and their rides, especially when she rode next to him.

Still, riding alongside the ocean was as wonderful as he could have hoped, on a Christmas day with the gray-blue clouds fading into the ocean, its color only slightly darker. The leader even got his horse to step into the surf, and the other horses, including Painterly, followed suit. Wade regarded Painterly with new tenderness. What a difficult life he must lead! He was a *good boy*.

When the ride ended, Wade asked if there were any treats he could give Painterly. When the owner apologetically replied "no," he found a feed store in Half Moon Bay, but it was closed. At the Safeway he bought carrots and drove back and gave one to each of the horses he'd ridden with. Painterly got four. Wade saved the rest for Gray Cloud and Artemis.

When he arrived back home, he listened to an excited voicemail from Amelia, asking him to call back. Maybe his gifts had brightened her day. When he called her, she did indeed begin by ticking off the presents he'd sent. "The sweater was beautiful, I love having cashmere next to my skin, and brown is the new black. I can't wait to use the gift cards." Wade loved hearing this, the effusive daughter she could sometimes be. She reminded him of her mother in better times.

But then Amelia revealed the real reason for her high spirits. "You won't believe what Tom and Mom bought me," she said, barely able to get it out, "a horse, a purebred Arabian!"

First, she didn't come for Christmas, and now this, he thought as he tried to understand why the gift bothered him so much. It wouldn't have if he weren't also riding now, but that made no sense. After a brief silence, he managed to say, "Amelia, how wonderful." He worked to remain cheerful but got off the phone as quickly as possible. Her words haunted him—"I always loved horses but from a distance. Now I will really get to see what it is like. I mean, owning my own horse, who would have thought, isn't that great, Dad?"

That afternoon Wade drove out to the ranch. He parked outside the barn and looked down the wide aisle between the rows of stalls. Artemis stuck her big cinnamon-colored head out of the Dutch door and, as Wade called her name, whinnied to him. The ranch felt strange without Diana. He missed her.

The tack room door outside the barn was ajar. Nicole, a slender high-school girl who worked at the ranch and had given Wade a lesson one day faced him in the back of the tack room.

"Hi, new guy Wade," she said with a smile. She was wearing a Christmas-tree pin on her shirt and ball-ornament earrings.

"Nicole, hi. You're right in the holiday spirit, huh?"

"Here on Christmas day? You're getting into this horse world, aren't you? Not many men do." She took a bridle off a hook and handed it to him. "Here, I cleaned Artemis's tack." She couldn't have been that much older than his own daughter. How he missed Amelia.

"Thanks, Nicole."

"Thank Jolene. She pays me."

Wade grabbed the bridle and a saddle and ambled down the barn to Artemis.

He broke off a carrot in the horse's mouth and stroked her long sleek muzzle. With his hand on her neck, he opened the door, walked into the stall, and fed her another carrot. Three months ago, he would never have let himself get penned up with a horse in such close quarters. He was careful where he put his feet. Was their sheer size and power part of the allure of horses?

He unlocked the combination padlock to her feed room. When he opened the door, Artemis shoved her big head into the tiny room, but Wade pushed her away. "Okay, okay. I've got a treat for you *right here*." The feed had a slight smell of molasses as he mixed it in with the remaining carrots and put the mix into her feed tray. Using a heavy brush that felt good in his hand, he groomed her as she ate. He patted her with his other hand, and she responded by moving her head toward him. "Good girl, Artie," he said. "You're the best." If only Diana was as easily pleased, or showed her pleasure so unabashedly, he thought. He didn't like thinking of her with her husband out in Dallas—let's face it, he thought, he missed her too.

He saddled Artemis up and rode to Gray Cloud's barn. After buckling the halter over Gray Cloud's head, he led Diana's horse out of the paddock. Holding the rope, Wade re-mounted Artemis and took both horses into a meadow. Gray Cloud followed alongside Artie, a few steps behind until they entered a field where they could graze. Two riders in Santa outfits rode by, Santa and Mrs. Claus. He had the same feeling he'd had at the Cliff House up in San Francisco, that these times were all about couples and families. The holidays were hard to face alone.

∞

It was almost dark by the time Wade arrived home. It was one of the shortest days of the year. He felt a long, lonely night coming on. Still, it was longer than the day before, which made him think of the far-off promise of spring. What was Shelley's quote, something about winter's wind and "can spring be far behind?" The poet found the universal winter hope that resonated as the sun went down.

He roughhoused with Keats until the beagle calmed down. Wade took his phone to the sofa and called Diana in Dallas.

Diana's mother's tone was controlled. "Diana's told me about you," she said coolly. "I'll get her."

Diana picked up the phone. "Wade, just a second. Let me duck into the study."

"What's with your mom? She seemed almost hostile."

"Don't mind her. She's never understood why I left Rob, so she doesn't like my talking about you."

Wade hesitated. Did this mean her mother would find him an intruder? "How is Christmas in Texas? Lots of great presents, I'm sure."

"The kids love being here, and, yes, we smothered 'em in gifts. I collapsed after a dumb dinner party last week, but today was a pleasure."

"A dinner party?" Wade wondered if Rob was there.

"I never mentioned the firm's annual dinner party to you?" Diana asked. "I'm sorry, Wade. It's an annual event at a local country club. They fly in partners and spouses from all over the world. There's been a lot of growth, especially in the Enersystems account. The firm has opened two new offices in Europe, bringing the total there to six, and one in Tokyo now, too. I thought about you a lot, wished you were with me."

"A lot of lawyers, all over the world."

"Oh, Wade, I love your humor. I was uncomfortable, I'll admit, although I tried not to show it. When Rob and I separated, since he'd pay all expenses, I agreed that I'd play hostess at company parties. It seemed like such a small thing until I realized Rob expected me to stand next to him like nothing had happened. My friend Jolene Tyler—Artemis's owner, I want you to meet her—hung in with me like a trooper while I stood by Rob like a . . . well, I don't know what I was supposed to *be* like, but I *felt* like a concubine."

"You mean everybody thinks you two are still together?" What bullshit, he thought but managed to not say that over the phone.

"They pretend to, at least. Who knows what they say behind our backs."

"There are parts of your life I'll never understand." Wade's words came out a little angry.

"Nothing's the slightest bit mysterious," she responded. "Black tie dinners are like theater. Rob's a bit of an actor. I had to duck behind the potted plants to whisper to Jolene about how much I missed you."

"That sounds a little better," Wade's voice grew husky.

She paused. "Thinking of you got me through that awful party. I pretended Rob was you a couple of times. You two don't look all that different from the back."

"Now, that's a little weird." Wade adjusted his phone as Keats came in and lay down on the rug.

"How about you, Wade? What are you up to? Have you been riding?" she asked.

Wade took a minute. *Settle down, don't show your jealousy,* he told himself. "Yes I rode Artemis and ponied Gray Cloud. That's what you call it when he walks next to us, right?

"Yep. You're turning into a real horseman. Did you go off on your own with Artie?"

When he told her no, Wade told her about riding that rent-a-plow-horse in Half Moon Bay.

"You rode on the beach on Christmas? *What* am I doing in Texas?"

"Don't get me started. I'm a little jealous of you having a home to return to. I haven't been back to Barrington in years."

"Your Christmas sounds a lot more exciting than mine. The only outing I had was to church yesterday."

"I went to church, too. Last night. The woman preaching there now is a hoot. I should go more often. She said Christmas was probably based on some pagan holiday, because Jesus was born in the spring. But she also said that shouldn't matter." As he was saying this, Wade wondered if it might offend Diana, but now that he'd started, he kept on. "She said no matter what, this is our culture, and it's one of our two big holidays. At the end she stood at the back of the church and had us all shout a Merry Christmas."

"Nothing questioning the date here," Diana replied. "In Texas, today is Jesus's birthday, you-betcha, no-doubt-about-it, as they say."

Wade wished he could see Diana's face when she said that. He couldn't tell how lightly she was saying this. And because he'd just like to see her pretty face. "Let's find something else to talk about."

He heard Diana take a deep breath before she asked, "You talked to your daughter? Did the sweater get there in time?"

"Yes, and she liked it. But her mother and stepfather gave her an Arabian horse."

"I hope you don't feel that you're competing with your ex's new husband," Diana said. "That wouldn't be good."

"I didn't think of it that way," Wade said, which wasn't entirely true. "Her new husband seems to be flush since his mother died. I have a hard enough time paying tuition."

"Well, I don't know what I'd be able to afford if it weren't for Rob." Then she paused and said, "I miss you," out of nowhere, which reminded Wade of just what he was missing.

He thought about how soon he would see her again and then told her he had a surprise for her. "We're set for New Year's Eve dinner at the Village Pub. I had to call twice and beg to get reservations for ten-thirty, the time everyone wants." In a restaurant he could not afford.

"Oh. Wade, I'm sorry, I thought you knew my flight is on New Year's Day. I wish I could leave and be with you, I do, but it just wouldn't work this year."

"Oh. I guess I assumed Friday to Friday. Sorry."

"The club's having a party for the teenagers, and Mom bought Beth a new dress for it. But I'll picture you riding on the beach or on Artemis. Maybe Gray Cloud, too. I hope you can get them out every day, and give them cookies and pats for me. I'm missing you all."

Wade couldn't help but ask, "Are you and Rob going to this club party?"

"No. Rob's chaperoning at the club. Mom and Dad and I are planning a quiet New Year's right here."

Wade lowered his voice. "I'll miss you."

"Well, I won't be with Rob. I begged off on those plans. I've lost all interest in him except as Beth and Robbie's father. And I'll make it up to you, I promise." She gave a suggestive laugh that made Wade think about how much fun they had together. Her laugh lingered in his mind well past the phone call.

Part II

All equestrians, if they last long enough, learn that riding in whatever form is a lifelong sport and art, an endeavor that is both familiar and new every time you take the horse out of his stall or pasture.

— Jane Smiley

8

Early on the morning of New Year's Day, when Diana was scheduled to return, Wade sent her a text. "Can I pick you up at the airport?"

She replied, "No need to do that, but it's supposed to get up into the sixties. Texas is still freezing, but it's clear out there, just high clouds, so I plan to throw on riding clothes as soon as I get home. Any chance you could meet me at the barn around two? Wouldn't that be a good thing to do on New Year's Day? There might be a surprise."

Wade went out to Jasper Ridge at one-thirty and drove to Artemis's barn, where she nickered at the sight of Wade's car. A first.

Artemis took Wade's mind off Diana as he fed her a carrot. Her head didn't move a whit when he snapped a carrot in her clenched teeth; she seemed so *massive*. Her lips were soft, dry, and surprisingly coordinated; gentleness itself. Wade checked her hooves and groomed her, spending time on her mane and tail before he brushed the "must do" part, her broad back with its dark dorsal stripe and her golden-red sides. Diana had taught him that anywhere the saddle would touch had to be spotless. He threw the blanket and saddle across her back and cinched up the girth.

Once Wade exchanged her halter for a bridle, Artemis would carry him wherever he wanted to go. She, who could overpower him in a second. *Do they even like us?* he wondered. If not, why had she nickered? Was that the lot of domesticated horses, to watch for their rider's car to approach their barn? *Why do they do our will?*

Planning to ride over to Diana's barn, Wade climbed the mounting platform and threw his leg over Artemis. He heard a woman's voice behind him, "Howdy, stranger."

She smiled broadly at him, looking beautiful and relaxed up on Gray Cloud. *God, he'd missed her.* He may as well tell her.

"I've missed you," he said.

"Same here. It's good to see you."

"What's in the saddle roll?" Wade asked.

She smiled again. "Just some stuff. A girl might have a welcome surprise. You'll see."

As they rode to the polo field, Diana held Gray Cloud to a walk. He was more skittish than Artemis, but when the horse rode too close, Artemis kicked out at him. Diana laughed. "Mares don't like other horses getting close. She'll settle down." Not thirty steps later, Artemis gave Gray Cloud a little love bite behind his saddle. Friends again.

Wade had kept up with his lessons and wanted to show Diana what he had learned. "Let's trot."

Diana pointed to Gray Cloud's ears, pinned almost straight back, and shook her head.

"He's nervous?" Wade asked. The horse's ears perked up and then went back again.

Diana nodded. "Horses aren't predators. They can be prey, so they're cautious. Thoroughbreds can be especially spooky. But Gray Cloud's even more of a nutcase today than usual. I wonder why."

When her horse's ears came up again, she said, "I'll just walk him until he settles down. Once he focuses on what he's supposed to be doing, we'll be okay." She scanned the field until her eyes stopped at a movement in the distance. She pointed to something fluttering in the wind on the far side of the field. "That's what it is, a plastic bag. Gray Cloud knows it wasn't there yesterday. Let's cut across the field and ride up to it."

"How can you tell what's bothering him?"

"It's what's *changed*. I could take him to a trail we rode last week and he'd shy at a replaced fence rail. They can only be confident when they know their environment." Wade tucked that away as something to know—it may even apply to more than horses.

Gray Cloud didn't want to walk anywhere near the plastic bag, but Diana took a short rein and forced him close so he could see it was nothing to be afraid of. Sure enough, he settled down. She and Wade continued at a quick walk, with Artemis lagging behind.

"C'mon, catch up!" Diana called.

"This is as fast as Artemis seems to want to go."

"Show her you mean business. Squeeze one leg at a time, left right, left right, move her along. Remind her that she's under tack. Let her feel you a little in the mouth, it's okay."

He nudged Artemis with his heels, but he didn't have any effect on her. Wade had been schooled on this. Still, she plodded on at her own rate. He didn't consider it sporting to pull too hard on the reins—they were, after all, connected to the inside of her mouth. Besides, wouldn't that stop her?

Diana said, "Use your stick."

Reluctantly, Wade raised his crop and gave Artemis a light smack on her shoulder. She quickly caught up. "I barely touched her," Wade said, pleased and relieved, but curious as well.

"Sometimes they just need a reminder. She can feel a fly anywhere on her body, you know, so even a little tap can do the trick. When Gray Cloud and I jump in shows, he knows me so well, I can merely turn my head to look at a new jump, and he'll change course."

"Incredible."

"Let's stay at a walk until they're settled down. We don't want a spill." With the horses stepping out, Diana seemed happy. "My favorite trainer used to talk about the best place from which to view the world. Where do you think that would be?"

"Maybe Mount Tamalpais, up in Marin, looking back at the Golden Gate and San Francisco?"

"No, the trainer would ask us where was best, and we'd pretend not to know. Then we all smiled when he'd repeat the adage *through the ears of a horse*. I miss that guy. He used a bit-less bridle—no hardware in the mouth—yet he could get a horse to do anything."

"No bit at all? How did that work?"

"For top riders, it's all in the seat."

Obviously, Wade thought, his seat was lacking.

When they got past the main road, they came to a trestle bridge made from a retired railroad flatbed car. Gray Cloud didn't want to go over it. This had happened once before.

"Let me lead him over," he said.

"No, I can't put up with this. Stay back." Diana led Gray Cloud to the bridge a second time, smacking his front shoulder with her crop a lot harder than Wade would ever think of hitting Artemis. Gray Cloud's legs locked just before the bridge and he turned away. After the third time, he emptied his bowels. The fourth time, Diana got a tough look in her eye, tightened even further up on the reins with her left hand and whacked his shank, hard. Gray Cloud walked across without hesitation.

Wade guided Artemis in behind Gray Cloud, wondering how well he understood Diana. "I'm not used to seeing you so tough."

"You sometimes have to have it out with them. He'll be fine the rest of the day, but I won't see how I've done until we go to the bridge next time. If he walks straight across, I've done my job."

The cloudless, crisp day made Wade feel lucky to live in California. TV news that morning had shown fierce snowstorms pelting the Midwest. Diana pulled off a few overhanging leaves and gave him some to sniff. Inhaling pungent bay leaf that sparkling winter day was one of those moments Wade had learned to remember even as they were happening.

As they rode through brush, hundreds of birds rose and scattered, flapping around them, but the horses didn't spook. "Why don't the horses react?" Wade asked.

"They're used to birds," she said. "They live with them in the barns. Okay, we're ready, let's trot."

Wade tightened up on the reins, kicked with both feet, and Artemis trotted alongside Gray Cloud. He posted as he'd been trained, rising and falling with each step.

"Good. You're getting the rhythm. Squeeze a little at the bottom of the step, let her know you like what she's doing."

Awkwardly, Wade tried to squeeze harder. "Like this?" He wanted to master this.

"Yes," she said, "but relax your heel, stay lower down, massage her belly with your calves. Pretend you're . . ." she hesitated. "Imagine Artemis is a woman. Pretend you're making love."

They laughed like kids. Then Diana got quiet. Without a word, she motioned for him to follow her along the trail by the creek. After a while she turned off the trail, bringing the horses up through dense brush into a secluded meadow. "Here, let's dismount."

Wade still couldn't figure out what the surprise was as Diana pulled two halters, a ground cover and two blankets out of her saddle roll. She wove the reins up in the bridles and put the halters on over them, so she could tie the horses to a tree branch. "Not many people know about this little meadow," she said, opening the ground cover. "It's my secret hideaway. It's invisible from any trail. Because of that rock and the patch of woods, nobody will know we're here."

"Is it only three months since you first put me up on a horse?" Wade asked as he helped her with the blankets. "I wondered where the safety-belt was."

Diana laughed. "I'd forgotten."

Once Diana spread one of the thick blankets on the ground and settled on it, she returned to the saddle roll and pulled out a bottle of wine and poured two glasses. Wade took a small notebook and pen from his pocket and started writing. Diana pulled some crackers and cheese from the saddle roll. She spread a cracker for Wade and fed him while he wrote. After the cracker, he lay on his stomach to finish.

What in the world are you scribbling?" she asked.

"I want to write down what you just said." He scratched words into the notebook, and finally, he read them to her—

Riding Lessons

She's teaching me about horses,
how riders hang halters next to
their stalls in case of fire, and that
those small English saddles leave
a horse free to jump, halfway
to riding bareback . . .

Wade let the words trail off, sat up and took a drink of wine before lying down to read the end of what he'd written. The place was completely private, allowing him to relax. He knew that while horseback riding may be considered analogous to being with a woman, it wasn't a very romantic notion. He continued—

She tells me to think of moving
up and down on a horse like
making love to a woman.
Perhaps, I think, a woman
you're not in love with,
but I am not yet a horseman.

"That's fun," she said. "Bringing you to my secret place is even better than I'd imagined." She kissed him, a lingering kiss. "And believe me, I've been imagining."

His face was inches from hers. Her hand rested on his back, and he felt her electric warmth. He asked, "Do I finally get to seduce you?"

She didn't say anything but returned his kisses with passion. When he began to unbutton her blouse, she watched his fumbling hands and helped with the last few buttons as she melted into him.

How quickly he was aroused. He loved feeling their bodies respond to each other, touching and being touched with only a blanket between them and the earth. She guided him to the warmth of her. He loved it that she closed her eyes to fully experience his touch as their bodies sought each other.

Once they began making love, he fell into a slow rhythm that built and built. He'd dreamed of this since he'd first seen her on the plane, yet her controlled passion went beyond his imagination. He wanted to tell her he felt like a teenager again, but without the fear before, the awkwardness during, and the guilt after. He wanted to say that she left him breathless, and had made him want her more than he could say.

Loving her was like that moment on the trail with the scented bay leaves, only stronger, a moment Wade would not forget. He looked over at Artemis and Gray Cloud. Perhaps horses and poetry could come together after all.

As their passions subsided, Diana spread the second blanket over them. As they snuggled under the warm blanket, he looked up at puffy gray clouds moving against a blue sky. Watching her eyes, Diana seemed to be as enthralled as he was by the fast-changing cloud formations. The clouds that seemed to be lower were almost pure white and moving faster than the large gray ones behind them. Birds flew across the clouds in a V-shaped formation, moving the opposite direction of the clouds.

Her head rested on his arm. He felt thankful and at home, and she seemed to as well. She looked at him in a way she never had before, an encompassing loving look with soft eyes. This is the vulnerable part of her she keeps hidden, he thought, honored that she'd shared it with him.

∞

In late January, the rains came. Storms rolled in from the Pacific, one after another, releasing torrents, until the last day of the month. The first morning the sun came out, Wade called Diana to see if she could meet him at the ranch during his lunch hour. She agreed.

Wade arrived early to find most of the trails closed. The lunging ring—where he wanted to turn Artemis out to help alleviate her pent-up energy—wasn't just muddy, it had standing pools of water.

After so many days without horses, Wade was all thumbs. He fastened Artemis's bridle before he removed her halter, so he had to undo everything and start over. Then he buckled her girth without looping it through the saddle pad. He was glad Diana was in the other barn and didn't see. These preparations seemed to take forever, but just as he got Artemis tacked up, Diana appeared. Soon they were riding together.

As usual, Artemis didn't like to keep up with Gray Cloud, but she didn't like trailing too far behind, either. She'd trot to catch up, and Diana and Wade could talk. But then she'd fall behind again.

When Wade caught up again, Diana said, "I've been talking to Jolene—she really wants to meet you. That's why the idea for the dinner party came up."

Artemis put her ears back. Wade tightened his legs around her wide belly, a lesson he had learned to use at the first sign of trouble. Artemis's ears straightened up again, and he relaxed.

"So, as I was saying, I want my friends, especially Jolene and Billy, to meet you," Diana said. "I'm thinking about a small party, on the elegant side. I like a party with a theme, so I thought we'd call it "Our IPO.""

"You mean like a new company IPO?" Wade asked.

"Yes, everyone's always talking about IPOs out here, and we're something new. Rob told me what it stood for, but I forget."

"Initial Public Offering, which generally refers to stock, but I like it," Wade said.

"Good. It'll be good to get our different groups of friends together. I'd love to cook the meal myself."

"You needn't go to so much effort," Wade said.

"Oh, I miss having people to dinner. I don't want to feel I'm sneaking around, so if I want to keep seeing you, and I do, I'd better have an introductory party. Sally says I should let my freak flag fly." She laughed.

"Jolene's husband works for Rob, right?" Wade asked. "Won't that be awkward?"

"Not for me. Quite the opposite," she said, as Artemis fell behind again. "It shouldn't be awkward for you, either. Jolene's like a sister to me. Her husband, Billy, and Rob met in law school and Billy's worked for the firm ever since. He even bought a house up by Rob in Woodside. And we should be thankful to her for Artemis." Diana put her hand on the back of the saddle and swiveled around. "I'm ready. I want you to meet my friends, and I want to meet yours. Invite whomever you'd like to our little IPO. Maybe you want to invite a poet?"

"No poets, no. I don't think so, although I'd hope you wouldn't have it on the first Friday of the month, when I go to Waverley Writers. But we poets don't socialize much together except for readings." Wade's thoughts ping-ponged between his immediate fear—Artemis had tripped twice—and the notion of a dinner party. Except for business, he hadn't been to many social dinners since his divorce. Wade missed the feeling of belonging that went along with a warm evening in a friend's home.

But would it work, meeting her conservative friends? He understood that she wanted to introduce him, but wouldn't they see him as a rather poor interloper? Artemis was so far behind that Wade had to almost shout, "Well, I still wonder how open they'll be to me, but an IPO dinner party sounds like fun. How about inviting Jorge and his wife?"

Diana stopped to let him catch up and, a bit reluctantly, nodded. "If they're your choice, fine, but I'm surprised. You always get this worried look on your face when you mention them. But, it's up to you. Billy and Jolene are Republicans, and, from what you told me about Jorge, he's on the other side of things. But it's fine. How's he doing, anyway?"

"He's still out of work. He started his job search late, so he's coming from behind."

"That's not good for him, I would guess. Text me the address, and I'll send him an invitation. It's time I sat down with them to get to know them. After all you *are* the godfather to their daughter, right? With Jolene and Billy Tyler and us, that would be six. Maybe someone else, too—I'm no good at small parties, the darn table's too big." She laughed.

"I'm a little out of practice on dinner parties. What should I wear?"

She paused. "I don't know. In Dallas the guys would wear ties, but maybe you can do without that. A jacket, anyway."

"I'd have a hard time talking Jorge into a jacket, but if you really want—"

"Sure, I guess we can skip the jacket, why not? I'll have to get used to California." She looked up at blue sky with a few puffs of clouds. "It's a lot easier to do on a day like today."

When they left paved roads for the only trail still open, the horses slipped so much in the mud that Diana and Wade turned around and walked slowly back to the blacktop. "No secret place today, I'm afraid," Diana said lightly.

Cliff, the guy who'd written the booklet about the ranch, came toward them in his beaten leather jacket. Wade whispered to Diana, "How about inviting Cliff?"

"I'd need to think about that. Not now," she whispered as Cliff approached. But after he and Diana laughed about the pitiful riding conditions, she said to Wade quietly, "Good idea. I have his address from the hunt roster. I'll invite him."

∞

Once the rains were past, he went out to the ranch three evenings a week and whenever he could slip away during the day. One afternoon, when Ray canceled a staff meeting, Wade called Diana and they agreed to meet there.

It seemed as if every local schoolgirl was riding that day. As he approached Artemis, she thrust her head out the Dutch door and nickered. Wade ruffled her mane. "You crazy lady, you're not even my horse, but I think of you all the time, I do."

Artemis was so full of energy that she trotted in place in the stall. Wade walked her out to an empty turnout ring, unhooked the lead line from her bridle, and watched her experience the freedom of setting her loose. There was a muddy pool in the turnout ring, but she nosed around the sandy surface until she found a patch that was dry enough so she could lie down and roll. On her back, she thrust her legs in the air, coming close to rolling completely over. Then she got up on her hooves and shook the dust off. From the center, Wade clucked and swung the lead rope around to get her going. She trotted briefly, then cantered around powerfully. Twice she threw her back legs into a buck that Wade knew could throw him off had he been saddled on her. Glad that she was doing this where she was supposed to, Wade called, "Good girl, Artemis." When she quieted down to a walk, he moved toward her. She came toward him and they met mid-ring—her way of saying she'd had enough. It was time to groom her and tack up.

Diana rode up on Gray Cloud just as Wade mounted. "Well, don't you look like an old pro up there," she said. "Smart to turn Artemis out."

"What's with all the kids?" Wade asked.

"It's Pony Club day," Diana said. "It's like 4-H, but for horses. Some of these girls will ride in the hunt next week."

"I've been meaning to ask you about that. You don't really hunt animals, do you?"

Diana laughed. "No. Well, not this time, anyway. This is a drag hunt. We lay down a scent from one jump to another. The hounds think they're hunting, but there's no game. When we do go after animals, it's coyotes we chase, and they always get away, you know, like Wile E. Coyote."

"Well, that's good. The word hunting isn't one of my favorites."

"Oh, Wade, we never catch 'em. It's not hunting like big-game hunting."

Soon they had the horses walking on the asphalt, with Artemis a few steps behind Gray Cloud. They veered off the pavement onto a trail.

"Come on." Diana said. "Let's trot. We must get you legged up. We'll ride third field, where it's almost all walking and trotting." She led him onto a trail they rarely took.

Wade prodded Artemis with his heel. The trainer had told him that Artemis would be more confident in him as a rider if he'd really kick her, but this time she responded to only a light kick with his heel.

"That's it," Diana said. "Just push up a little with every step. Go with her rhythm."

He recognized a distinctive rock on the left side of the trail that led to the place they had made love. "Isn't that rock the other side of what you called your secret place?"

Diana laughed. "As a matter of fact, it is. It's remarkably well hidden, isn't it?"

"Really," Wade said, flicking an imaginary cigar like Groucho Marx.

"Sorry, big boy, no romance today. I brought you here because we need to talk about something." Following Diana's lead, he tied Artemis to a tree. Diana dismounted, sat down on a log, and motioned to him to join her.

"I've been dying to kiss you," Wade said, moving his head toward hers, seeking her lips.

"Wade, Wade," she said, kissing him, and for a moment they blended into each other. Then she gently pushed him away. "Today's not a good day with all these kids around. Some hapless Pony Clubber could wander over the wrong hill."

As he withdrew, Diana said, "Not that there won't be plenty of time for that in the future. I love kissing you, just not now. There's something we need to discuss."

"Okay, you've got my attention."

She rose to stand right in front of Wade, and she looked very serious. "It's about Jolene and Billy. I've known them a long time. When Rob was in law school, we'd double date. Jolene only finished Dallas Community College, so Billy, who was on Law Review, was quite the catch for her. Law Review impressed Rob, who squeaked through. Now Billy manages the Enersystems account, the biggest in the firm. He can be a character, but be nice to them. Please, for me. They truly are like family. I want you to be part of this."

Wade thought he could get along with just about anyone but had to admit that a conservative high-powered law partner from Texas might be a challenge. No wonder Diana had at first hesitated to let Wade invite Jorge. After all, when it came to politics, his dear friend could be a loose cannon. Wade looked over at the tied-up horses as she talked. "Maybe you think I am too different for your oldest friends?"

"You're just fine. I don't worry about that. I want you to know how close Billy is to my family." She stood up and dusted off hands, clearly finished with the subject. "The kids are coming at five, and you and I have work to do—to get you ready for the hunt. It's a week away. Let's work the horses a bit longer."

Wade pulled her toward him for a last kiss before they remounted their horses. As she threw her leg over Gray Cloud, Diana's movement triggered a wave of thoughts, and Wade took a sharp breath. Diana's beauty hit him again so hard that he wondered if he could keep his head about him.

She nudged Gray Cloud out of his walk. "Let's trot to the end of the fence."

When Wade followed her lead, she said, "That's the way." Artemis caught up. "She's got a strong trot. Now control it—lean back a little and pull ever so gently on the reins. Come to a full stop at the end of the fence. Show her you're in charge."

Wade wondered if Diana wanted him to be the guy who would show *her* he was in charge. "Whoa," he said as he tightened his upper legs and pulled, so Artemis slowed to a walk for two steps before stopping. They practiced like that, with Diana even having Wade canter.

Later the following week, Diana said Wade was ready to hunt. "We'll take it easy on you this time. You're not quite ready to chase directly behind the hounds, but you'll do fine in third field, also known as hilltoppers, because where we often end up watching the hounds and the first two fields from a nearby hill."

That will be a real hoot, Wade thought, thankful that Diana had brought him along so quickly. He could even imagine getting a poem out of his experience—time would tell. Imagine, he thought, I'll be riding as part of a group out with the hounds. He'd take a major step into a life he'd only dreamed of. With Diana.

9

Wade almost didn't go out with the hounds on the day Diana had planned. He'd forgotten it was Jorge and Marita's wedding anniversary, and they always celebrated with a dinner. He hated to cancel on Diana, but he wanted to keep up his friends' tradition and see how Eva was doing. But, when he called Jorge, he and Marita had decided, with Jorge out of work, that they'd complete that San Antonio trip Lydia had canceled. So, Wade would get to *ride to hounds* after all.

The night before Wade was to go out, Diana invited him to stay over at her condominium. "I know I may sound forward," she said, "but it's mainly practical—we both have to get up so early, and I know you'll need help with the stock tie and all."

She made dinner for him that evening, a flank steak and Brussels sprouts with almonds and cranberries. After the chocolate torte dessert accompanied by a late harvest Zinfandel and coffee, she asked, "Are you nervous about going out with the hounds tomorrow?"

He was quite nervous but wasn't eager to let her know. "Should I be?" he asked in a casual way.

She took a sip of her wine, finishing the glass. "I don't agree with Billy that horses are dumb, but there's no doubt they're big. It's okay to be a little scared—it might keep you from doing something foolhardy."

He told her he appreciated her concern.

"I'll ride with you in third field. I know some good places we can view the first and second fields. First field jumps, second field goes close behind them but avoids jumping by going through gates."

"Which field," Wade asked, hoping his terminology was right, "do you usually ride in?"

"Sometimes they ask me to lead second field, but most of the time I'm up front with the master."

"I know so little, but that's what I would have guessed. I thank the hunt for my getting to stay over with you."

Getting ready for bed with her felt awkward. They were nowhere near a "your place or mine" kind of relationship, so he took nothing for granted. "It's the first time you've actually invited me," he said. "Before, it just kind of happened."

Diana put her finger over Wade's lips. "Perhaps some things are best left unsaid." Then she took her finger away and reached up and kissed his cheek. "But this is the night before the hunt. Tonight isn't about romance. We're only a few hours away from loading the horses into the trailer in the dark."

Wade watched Diana take her excess pillows, some of which had pictures of horses jumping fences on a sunny day, and pile them on her dresser. The room was feminine without being frilly. The walls were painted a soft peach color and the furniture seemed to be antiques. Her riding outfit hung on the bathroom door—all was in readiness for the big event. When she pulled the blinds, he realized he was watching her nighttime ritual. He compared it to his nightly plopping into bed and thought of the differences in the habits of their lives. Would he fit into such an ordered life? Compared to her, he saw his life as a chaos of disorder.

When she lay down beside him Wade pulled her to him, but she rolled out of his grasp, saying, "I've set the alarm for five. We need sleep."

In the depth of the night Wade woke up to Diana's touch. She'd snuggled up behind him and pulled him close. Wordlessly, Wade turned toward her, and they made love as if their bodies knew what they needed more than they did. This time was strong and slow, almost as if they were in each other's dream. After they made love, he remembered his thought earlier, wondering if she'd wanted someone to take charge. Perhaps he was right.

∞

It seemed like he'd barely slept when the alarm jangled. Diana sprang out of bed. Wade played possum. She was only partially dressed when he caught a glimpse of her turned toward the mirror. Her profile was most revealing and alluring. God, he thought as she brushed her hair and the image of *Diana, the Huntress*, a life-sized nude Wade had seen in New York City long ago flashed into his mind. *I want that woman.* "You look lovely," he said.

"Get up, lazybones." He saw her smile as she chided him. Diana fixed her stock tie so that it jutted out from its pin. She donned a white smock as a cover-up, making him think of a doctor about to make morning rounds.

"Come on, get dressed. I'll fix your tie after we load the horses."

They drove to the ranch in the pre-dawn and worked in the dark to attach the trailer to her SUV. Artemis and Gray Cloud didn't want to get in, so Diana positioned Wade behind them while she pulled Artemis into the trailer, then beat a hasty exit through a side door as the mare lumbered up the ramp. Once Artie was in, Gray Cloud followed easily.

∞

They drove across Alpine Road to a dirt road in a grassy field already dotted with trailers, unloaded their horses, and tied them on opposite sides of the trailer. Everyone, including the experienced male hunters in red coats, and the young riders, both men and women, worked to get their horses tacked up and their riding outfits in order. The scene made him think of actors before a performance.

In the first light of dawn, Diana helped Wade with his stock tie, explaining that the wide soft ties serve a valid purpose. "In an emergency it can be used as a bandage."

Wade enjoyed learning all the ins and outs of this ancient sport. A man, dressed like Diana, wearing a white doctor's smock as a cover-up, came by their trailer carrying a silver tray with plastic cups of port wine.

"Good morning, Master," Diana said, and introduced him as Jack. He was a little taller than Wade, about his age, with a long-limbed frame and close-cropped brown hair.

"Stirrup cups," he said as he offered the tray to the two of them. "Liquid courage."

Diana demurred, but Wade took a cup. It tasted powerful so early in the morning, but it took the chill off.

"Diana, can you lead second field?" the Master asked. "It shouldn't be a long day. They're only laying the drag for eight jumps."

"Gray Cloud's acting up, so I think I'd better hilltop today," she said.

Jack seemed to know immediately why Diana was dropping back to a lower field. Wade wondered what Jack thought as he looked him up and down. "Nice to meet you, Wade. You're a lucky guy."

He turned back to Diana. "Why don't you lead third field, and I'll have Richard take second. Don't tell him he was my second choice, okay?" He winked.

Diana laughed, saying, "Yes, Master." As he started to walk off, she asked, "Could I get a look at the trail map?" He pulled the paper from his smock's pocket and unfolded it so she could see the day's planned course.

After Diana led Wade on a few short trots, Jack called out, "Field please," and forty riders circled around him. Intimidating now on a tall white horse, Jack had exchanged his doctor's smock for a bright red hunting coat and carried a bone-handled whip. He emphasized the importance of closing all gates after everyone went through, and then he thanked the landowner, a smiling gray-haired man, also in a red coat, who nodded his appreciation.

Wade's stomach turned uneasily. Maybe he shouldn't have had

that port—he didn't remember ever drinking before noon.

The huntsman opened a trailer and shouted out, "Twelve and a half couple, Master." Out bounded the hounds, taller and whiter than beagles, wagging tails that seemed to stand straight up. The hounds reminded him of Keats. "I hope the teenager next door remembers to feed Keats," he whispered to Diana.

Diana, right next to Wade, whispered, "He'll be fine, don't think of him now. The hounds are counted two by two. Twelve and a half couple is 25." The horses moved nervously as the riders organized themselves into three distinct groups behind the hounds. The horses' ears swiveled severely, almost mechanically.

With Wade by her side, Diana led the largest group up a hill to the left. Morning mist rose off the grass. She stood in her saddle and turned around to speak to the field. So confident. Wade felt proud to be there with her. "We should have a great day," she said. "I'll try to get us some good vantage points. See those two riders across the way? They're laying down the scent. Hounds and riders will follow that path." After a few moments, she spun in her seat again and asked if the group was ready for a trot.

The woman behind her, on a spotted pinto, yelled, "Sure, let's go!"

Diana kicked Gray Cloud and led the horses onto a small knoll. Soon the hounds appeared and scrambled along the scent path, followed by what Wade figured must have been the first and second fields, more than twenty riders.

"For those of you new to hunting," Diana said, "The hounds are giving tongue. They're on scent." The riders behind the hounds were cantering at full speed. The spectacle was breathtaking—black-coated riders with a few red coats mixed in, on spirited horses behind the yelping hounds.

The hills behind the Stanford campus, dotted with houses, were a vibrant green. After the hounds and hunters disappeared around a bend, Diana pointed off to another hill and said to Wade, "Let's go over that way, so we can see two jumps from there. We'll need to hurry, since they'll get to the first one pretty soon now." To the group, she said, "Everybody up for a canter? Let's go."

The hill she pointed to was at least half a mile away. Riding there, Wade was quickly winded. When he caught up to Diana, who didn't seem to be winded, he said, "Wow, this is work."

"Aww, this is a walk in the park. You're not legged up. Wait till you're up with the hounds."

She turned to the others and said, "How about a controlled canter up that next hill?"

She led them in a trot until the grade got steeper, where Diana kicked Gray Cloud into a full canter. The horses seemed to go into high gear all at once. It reminded Wade of those cowboy movies in which the good guys fly across the plains after the bad guys. He tried to figure out why cantering uphill felt safer than on the flat and guessed that it was harder for the horse to run away on the rider, who was closer to the ground. Wade worked to keep Artemis's head up and his to stay down on his horse. He wasn't as scared as he was winded. He knew he was flopping around on his horse and hoped no one would notice.

"Tuck in like a skier," Diana yelled across to him. "Heels down, weight back. Let Artemis do the work. She doesn't mind. This is what she lives for."

Wade settled in. His ride smoothed out.

∞

As they stood on the hill, Wade studied Diana. Her tack was immaculate, with the end of each leather strap secure in its keeper. Gray Cloud looked as if he were born to hunt, a fit dappled gray thoroughbred from central casting. The white form-fitting saddle pad on his back was whiter than Diana's knit gloves. Unlike Artemis, Gray Cloud didn't seem the slightest bit winded. Diana turned around and said, "Perfect weather. Sit straight in the saddle. You're doing great."

"I'm glad there's a chill in the air or we'd all be dying of heat," Wade said.

On Diana's command, it seemed, their group would trot, canter up a new hill, and the spectacle of the hunt would appear magically before them. She was so skillful that Wade felt like a member of a medieval court for whom the field riders were being presented for his amusement.

He found foxhunting, even without a fox, to be as colorful and entertaining as any movie on the big screen. The sport was all form. Except for the huntsman, who directed the hounds, and the whippers-in, who kept the hounds from running off, not one of the riders was necessary. In their finery, the first and second fields provided little more than pageantry and excitement for the riders. When the woman next to him, wearing a yellow vest under her black jacket, was asked what those following the hounds do, she said, "Logically, theirs is the least-needed position in all of sport, of less use than a batboy. But I'm going to be one of them by the end of the season, no matter what it takes. Imagine tucking in behind the master, right behind the hounds. I'll do it."

These riders were most aware of form. "You look *fantastic*," he'd heard one rider say to another in greeting that morning a line from a movie actor, "It is much more important to *look* good than to *feel* good." Each of these riders had risen long before dawn for the excitement of being part of this scene. Is there any way, Wade wondered, that a hapless kid from the Midwest, faced with this elaborate pageantry, could not be moved? Now that he had smelled the bayleaf and felt the physicality of a canter, he wondered if he ever had a prayer of not falling for the woman who showed him this world? He would have been attracted to her even without this, but with it, he knew he was putty in her hands.

He was thankful for a rest at the top of the hill. He couldn't imagine how the riders who followed the hounds maintained their pace. Except for an occasional stop, which they called a check, they just rode and rode full-out.

∞

Wade was relieved, hours later, after two more hills, when Diana said, "I think the first field is already hacking back. If we trot over this hill, we should meet up with them." It was almost over. Wade loved it, but he was dead meat. Soon the three fields joined together, the horses walking back in from the hunt behind the hounds.

When they came within sight of the trailers, the huntsman vaulted off his horse like a gymnast and handed his reins to the master. The huntsman talked constantly to his hounds, who followed him as he briskly walked. He called out miscreants by name, "Whiskey, get back in here. Winner, off that squirrel. Wishlist, down." Walking briskly, surrounded by his hounds, the huntsman appeared to be the very picture of hunting tradition.

It was just after noon when they sponge-washed their horses and put cotton blankets over them. At last they could eat. Diana had brought two folding chairs, which Wade set up in the circle where people shared food and wine. The riders, whose outfits were now disheveled and spotted with mud, seemed exhausted but talked excitedly of the day's spectacle. An older friend of Diana's had come off her horse at a jump, but she was unhurt and said casually, "Blackie and I were together over the coop, but when we landed on the other side, I went left and Blackie went right." She laughed and took a large swallow of wine.

Jack, who had traded his red coat for a belted green heather wool jacket, and his helmet for a tweed driver's cap, congratulated Wade on his first hunt. "I hear you did well."

"Thanks. Great fun," Wade said, truly enjoying his accomplishment.

"Breakfast is one of my favorite parts of the hunt," Diana whispered to him. She had encouraging words for everyone who joined the circle.

Sitting next to her, he downed his second glass of Chardonnay. "Honey, this roast beef is delicious, but it's almost noon—shouldn't we call this lunch? People laughed as they told him that even if it were four in the afternoon, the meal after a hunt is always *breakfast*. Their words and good humor gave Wade a sense of belonging, even though he was a newcomer.

After they ate, Diana, all waves and smiles and quick to leave, stood up, turned to him and said, "The kids are coming in a couple of hours and we have so much to do." She and Wade gathered their gear and loaded the horses for the short drive back to the ranch. Gray Cloud and Artemis must have known they were headed back to their barns because they marched up the ramp into the trailer without hesitation.

At the ranch, Wade and Diana put the horses up, washed their tack, and put everything away. Diana touched his arm. "I wish we'd planned and you could at least shower at my place. But the kids will be coming by any minute."

After they cleaned out the trailer and unhooked it, it was time for Wade to get into his own car. She hugged him and pulled away. Then she moved close again and kissed him on the cheek. "You're *sweaty*. Actually," she said, coming back for another kiss, "I like salt."

10

Before Diana's dinner party, Wade called her to see if there was anything he could do. "Maybe set the table?"

"Oh, I finished that long before noon. But maybe you could pick up a couple of packs of party ice. Those tiny cubes, you know. Jorge and Marita are still coming, right?"

"Yes, I called them. Jorge said Marita's mom used to throw fancy parties in Havana before Castro, so she's looking forward to it. They had some upset over what she's wearing, but they're coming."

"I never thought about fancy parties in Havana, but . . . of course. Forced to leave her own country—that must have been terrible."

Wade explained that Marita's father was a doctor who taught at a medical school in Cuba. "When they escaped to Florida—Marita was in junior high—Florida wouldn't recognize his medical license and he had to drive a cab. It killed him, literally. He drove a double shift and had a heart attack coming home. Jorge thinks that's why Marita's so pushy for Eva." Wade paused. "He thinks that Marita wants to give her daughter the start her father had tried to give her before things fell apart. That's more than you want to hear, isn't it? Anyway, they'll join us for sure." He ended the call and set out to find party ice.

∞

Diana, looking crisp and pretty in a navy blue blouse and white wool slacks under a red apron, greeted Wade at the door with a warm but too-brief kiss. If it weren't a party, since they were still alone, he'd tousle her hair and perhaps her blouse, too, but tonight he stayed demure. In addition to the ice she had requested, he brought a bottle of wine—a Chardonnay, much fancier than what he drank at home. "Let's get that on ice," she said, leading him inside and taking off her apron. In the guest room she shooed Micah off the bed. "I'd better throw a sheet over the cat hair. This is where I'll have them put their coats."

A silver place card holder indicated to Wade his place at the head of the table, an honor that both pleased and bewildered him. He didn't feel quite like the man of the house. Two tall crystal vases held roses at the center of the table. Wade had to look twice at the large plates at each setting. Were they silver? Yes. "Is it safe to eat off metal?" he asked.

"Those are chargers, silly. The plates will go on top." The phone rang. "It's the Tylers," she said.

Billy and Jolene, Wade reminded himself as she buzzed them up. Billy had a short haircut and bulldog face and the swagger of a man who was used to getting his way. He came bearing two bottles of white wine. Wade, reminding himself this is who Diana wanted him to get on with, steeled himself. Jolene was a well-put-together blonde woman who seemed at home on Billy's arm.

Once they settled in, standing in the living room, Diana asked Billy if she should open some of the chilled wine Billy had brought. "Good wine," she said. "*Far Niente*," a more elegant Chardonnay than Wade had brought. In fact, it was much fancier than any wine Wade had ever bought, which made him a bit insecure.

"Wine's definitely cheaper out here," Billy said slowly, with a drawl. "That's a good thing about being so close to Napa Valley."

Diana turned to him, "Napa. Remember that partner's meeting at Silverado when we wondered what it would be like to live out here? No one took it seriously. Could that have been only two years ago?"

"I'm liking California more than I thought I would," Jolene said. "Wade, you're going to have to get used to how crazy we Texans are about our state. When I said I was moving out here, my friends went into mourning. But over the holidays back in Dallas, I found myself missing California, anxious to get back. You were brought up here, right?"

"Wade's from the Midwest—Illinois," Diana said.

Wade looked at Billy and said, "I haven't been back to my home town for years. I like it here." Meanwhile, he thought, maybe it's time I *do* touch home base. This new world had Wade wondering who he was—what better way to ground himself than to return to his roots?

Jolene motioned toward the window, which framed the red roofs of Stanford. "And it's hard to argue with this weather."

Billy shook his head and frowned. Wade took it that he didn't like California as much as his wife did, and he wanted people to know it. Happily, the phone rang and Diana buzzed someone else up the elevator.

"It's Cliff. He rides with me, Billy," Diana said. "You'll like him. He hunts. Plays polo, too."

Cliff removed his trademark leather jacket when he came in. Wade turned to Billy. "This guy has written the most interesting book about the ranch where Artemis lives. Cliff brings the place alive. Great photos. Did you know Leland Stanford bought the ranch, possibly on his deathbed?"

"I've thought a lot about that guy since I moved out here," Billy said. "Talk about strategic thinking."

Wade didn't like Billy's tone—was he trying to make Leland Stanford into an early venture capitalist?—but Wade was circumspect. "He left a legacy, for sure," he said.

Cliff turned to Billy. "I wanted to thank you for letting me ride Artemis. And Wade here's been getting her out even more than I have. He even took her out with the hounds last week."

Billy looked at Cliff, then Wade. "We worried Artemis wouldn't get enough work. We'd hoped the kids would ride her, but no. You two are doing us a big favor."

"Did you know the ranch was used for artillery practice in both World Wars?" Wade asked Billy. "It's in Cliff's book."

"How did you dig all this stuff up, Cliff?" Billy asked.

"Local libraries, mostly. They've been helpful at Stanford, too."

Billy shook his head. "One of the best things about being a senior partner is I don't have to do my own research anymore. I did it for years, but I never really liked it. What's this about a nearby hunt? I met some of the hunt crowd in Dallas—good people."

"There's a club here with over fifty hounds," Cliff said. "We go out two or three times a week in the winter."

Diana and Jolene moved toward the men. "He took to it like a fish to water," Diana said lightly.

"I'm just learning my way around horses," Wade said.

Cliff shook his head. "It's the best way to get to know Diana, I'll tell you that."

Diana grimaced. "Cliff, back off," she said good naturedly. "Let Wade be Wade. He's a poet, you know."

Billy regarded him with renewed curiosity. "Poetry? I hope you're not one of those flaming liberals."

While Diana refreshed glasses all around, Wade thought, *Why did Diana have to bring up poetry?* "Poets come in all stripes," he responded. "In politics, I'm what they call out here a *Declines to State*, an independent voter. The major parties try to make it sound as unattractive as possible." After he said it, Wade wondered if he was kowtowing to these people on the right. He liked to think of himself as a centrist but had never voted for a Republican president. A governor, once, and he was sorry afterwards. Calm down, he said to himself. Blending in wasn't a crime. Was it?

"Hah," said Billy. "So you write poems. Do you publish?"

"Only in little magazines you've probably never heard of. I'm a local poet, meaning no one has heard of me locally. As opposed to the national poets, who no one has heard of clear across the country."

"He's making a joke, Billy," Diana said. "Laugh, okay?"

"I might need a lot more wine before I start laughing at poet jokes," Billy said.

"Let me refresh that drink," Wade said, happy to have an excuse to leave the conversation.

Diana's phone rang again. "That must be Jorge and Marita."

He excused himself and headed for the door.

Diana joined him just as they got off the elevator, saying, "Nice of you to come, Marita. And daffodils! Let me get them into some water." She turned her wide smile on Jorge. "And you must be *the* Jorge who Wade always talks so glowingly about."

"We've been friends for years," Jorge said. "He's my daughter Eva's godfather."

While Diana dealt with the flowers, Wade walked Jorge and Marita into the living room and introduced them to the Tylers and Cliff. Jolene raised her hand and waved horizontally when her name was mentioned, the way James Dean swept his hand in *Giant*.

Diana came in and placed the daffodils on the piano.

Billy said, "We were just talking about how different California is, compared to Texas, that is. Where are you two from?" he asked Jorge and Marita. Wade noticed that Billy's eyes lingered on Marita.

"I'm from El Paso," Jorge said. "Marita's from Florida—originally from Havana."

Marita extended her hand. Rather than shake it, Billy lifted it to his lips, Wade could not help but notice. Marita surprised him by curtseying. "Jorge used to work with Wade here, but he's between jobs now."

Wade brought in a tray of wine glasses and two newly-opened bottles. As people moved into the dining room.

Looking over the place cards, Jorge nudged him, "Man, she has you at the head of the table. The big Kahuna."

Wade shrugged, trying to be cool. But maybe Jorge was right—as he had suspected when he first saw the silver place holder with his name on it at the head of the table—maybe Diana had intended to make Wade feel like the man of the house. This must be part of the idea they were 'coming out like an IPO.' Relax, he told himself. Go with it. Isn't this what you want, anyway?

Marita laughed as she pointed to Jorge's place card. "And we're seated across from each other, just the way Mama used to do."

"Cuba. Looks like those Castro brothers are going to hang on forever," Billy said. "They've driven that island right into the ground."

Marita smiled at him. "I'm with you, Billy. Americans don't realize how quickly freedom can disappear." She snapped her fingers. "Overnight."

Billy reached out and touched Marita's arm. He turned his attention to Jorge. "That's a smart little lady you've got there, buddy."

"I've had friends go to Cuba in the last year," Wade said, uneasy with where Billy was going with all of this. "They say it's not as bad for the people living there as the press makes out. I think opening it up is good."

Billy shook his head. "Nah, not until they change. The government has to get out of the people's way. Like Marita said, let freedom ring."

"Wade's just talking about his poet-friends—I'm sure some have visited Cuba," Diana interjected. "From what I've seen, some of them will do pretty much anything." She was getting a little testy, Wade thought, especially for her. "I know they'll *say* anything, that's for sure."

Jolene looked lovingly at her husband. "Like Billy said, it's very poor." Wade saw that Jolene didn't seem to have noticed how blatantly Billy had been flirting with Marita. How could she miss it? Could she have noticed and not have been bothered? Long ago, Wade had seen that long-term marriages develop rules all their own. Perhaps that was what was going on.

Billy stared straight at Wade. "I can't believe what you said about Cuba. It's a communist threat, ninety miles from our border."

Marita looked at Billy. "Mom goes on and on about the days before Castro took over. They were so happy there."

"Of course, Marita," Wade said. "But you don't deal with the leaders by ignoring them."

Billy shook his head. "We could improve those people's lives in a weekend if we had the guts."

"It is a beautiful island," Jolene said. "No one's going to argue with you about that, sweetie."

Billy raised his drink to his wife. "That's my girl. Hell, we could go down there and the next thing you know they'll be eating Big Macs and speaking American." He glanced at Jorge and Marita awkwardly. "No offense, but English is ten times better. We have over a million words; they don't have a hundred thousand. Check it out."

Wade saw Marita frown and shake her head when she heard this, but she didn't go against Billy.

"Scary," Wade mumbled, almost audibly.

Billy looked at Marita. "You must be hot in that jacket."

She frowned at Jorge and said, "He made me promise I'd leave it on."

Jorge shrugged and nodded, seeming to give her permission to take it off.

"W-e-l-l-l," she said, spreading the word out to make her husband's nod seem like a dare. Starting at her waist, Marita slowly unbuttoned her jean jacket. Her hesitancy added drama, and soon all eyes were on her. Her blouse was so transparent that her red bra was as prominent a feature of her outfit as the blouse. Wade noticed that everyone but Billy quickly looked away.

Diana's jaw was clenched, her lips tight. Watching her, Wade thought of what sailors say before a storm. *Batten down the hatches. Stand by for large seas and heavy rolls.*

∞

By the time Diana served dessert, Wade was thankful the discussion had moved back to horses and the hunt. Cliff said to him, "So now you're a foxhunter as well as a poet?"

"I've really only ridden with the hounds once, Cliff, in third field,"

Wade said. "It hardly counts. And I'm only a part-time poet."

"Third field can be pretty crazy with all those nutsy horses," Cliff said. "I heard you did well."

Billy seemed to have cooled down after the Castro conversation. But Wade noticed he still couldn't keep his eyes off Marita, who was seated beside him.

Jolene moved her gaze to Wade as she passed a bowl of fruit and a plate of biscotti. "I'm so glad you're getting Artemis out. How did she behave with the hounds?"

"We were hilltopping, so she didn't have much interaction with the hounds. I'm not ready to tear off behind the master yet, but if I were to do it, it'd be on Artemis."

Cliff interjected, "You'll get there. There's nothing like it, except possibly polo. I do miss polo."

Jolene had a smirk on her face. "Diana is all about the hunt, not polo. Artemis *told me* she loves that you take her out with the hounds."

Billy piped in. "I don't know. Horses are damn big and not real smart." Just as Diana had said, Wade thought, Billy did not think much of horses.

Jolene glared at her husband. "Wade *likes* Artemis, and the big girl likes him. Just because she bucked *you* off, sweetie—"

"Well, I'm right," Billy said, interrupting. "Cliff, name one person in the hunt who hasn't been seriously injured."

"I broke both my collarbones," Cliff admitted. "One hunting, the other playing polo."

Marita leaned toward Billy and whispered something. Wade watched Jorge, who kept his eyes on Billy, who in turn, was intent on Marita's cardinal-red bra and impressive cleavage. Wade concentrated on not looking her way. He was surprised that Jolene and Diana seemed to be ignoring Billy's keen interest in Marita.

Diana stood and picked up her plate and then Wade's. She seemed anxious to get away from the table. Maybe he was just imagining it, but he thought he noticed Diana repeatedly looking over at Marita and then looking away with what seemed like disgust. He wondered if Diana might be threatened by Marita's brazen sensuality.

Marita said to Billy, "We should help her clear."

Diana said, "No need to do that. I'll get it."

Marita didn't give up. "Please, let me help you." She picked up Billy's plate, then Jorge's, and moved to the kitchen.

Billy picked up a salad plate and followed her. Wade noticed everyone stopped to listen to what was going on in the kitchen with Marita and Billy, who spoke in low tones. Marita's voice was louder and broke the quiet, rising from behind the door in a loud suggestive laugh. Diana winced. Cliff and Wade looked at each other. Jorge suddenly stood, his face scrunched up in anger. He grabbed Marita's jacket from her chair and strode into the kitchen, the door swinging behind him. Wade heard him say, loudly, from behind the door, "We're going home, Marita."

"Relax," Marita said.

The door opened and she came back into the dining room, followed by Jorge, who was attempting to drape the jacket over her shoulders as she walked.

Billy followed Jorge back from the kitchen. "Don't leave too fast, *compadre*," he said. "Your wife's been telling me great things about you."

Jorge's face flushed as he returned to his seat.

"Maybe we should have a talk about you and Enersystems," Billy said calmly. "They're always on the lookout for good people. Sometimes they use me as a scout."

It looked like Jorge wanted to punch Billy in the face and give him his phone number at the same time. Then he went limp, his body language saying, *where do I go to surrender?* "Okay," he finally said, shoulders slumped.

Billy nodded. "I'll make a few calls on Monday. Come on, Jolene, we'd better get going. I have an eight-thirty tee-time, and if I don't hit a bucket of balls beforehand, I'll duff around the first five holes."

As soon as Billy said that, Wade watched Jolene stand up. Soon, she and Billy were out the door. Jorge and Marita followed close behind. Marita attempted to gush to Diana about the wonderful evening—she came up with the appropriate words, but Wade could hear her voice was nervous, almost singsong.

Cliff followed behind them as if nothing had happened, so casual that Wade wondered if he'd exaggerated the drama. No, he decided, with Billy, Marita and Jorge, there'd been drama. Where Diana stood on all of this was still a question.

∞

Once they saw Cliff to the elevator, his leather jacket slung over his shoulder, Wade and Diana were alone. Wade helped her move a few more dishes into the kitchen, hesitant to start a conversation. "We can leave the rest on the table while the dishwasher runs," she said over the whir of the machine. "Let's sit down."

She led Wade to an alcove next to the window overlooking Stanford and the lights of the houses in the foothills.

"Sorry about that scene," he said. "A bit of a mess." After he said it, he wondered why he was always apologizing.

"Yes. An embarrassment," she answered tensely.

"That Billy's a piece of work, for sure."

"Billy?" Diana asked incredulously. "It was that woman. She was half-naked in *my* dining room. And who knows what went on in the kitchen. That Cuban laugh!"

"I thought Billy was a little overwhelming, too," Wade said, wondering again if Diana might be jealous.

Diana took a deep breath. "That's just who Billy is. He flirts, There's no denying that. I've had long discussions with Jolene. She says she's come to grips with Billy's flirting. First she told Billy to look but don't touch. 'But now,' Jolene told me, 'I figure whatever he does is okay. He works so hard, and he's always treated me as the most important thing in his life, so let him have some fun.'"

"Don't get me wrong," Diana told Wade. "That would never

meet my standards for a marriage, but remember Jolene comes from a different background. I'm not sure what the Catholics believe. But I support her, I do. And Rob absolutely loves Billy. He was best man at our wedding."

Wade frowned. He walked to the window and stared out into the darkness. He wished Diana could finish two sentences without talking about Rob. He said, "I see, so even with what you've been through, you can overlook Billy's faults?"

"Yes, absolutely. I don't understand you. Sometimes it seems you go out of your way to make me uncomfortable."

Wade wasn't sure what to say. From all of their conversations, he knew Diana was, at her core, a warm person. But sometimes she could be so cold. He hadn't intentionally made her uncomfortable, so what could he say? He didn't look at her when he said, "I'm thinking about taking a trip back to the Midwest."

Diana reached out to take his arm and turn him to face her. "Where'd that come from?"

"I haven't been back in . . . whew, over twenty years, and SnyderSound has a sales prospect in Chicago. Ray found some hot potential customer. It may be time for me to return to where I grew up. I have a lot to figure out."

Diana looked out toward the lights in the hills. "About us, you mean?"

Wade didn't want to say yes, and resorted, for good or ill—to poetry. He recited the lines that had come into his mind as he wondered what to do—

"Should I part my hair behind?

Do I dare to eat a peach?

I will wear white flannel trousers, and walk upon the beach.

I have heard the mermaids singing, each to each."

"I like you very much, Wade, you and your poetry world, but you may be right. Perhaps we *both* need time to think."

Rather than respond directly, Wade took the coward's route and quoted the next of Eliot's lines: "I do not think that they will sing to me."

They sat silently for a few minutes overlooking the foothills until they both stood up at the same time and she walked him to the door. They stepped into the entryway. Without touching, Diana walked Wade to the elevator. After he pushed the button, they hesitated before they embraced. Wade half-expected to feel a brass breastplate, but she was as soft as his memories of her.

She gently pushed away, slowly. "Part of me is dying to invite you back in."

Even though she felt wonderful in his arms, Wade kissed her on the forehead, dropped his hands from her waist, and left.

11

Wade didn't like to think about why he'd waited decades to return to Barrington. A business trip put him so near his home town that a visit seemed almost unavoidable, but he couldn't keep his high school thoughts away. His mother had abused prescription drugs and alcohol, and his father, even with his Ivy League education, had a hard time keeping a job. Could high school memories have been anything he was eager to revisit? Leaving from the airport in San Francisco, Wade scribbled down the start of a list, or even a poem, about how to return home, *Step One: Wait Twenty-two Years*.

The expensive suburb of his youth made him think of his last name—Middleton—the guy in the middle. He wasn't poor but he certainly wasn't wealthy like the family of his first love, Barbara, who had left him when he was twenty. He wondered now if he found Diana to be like Barbara, as they were both from wealth. Diana seemed a warmer person, but his memory of his college girlfriend could be colored by how she'd left him. One way or another, he didn't want to return to Barrington feeling inadequate. He had used frequent-flyer miles, once again, to upgrade for this trip home. *Step Two: Go First Class*.

His first sight was of a lush green landscape as the airplane descended into O'Hare airport, an unexpected nostalgia overwhelmed him. His eyes filled with tears and he felt a little woozy. When he deplaned, a late model blue sedan waited for him, trunk raised for his luggage, another frequent-flier benefit.

He drove to Hinsdale, a suburb twenty minutes south from the airport, where he was to meet with a group of local investors who wanted to refurbish nine theaters. Wade's job, theoretically, was to introduce them to the company's sound systems, but he knew his real job was to sell. During his presentation, he thought he impressed them with his thorough knowledge of the theaters in their present state and what the SnyderSound product would do to improve them. When they responded with enthusiasm, Wade called Ray to negotiate a price and presented it to them. Pleased with his success, he hopped in the car and drove thirty-five miles north to Barrington.

Rather than cut over to the toll road, he took surface streets through the towns he'd grown up around, like Arlington Heights. Forests, thicker than he was used to seeing in California, often flanked his car as he drove. Wade had heard of a new physics theory that people are connected to their place on earth through patterns in the earth's molecular structure and wondered if that might be affecting him. He guessed that the huge cumulonimbus cloud he saw out the right window had formed itself over Lake Michigan, which couldn't have been more than fifty miles to the East. He wasn't sure what seemed so familiar, the thick forests, or this molecule thing or the big sky with towering white clouds. One way or another, far from where he lived in California, Wade felt remarkably at home.

He first drove into the center of Barrington, where the forests had given way to strip malls, little developments, and, near the train tracks, a small downtown. He was in two worlds—real people were out buying things and going to jobs, looking like the people he'd seen in California that very same morning, but they were walking on streets that belonged in his childhood. Wade suddenly knew *Step Three: Hit All the Old Haunts.*

He passed the barbershop, its red, white, and blue striped pole still swirling exactly as it had when he was young. On haircut days, he'd run the six or seven blocks from high school into town to get a jump on the other boys. It was an early brush with *tempus fugit;* five minutes could save him an hour.

Wade drove past his old high school, situated on acres and acres of surrounding farm country, so it seemed large for the town. The school's clay-colored brick core stood three stories, with wings of classrooms protruding out into the northern Illinois plains. He spotted Mrs. Hautch's social studies classroom where, buoyed by her encouragement, he had worked hard the first semester of his senior year to get into college, and earned top marks. When he had slacked off second semester, she'd looked pained when she handed the first quiz back to him with a 'D' at the top. He'd managed to get into college, but years later, the memory still nagged at him.

Wade made a U-turn and headed into town, where he searched for the drive-in burger place, The Spot. It was the place he thought of every time he had watched *American Graffiti*. That would be a good feeling to recapture, he thought. Long before Lucas's movie, Wade had enjoyed cruising past The Spot in his father's emerald green Pontiac Catalina, purchased with inherited money right before his father had lost his last job. He wondered what effect his father's failures had on his own choices now. Perhaps Wade was a little too risk-averse for Silicon Valley.

When he arrived at the Spot's location, the drive-in was gone, replaced by a Ten-Minute-Lube. Wade inhaled the sour odor of discarded motor oil instead of the sweet smell of chocolate malts and hamburgers and sighed deeply. The disappearance of the drive-in saddened him. How could an oil-change business could hold the same memories as the drive-in?

∞

As the sun set among the massive puffy white clouds, Wade drove away from town, toward his old neighborhood, turning in to North Barrington Elementary School. From there he traced the path he used to walk to his house with his grade school friends. Ancient conversations came back to him: *What about the Giants swarming out of the dugout to throw punches at the Dodger pitcher? Normal adults don't beat each other up, do they? Why did God put sex in the same place where you go to the bathroom? And why did Jimmy's mom meet him at the door in her lacy underwear and slip? The bra was unlike any he'd ever seen—no shoulder straps! And when he stared, trying to understand what magic held it up, did she have to smile so directly at him?*

Unlike those slow walks, the drive from school to his old house took just minutes. When Wade saw his childhood home, he almost turned around and left. The original small building sitting on almost an acre of lawn was now painted white and had several additions. Two Honda sedans were parked in the driveway. He hesitated. But this was why he'd come, right? What he should do is knock on the front door. Who lives there now? Would there be any chance they'd let him in?

Step Four: Knock on the Door of the House Where You Lived. When Wade stepped onto the porch and worked up his nerve to rap on the door, he heard a woman's voice answer from a distant part of the house. "Who is it?" Wade took a step back when a woman opened the door a crack. Her pixie-cut gray hair framed a pleasant, kind-eyed face. He extended his hand and introduced himself, "My name is Wade Middleton. I used to live here, in the long bedroom over the garage, the one you have to go through the other bedroom to get to."

"Martha's my name," she opened the door wider and shyly returned his handshake. "When did you live here? We came in ninety-four. Please, come in."

"I left for California in the early eighties, just before they widened the road. You've kept it up nicely." Wade nodded as he stepped into the foyer off the living room.

A man with rolled-up shirt sleeves and a pair of wire-cutters in his hand stared out at Wade. He put the tool in his back pocket and came forward to shake Wade's hand. "I'm Tom," he said. "You say you're from California?"

"Yes, on a business trip." Wade looked around at the intricately patterned wood ceiling and stone fireplace and said, "I don't remember it being so elegant."

Tom smiled at the compliment, "Well, I spent three months sanding down the ceiling. It had been painted over. Everything needed work. The toughest was the crawl space—the lightest rain would fill it up." Wade remembered the drainage problems his father couldn't fix.

Martha motioned for Wade to take a seat and bustled off to the kitchen to start a pot of coffee. Tom settled into an easy chair as if he had no other plans than to have a pleasant chat with a man from California. Tom asked what had brought Wade out on a business trip.

"Oh, I work for a company that wires movie houses for sound, and I just closed a deal over in Hinsdale. That's my day job anyway. I also write some poems."

"Is that so? Well, I'm the vice-principal at a high school on the North side, where Martha teaches English. It's a long commute, but we love the rural feel out here. How about you?" He snapped his fingers as if he had just remembered something. He called out, "Martha, where's that old book I found?"

"It's around here someplace. I saw it just last week. Tom, why don't you take him upstairs?"

Wade followed Tom up a short stairway to a small room set among the sloping roofs. "This was my sister's room. She lives with another woman now, but it was young guys who'd come around in high school. It's strange to be in here." The room had a small balcony overlooking the front yard. "She was a live wire in those days. I think she might have snuck out down that trellis once or twice."

Tom chuckled politely. "We raised a daughter in here, too. Never thought about it, maybe she did that as well."

The two men walked into Wade's old room built over the two-car garage. He could almost touch the plasterboard ceiling. "As I was growing up here, an aspiring basketball player, I used to jump to the ceiling, no more than, oh, ten or twenty thousand times."

Tom laughed.

Wade had loved basketball in eighth grade, when he practiced endless shots and made the team. He'd found his moment of glory when he fashioned an improbable hook shot—the specialty of taller guys—to win a game. But he never grew past five foot nine, and when he got to high school the townies, bigger boys from a bigger school with real coaching, ran circles around him.

He stopped in the hallway up on the next level when he saw his parents' room, where his mother often lay in bed when he came home after school. Each day was slightly different. Sometimes she was lucid but argumentative. On the worst days she lay barely conscious, sometimes half-dressed, her speech slurred.

The thing that Wade learned was that he was less important to his mother than her next drink. These memories could keep anyone away, probably forever, and he questioned why he'd decided this time to come. He stopped talking to Tom—he couldn't be social any more. He followed Tom down the stairs without a word.

In the kitchen, Martha had filled three coffee mugs. "This house had five or six owners in just a few years, and two divorces. The neighbors called it the troubled house. Tom and I bought it after the young man who lived here died in a car wreck." It certainly was troubled when we lived here, Wade thought, and was glad when Martha interrupted his thoughts by handing him a book, an old paperback with cardboard covers.

Tom told Wade, "I found it between joists in the crawl space off your old bedroom."

Wade turned its fragile pages. "*101 Favorite Poems*. It's a wonderful find. I vaguely remember it, but I'm pretty sure it was mine."

Martha topped off the mugs. "Read it and see if it brings back any memories."

Wade thought he might have remembered his father reading "Jest 'Fore Christmas" by Eugene Field aloud to him and his sister. Could it have been from this book? Then he spotted his carefully-inscribed initials, WM, one the upside-down of the other, on the flyleaf. It was his. He kept reading.

Martha asked, "Are these the kinds of poems you write?"

"I don't rhyme mine very often. Sometimes. But these are great.
Here, listen to the way Kipling starts 'If'"—

> If you can keep your head when all about you
> Are losing theirs and blaming it on you,
> If you can trust yourself when all men doubt you,
> But make allowance for their doubting too.

Martha smiled warmly. "This book should be yours."

Wade shook his head. "No, I couldn't take it from you. But here's the part everybody remembers, the last stanza—

> If you can fill the unforgiving minute
> With sixty seconds' worth of distance run,
> Yours is the Earth and everything that's in it,
> And—which is more—you'll be a Man, my son!

Wade remembered wishing his father had been the kind of father who would talk to him like that. But now a father himself, he thought perhaps children ask too much of their parents. For the first time he realized that the birth of his daughter had allowed him to forgive his own parents, in a way. He looked at his hosts. "Maybe I should work on rhyming mine more—there's power in those rhymes."

"It's yours again." Martha looked at Tom, who nodded in agreement.

Wade started to refuse the book, but remembered the old adage that to accept a gift is to give a gift. The next step came to him. *Step Five: Accept Life's Gifts.* "Well, thank you, I'd love that."

∞

Wade drove west along a winding country road dotted with meadows. He soon entered the horsey-estates side of town, Barrington Hills, where his ex-girlfriend Barbara had lived. He passed the country club where he'd worn his first tux to escort Barbara to a cotillion. It wasn't until he took a right turn on Otis Road that he realized he was headed for Barbara's house. *Step Six: Ferret out the Pain.*

That summer when she was home from Bennington and he was home from the University of Washington, Wade and Barbara spent many evenings together. She pretended that she was headed for bed, and, with two sheets she had sewn together, slipped out her first-floor window and joined him in the barn, which wasn't visible from the house. He thought of the nights he gathered dry straw and Barbara stuffed it into the sheets, handful after handful. Wade had never been happier than when he drank in her nakedness, or better still, held her, made love to her. He loved the way she was confident and vulnerable at the same time—she opened herself to him without fear. In her warmth, his concerns about his family and his future faded. They were in love. What else could it be? That made everything right.

He never understood why, the following year, she broke up with him. The thought still stung. They were going to colleges on opposite ends of the country when the phone calls grew less frequent, and her letters, which had been filled with details of her days and specific longings for him, stopped altogether. Barbara's father, a prominent banker, hadn't liked Wade. Perhaps it was her father who had convinced her to stop seeing him, maybe even with a reward. Wade couldn't know for sure, but that spring Barbara's father did give her a new yellow convertible. Wade's letters to Barbara, compared to hers, were short and sketchy. Maybe he hadn't let her know how special he thought she was. Maybe a little acknowledgement might have helped with his ex-wife, too? Perhaps these were lessons he still needed to learn.

Barbara was a raw memory now, the girl who walked away. When Wade arrived at Barbara's childhood home and got out of the car, the sight of her father's name on the mailbox made him feel as uneasy as he had in his mother's room.

Lost in the memory of the times he'd met Barbara in the barn, he walked toward the dark structure. Suddenly lights went on everywhere, and a bell clanged. Dogs howled. Wade sprinted back to his car, slipping on the gravel and scraping his hand so it bled. He sped off. When he was well down the road, a police cruiser passed him headed the other way toward Barbara's house, its red and blue lights pulsing.

∞

On the night flight back to San Francisco, Wade was seated again in first class, next to a woman who appeared to be his age or slightly older. As he watched her remove her heels and change into slippers she carried in her briefcase, he thought what a seasoned traveler she must be. Wade admired how relaxed and graceful she seemed. Her black hair showed a few gray hairs that she had not dyed. Her elegant real-worldness blended well with her professional blue suit image, and her string of pearls. Wade made a mental note about carrying slippers in his briefcase. That would feel good, especially after a long day.

Glancing at her as the plane took off, the term "earth mother" came to mind, putting him at ease, but, elegantly dressed, she appeared a woman of power as well. After the painful trip to Barrington, Wade thought she might be a good person to talk to. He managed, with some delicacy, to strike up a conversation. After some gentle prodding, the woman said her name—"I'm Nicola Beldner, but everyone calls me by my initials, 'N. B.'" She said she was a university provost, which sounded vaguely powerful and learned. This seemed right—Wade wouldn't have been at all surprised if she had said she was a partner in a law firm or a powerful politician.

When he pulled out the book Martha and Tom had given him, *101 Favorite Poems*, N. B. said, "That book looks familiar. May I see it?"

Wade handed it to her.

"I had a book like this back in high school." She handled the volume carefully, like a curator. "Mine wasn't this tattered, but close. It's a classic, with Wordsworth, Shelley, Lord Byron. Look, first copyrighted 1873. Almost 150 years ago. Imagine how much things have changed, but somehow these seem fresh." She handed it back. "So, tell me about yourself."

Shyly at first, since N. B. seemed so accomplished, he described his life in Palo Alto. "And lately I've been seeing a new lady. I might have finally found the right one, a lovely horsewoman, but right now we're apart," Wade concluded. He quickly chided himself for revealing too much.

"Palo Alto's a nice town. It's where I met my partner, actually my wife." At Wade's surprised glance, she smiled and said, "We're one of those gay couples you read so much about."

"Oh, my sister is in a relationship with a woman," Wade said. "She was married to a guy, which was a bit of a mess, but we all got through it, and so did she. The two of us are closer now than ever." He reached out to shake N. B's hand. "Well, congratulations." She smiled as they shook.

Wade took a deep breath. He felt the same urge to take a chance that he did when he stood outside his old house. "I hate to impose," Wade blurted out, "but I'd like a little help here. I have seven steps for a poem or article on *going home*. I need one more."

"Steps?" she asked, shaking her head. "I don't know what you mean."

"Pretend you had to choose one pithy thing to say to people who are returning home after a long time. What would it be?"

"You want me to distill life into one statement?" she laughed wryly and shook her head. "All right, what have you got already?"

Wade talked her through the steps. She smiled when he told her *Wait Twenty-two Years, Go First Class, Hit All the Old Haunts,* but looked apprehensive when Wade mentioned *Knock on the Door of the House Where You Lived.* She smiled again at *Accept Life's Gifts,* and said, "Good advice there, people have the hardest time accepting gifts, but they resent it when they don't get them!" She laughed.

When he came to *Ferret out the Pain,* N. B. looked at him like a country doctor making a diagnosis.

Wade didn't want her analysis. He wanted a last step. "Whatever you say the last step is, N. B., that's it. I won't argue."

She said, "Okay, I'll think about it," and returned to the poetry book.

A half hour later, as the pilot announced the plane was on final approach, Wade's seatmate looked at him. He quickly asked, "So do you have one for me?"

"I might," she said. "This guy's confidence ebbs and flows. The trip home brings out his insecurities."

Wade didn't want to push deeper. "Yes, that's true. So, what's the last step?"

"This isn't going to end up in some newspaper as what the provost says, right?"

He laughed. "No, I'll steal it as my own, I promise."

"We need to buck this guy up. Kipling's poem encourages trust. 'Trust yourself when all men doubt you.' Things have always gone better for me when I do that. How about just *Trust yourself*?"

Wade hesitated. The step didn't sound as final as he had hoped, and too *easy* somehow. But he had told her he would accept her answer, no matter what. And this was a gift, and one of the steps was *Accept Life's Gifts*. If he took it, the list would be complete. Done.

In the terminal, just beyond the security exit, a muscular driver in a navy-blue sport coat and red tie waited for the provost. Wade thought he saw the bulge of a gun near the driver's shoulder as he welcomed N. B. to San Francisco.

"So it's *Step Seven: Trust Yourself?*" he asked her.

The provost nodded. She said, "I fly quite a bit, so I've had some strange things happen on planes, but none stranger than this. Still, I'd like to read what you finally come up with." With that, she handed Wade her business card, clapped him lightly on the shoulder, turned, and walked off with her driver.

12

Wade arrived home that night to find that Jorge had left three short voicemails. The last one ended, "Call me when you get in, no matter how late."

It was after eleven, but he did what Jorge asked. "Hey buddy. What's going on?"

"Eva's sick, that's one thing. She's had a cough for two weeks and doctors have run two sets of allergy tests. They can't find anything, so we're back to square one. She woke us all up this morning at four. It's pretty bad."

"Is she going to school?"

"Well, no. Not since Tuesday when the school called and asked Marita to come in and pick her up. The weird thing is, when the doctor's tests didn't turn up anything, he asked if there were any problems at home." He lowered his voice. "He wondered if it was, you know, emotional."

Wade grimaced, and was glad Jorge couldn't see him through the telephone.

"But the real problem," Jorge continued, "is Billy the Kid. He called Friday afternoon and told Marita to ask me to call him first thing the next day. I haven't called him because I wanted to talk to you first. Marita thinks he has a job for me."

"Well, you need a job, right?" Wade knew what Jorge was asking and didn't like how he'd responded.

"I don't know." Jorge took a deep breath. "Okay. I guess you're right. I have to call him."

Although it would later become one of those memories Wade would beat himself up for, he didn't take much time in replying. "I don't see what harm talking to him can do." Wade knew guys like Billy could do harm, a lot of harm, so what he said to Jorge was a lie. A white lie, but still a lie.

"Marita said he wants me to come to his offices," Jorge said. "*Offices?* I swear there's something very weird about that guy. But you're right, Wade, I need a job."

After a long pause, Jorge finished by saying, "I'll call him."

Long after this conversation, Wade wondered if he'd done the right thing by his friend. His gut told him otherwise. But his gut also knew Jorge badly needed a job.

∞

Three days after Wade encouraged Jorge to call Billy, as Wade was driving to work, his cell phone rang. Jorge. Wade put the phone on speaker to hear, "I'm sitting at Whileaway Circle, in Woodside. Seven names are nailed to boards on a tree, showing who lives there. The list includes both Buchanan—that's Diana's ex, right?—and Tyler. This is where the hotshots live. The lots must be five acres or more."

"Yes, they've got the long green, for sure. It's easy to say money isn't everything, but it sure takes the sting out of things. Why in the world are you there, Jorge?"

"When I signed up for the interview, I went to the Internet to check around. The search for 'Billy Tyler' produced four entries, a public relations announcement of his transfer to California—that law firm is a real powerhouse, then articles about two of his law cases, and a recent entry—something where he'd donated to a political group, not one I'd heard of, something about Freedom—that gave his home address here on Whileaway Circle. The online map guide showed me it was close to the office where I'm supposed to meet him later this morning, so I thought I'd see how these guys live. Top-drawer."

"I guess," Wade said. "Joan Baez lives up there in Woodside. And the founder of Oracle, Larry Ellison, has a house there. He's on all the too-much-money-to-count lists. Woodside is the place I'd wanted to take Diana for New Year's dinner. Yes, as you'd guessed, her husband or ex or whatever is the Buchanan name you saw. He has a place near where you are. He's Billy's boss."

"Oh, so Diana's into the big big money—I didn't quite get that. I'm heading out, but I can see a couple of the houses. One's modern, the other traditional, both huge of course, with barns and rail fences that go on and on. One house had at least twelve guys laying sod and building a fence. Another world. I think I'll go into that little village I passed on my way in here and grab a cup of coffee before I see Billy."

"I just pulled into the parking lot here at work, Jorge, and I need to get upstairs to make a phone call back East. But that will only take a few minutes, after that I'm free all morning. Sure, go into Woodside and grab a cup of coffee at Buck's to settle down, and then go see Billy. Buck's is a coffee shop the way the old Schwab's on Sunset was a drugstore. Sometimes it seems like it's action central for Silicon Valley. Call me when you get out. Don't let their mansions intimidate you. As the saying goes, they still have to put their trousers on one leg at a time."

"I don't know if I'm intimidated, but I'm starting to understand this valley is all about money. In that world, I'm nothing. Why don't you come up to that Buck's place in two hours, I'll go there after my interview."

"Don't get overwhelmed by their money," Wade said. "It's as much circumstance as anything else. I mean, look at Rob—that's Diana's ex. He inherited the firm from his father."

Wade finished off the conversation by saying, "Okay, see you at Buck's around eleven." When he hung up, he said a little prayer for his friend and his meeting.

∞

While waiting for Jorge at Buck's Restaurant, Wade thought it wasn't the kind of place where one would imagine deals got done. He stood beneath the most famous of its hundreds of decorations, a mounted buffalo head. Wade had been introduced to the owner of Bucks—Jamis MacNiven—and respected him and the quirky, remarkably well-liked institution he'd created. Just as he had begun to realize on his trip back to Barrington, he was just like his last name, he thought, neither rich nor poor—he was mid-peninsula, midtown in Palo Alto, *Middleton.*

Wade took a seat in a booth and read a morning *San Francisco Chronicle* that had been left on the table.

When Jorge came in, he sat down. "Billy pretty much offered me a job with stock options. He's focused on security and thought the options would tie me to the company."

Wade didn't receive stock options—typically they came with executive-level jobs—and was surprised they were offered to Jorge. "Tell me more," he said.

"I will, but first, did you see that huge buffalo head on the wall over there? I swear its eyes move when a customer goes by. It must be some kind of trick."

"Sure, the eyes move. Nobody's sure how the owner does it. He's a character. That's him over in the corner—I'll introduce you. But first I want to hear about your meeting."

"Billy's office is amazing, the whole building. Tall ceilings, French furniture, big plants everywhere. His offices, as he says. Always with an *s* at the end."

"I hear that the suite is actually leased by Diana's husband, or his father. Everyone there works for Buchanan, including Billy."

"At any rate, impressive. This knockout redhead met me in the lobby. Robin. She fit right in with the place. Could have been a model. The law offices were nothing like SnyderSound. Billy's office has a view of San Francisco Bay, with a carpeted putting green in one corner."

"Whoa," Wade said.

"Robin is a personnel specialist. Billy said Enersystems would have to make the actual offer, but that Robin was taking notes, which she was, furiously. She handed me some brochures about the company. From there on, Billy didn't say too much. She kind of ran the meeting, taking notes and going over lists she'd made. Afterwards she said she'd fax her notes over to Enersystems and they'd probably make an offer."

"What's the job?"

"They're making a lot of presentations, especially to the Energy Commission in Sacramento. Most of the pitches have graphics and video in them. I'd be the part of the team that makes sure nothing goes wrong. Presentations with no glitches, he said. Troubleshoot technically, you know."

"That's all? You could do that with your left hand."

"It sounds like something they could hire a contractor for. I asked them about that."

"Gutsy, when they're dangling a job." Wade looked at the buffalo head, trying to figure out how the owner, who was slowly moving toward them talking to his customers along the way, managed to get the eyes to move. "How did Billy respond?"

"He said that the job's all about confidentiality. Only trusted Enersystems employees can attend these meetings, no contractors. That's when he said the job would have stock options to tie me to the company. He claimed I could make thousands of dollars on them. He actually said hundreds of thousands but I'm not about to believe that. He explained I could sell the shares or borrow on them—some in twelve months and some in twenty-four months. Seven thousand shares each time, with a strike price of twenty dollars. It was a little confusing—"

"It means you have to pay twenty dollars a share," Wade interjected. "The question is what the shares are worth. Let me check." He thumbed to the business section of the newspaper he'd been reading. "Holy shit, Enersystems is selling for just under forty dollars. I'm sure yours don't vest right away—next year or so—but if they did, you'd make almost twenty dollars a share. Seven thousand shares today would net you, let's see, a hundred and forty thousand dollars, like Billy said. That's hard to believe. Are you sure he said twenty a share?"

"I wrote it down," Jorge said, pointing to his notes. "Look."

"Did he talk salary?"

"At least twenty percent above what I made at SnyderSound, he said. They didn't mention a specific number."

"Why aren't you walking on air?"

"There was something he said at the end. He told me that my political views made him nervous, but it helped that Marita seemed to have her head screwed on right."

"That's not a problem, is it?"

"If it ended there, no. But he went on. He said he wanted her to come into 'his offices' for a private conference. Billy said he'd get everything started with Enersystems, but he wouldn't sign off on it until Marita came in for a private meeting. Wade, you have more business experience than I do. That's strange, right?"

"It sure is," Wade blurted out. "Beyond strange." It made Wade even more suspicious of Billy's intentions. Why was he offering to pay Jorge so much? Marita was an attractive woman, but if that was what this was about, the amount of money they were discussing seemed like overkill.

"The next thing you know," Jorge said, "I was following Robin out past the leafy plants and fancy furniture. It wasn't that long ago that I was following Günter under very different circumstances. Things look a lot better when people are hiring you than when they're firing you, that's for sure."

Wade took a deep breath. His gut knew he should tell Jorge to forget Enersystems right then and there, but before he could say that, Jorge took Wade off the hook by bringing up a new subject. "This restaurant is filled with people talking about startups and financing deals. Before I went to see Billy, I asked this guy next to me—he's gone now—if he'd heard of Enersystems, that I might work there. He said he knew them, and that they were very slick. 'Everybody's political, but Enersystems is even more so,' he said. When I asked him what he meant, he shook his head and said, 'You'll see.'"

Wade waited a beat before he responded. "Let me think all this over."

Jorge said, "At the very least, if I take the job I can get Eva her own room. There's a two-bedroom unit available in our building. That *would* be great."

"True," he said. The restaurant's colorful owner came by wearing an outsized cowboy hat and outlandish shirt stitched with bucking red cows. When Wade introduced him, he noticed Jorge's plate and asked, "Good pancakes? They're our specialty, a secret recipe," and shook Jorge's hand. The owner had one of those novelty joke buzzers in his palm. Jorge, taken completely by surprise, jumped a mile. He shook his head after the owner left.

Wade shrugged and said, "So much for local color. Where were we? Oh, yes, Billy. For all the good in this, buddy, I have to be honest with you. You're being offered a lot of money. It might make you wonder exactly what Billy is up to." As soon as Wade said it that way, he was certain they both knew exactly what Billy was up to, words they could never say to one another.

Jorge wanted to pay the bill, but Wade insisted. On the way out, he went into the restroom and washed his hands. Leaning down over the sink, scrubbing his hands more than they needed, he could not help but think about Pontius Pilate and Lady Macbeth and all the hand-washers before him who could not erase their fate. Wade kicked himself for not telling Jorge to get out while he still could.

13

Wade worked himself up to call Diana a few days after he returned from Barrington, not knowing what to expect because of what she had said after the dinner party, that they both needed some time apart. On the phone, though, Diana was her gracious self, which relieved him. Had she forgotten their little fight? She laughingly told him Artemis missed him.

Wade took a chance and asked her out to coffee. She agreed to meet him at the Palo Alto Café, their regular spot. She wore the same creamy silk blouse he'd noticed the first time he'd met her. It was particularly flattering on her slim torso and gave her an alluring look of womanhood and sophistication. If she wore this to draw Wade in, she succeeded. But after small talk, he made the mistake of bringing up Jorge and Billy, which turned her smile into a frown. Still, he pressed. "Don't you think that Billy wanting to meet with Marita is strange?" Wade asked.

"No, it's not strange. It's business. Jolene explained this to me," Diana said quickly. "Billy wants to hire Jorge as a favor to, well, to Marita and her daughter Eva and all of us, really. We all want the best for them. But he wants to be sure of his loyalty before he brings him onto the team. Enersystems is involved in some critical talks, very political, and the last thing they need is a loose cannon. And although Marita has her idiosyncrasies, her politics make him more comfortable about Jorge. I'm even feeling better about Marita. Perhaps I shouldn't have reacted so negatively after the party. Billy certainly warmed to her, and he's no fool."

Who could forget? "You really think that's all there is to it, a question of Jorge's loyalty? I could testify to that. He's a straight arrow."

Diana changed the subject by saying, "Tell me all about your trip."

Wade took a deep breath and told her he'd visited the house of an old girlfriend. "She broke it off, and she's married now, so it's not like I'm trying to rekindle an old flame, but it was interesting to think of how much the two of you are alike. Barbara reminds me of you in a lot of good ways. She had horses, Arabians, like Amelia's new horse. She wasn't as petite as you are, and her hair was longer, and Barbara had none of the red of your hair. Still, there's a similarity."

The café was almost deserted. She scrunched her face to show Wade she thought this was a strange thing to bring up. "Was she at the house you visited?"

"Oh, no, Barbara's long gone from Barrington. I hear she lives in New Mexico. I don't know if anyone lives in her parent's house now. It's an estate really, with a covered ring and a barn. I'm pretty sure there was no one home. I walked out to the empty barn and tripped a security alarm. I jumped like a jackrabbit." He laughed at himself and showed where he'd scraped his hand, hoping Diana would laugh with him.

"That *is* strange." Diana shook her head and then looked at him directly, so that the imperfection around her eye stood out. "Why are you telling me this? Are you planning to see her or something?"

"No, no. I haven't talked to her in years. If it weren't for you, I wouldn't think about her at all. The fact that you two are so similar gives me a little pause. She wounded me."

"That might have been her loss, Wade. I've been thinking a lot about you, too. Good thoughts, mainly, and I made a decision that will help me to break my ties to Rob."

As they sipped coffee, her hand moved nearer to his on the table.

"Yesterday I told him I wouldn't play hostess at the partner's retreat ever again. No more Wifey. That Christmas party was my last. End of discussion."

Wade moved his hand closer to hers. "How'd he take it?"

"Not well. He was dropping the kids off, happy as can be, until I said no more partner parties. He looked like I punched him."

"I'm sorry," Wade said.

"We're both so committed to the kids, but I can no longer pretend that nothing's happened. I almost mentioned the D word to him."

"You're afraid to even say the word *divorce?*"

"Not now, Wade."

He moved his hand the last few inches to hers, wondering, but not asking, why she didn't broach divorce with Rob. Probably to protect the kids and because he was so generous financially. But then he wondered if it may have had to do with religion. "With your religious beliefs, is divorce possible?"

"Oh, sure," Diana said. "Evangelicals don't like divorce, but they *can* remarry afterwards. It's not like the Catholics, who frown on remarrying. It's not a no-no, but we try to avoid it."

Her staying married shouldn't bother him, Wade thought. After all, was he ready for a fully committed relationship? He knew his attraction to her was real, and it was not only a physical one. Who understands these things, really?

∞

Once back home, Wade checked messages on his landline. He had a voicemail from Amelia. When Wade called her back, he could hear music—something metallic—blaring. He sure wished her cell phone worked in the dorm. The phone she called from in the hallway was a pain.

"Just a second," she said. A door slammed, and the noise hushed. "I wanted to talk to you more about horses, Dad. I'm so excited you're riding. I'm getting serious about bringing Ahab down to Bard. I could stable him across the street from campus."

"Don't you think Bard seems more artsy than horsey?" Wade asked. He was standing by the kitchen counter, sorting mail with his iPhone on speaker.

"They're not mutually exclusive, Dad. In those old French caves, what's the oldest art archaeologists find? Horses have inspired art for a long time. And, to change the subject, there are a lot of horses in Mexico. I hope we can go."

"Are you going to use Ahab as a subject for your photographs?"

"I hadn't thought about it—that's not my kind of photography. Still, that's an interesting idea." After a pause, Amelia asked, "Do you canter?"

"Some. Mainly we walk and trot." Wade realized he'd never told her about going out with the hounds, but that was a subject that would take a while so he didn't mention it. "Diana's afraid I'll stop riding if I fall."

"I almost quit the first time I came off. I cracked a rib," his daughter replied.

"You cracked a rib!" Wade dropped the mail and sat down on the sofa. "When?"

"Last summer. Not on Ahab, but with a rent-a-horse at a place I found with Mom. It was before Christmas. Mom and I agreed not to tell you so you wouldn't worry."

Wade felt a flash of anger at Liz. Not only did this make Wade wonder what else he hadn't been told, but he had thought the rent-a-horse excursions he used to have with Amelia were reserved for the two of them only. He worked on holding his tongue.

Amelia quickly filled the silence. "Dad, are you riding horses just to get close to Diana, or do you really like it?"

"I love it, honey. Sometimes I go out to the ranch even when I don't have time to ride, without Diana, just to feed Artemis. Groom her, give her a carrot, talk to her, all those things."

"I was hoping that was true, Dad. That's one of the things that made me call. You may not realize this, but it was you who got me into horses in the first place. Those times you took me to Half Moon Bay. And this weekend, I rode Ahab three times and I cried when I had to leave him up there. Mom feeds him and everything, but he hardly ever gets ridden. Horses need to get out. What breed is Artemis?"

"Diana tells me Artemis is a Percheron-Thoroughbred mix," he said. "Everybody says she's very much the mare. She's particular about who rides her. She's bucked a lot of people off, but she and I get along fine. I spoil her."

"Why am I not surprised, Dad. Maybe I can get out to California and we can ride together."

"You *should* come. I want you to meet Diana and her kids. You could give Beth some tips on getting through Paly."

"Well, I was thinking about something else for spring break. Remember we talked about going to Mexico together? I want to learn Spanish over the summer in some out of the way place—perhaps we could visit a few likely towns?"

"That'd be great, and I'd also like you to meet Beth."

His daughter didn't respond, which didn't cheer Wade at all.

Finally she said, "Well, what do you think about Mexico?"

"I'd love that, honey," Wade said. "Let's do it. Get tickets in and out of Guanajuato—it's central. Use that credit card number I gave you. We can go from there. Send me the dates and I'll meet you there and rent a car. Make sure your passport's up to date and good for six months. I love you."

She closed off by saying, "Me, too. Thanks, Dad."

14

Even as Wade continued his ambiguous relationship with Diana, he realized, at least for now as they were each figuring things out, his higher responsibility was to Amelia. First things first—his flesh-and-blood. If she wanted to go to Mexico, he would make it happen, and he did.

He and Amelia spent their first two days in Mexico in the colonial mountain towns of San Miguel de Allende and Querétaro, but Amelia never warmed to them. "Too touristy," she said.

Their travel plans took them to Acapulco on their third day, but they got a late start, and it took forever to get through Mexico City. By seven o'clock the sun was setting, and they were still hours from the Pacific. When they came to the town of Taxco, "Mexico's Silver Capital," they agreed to stop for the night. He parked their rental car near an intersection where a policeman directed traffic from a stand and approached to ask directions. The officer stepped down from the stand so Wade could talk to him over the traffic noise.

"Hotel?" Wade asked, working to drop the "h."

"*Si, Santa Prisca,*" he said, pointing down the street. "*Es muy bonito.*"

Wade pressed a small coin into the policeman's palm. When he thanked him with the Italian phrase, *Grazie,* Amelia rolled her eyes.

"*Gracias,*" the cop said without changing his expression, and re-mounted his stand.

The courtly man behind the desk at the Santa Prisca told him neither they, nor anyone downtown, had rooms. But his cousin had a place on the edge of town. After making a phone call, he said, nodding, "He's away this weekend, but they still have an opening."

The hotel was a run-down three-story gray box across from a deserted gas station. Wade and Amelia climbed to the third floor to find that the only room available was only big enough to contain two simple beds. A small porch overlooked the gas station. Half of the tile bathroom was a shower with no curtain, something neither of them had ever seen before. A bare bulb hung from the ceiling. He and his daughter looked at each other and shrugged.

Wade paid the young man to carry their luggage upstairs. At last they could head out and find dinner.

He loved the ubiquitous town squares of Mexico, where people go to see and be seen, especially as the evenings cooled. As they walked up a street and across a square to dinner, Wade noticed how grown up and pretty Amelia looked. She had styled her hair in a buzz cut the last time Wade had seen her, but the sides had grown in, so it had lost its shock value. When the young men on the square couldn't keep their eyes off her, he felt half protective of her and half proud that he had raised this lovely young woman.

During their meal at a charming restaurant, Amelia said she didn't think she wanted to stop in Acapulco the next day.

"No?" Wade asked incredulously. "I've always wanted to go there."

"Dad, maybe I could learn Spanish in some place like we visited last night. Querétaro, right? But I saw license plates from Idaho and Georgia. I'd like to experience the local culture. I imagine Acapulco will be worse. Let's get on to Oaxaca. That's the town my friends talk about."

"I've read about Acapulco all my life," he said. "I'd really like to see it."

"We've lost a day, Dad. What kind of photographs am I going to get in Acapulco?"

A gaunt middle-aged man with a peaceful-looking face and wearing a necktie shyly angled toward their table, looking longingly at their plate of bread. Wade wrapped the bread in a paper napkin, moved it to the edge of the table near him, and motioned.

The man in the necktie grabbed the bread and quickly disappeared from the restaurant.

"Good job, Dad," Amelia said. "I wish I had a picture of his face."

"A camera would have scared him, I'm sure. But I love it that you always think in photographic terms."

"Yes, it's not all about capturing moments, but that's part of photography for sure. Speaking of capturing the past, Dad, there's something I have been wanting to ask you. Looking back, how do you feel about the divorce? I know you loved Mom."

Wade was slightly taken aback at his daughter's directness and shift of subject matter. "Oh, sweetie," he answered, "I'm finally over it. I know your mother is wonderful to you—she always has been. How about you?"

"Yeah, I'm glad those days are behind us. I was so mad at each of you at different times. But, here in Mexico, I'm have pangs of guilt. We don't feel rich in Palo Alto, but compared to how people live here, we are. Practically nobody here has cars. Except around Mexico City, the highway is mainly for trucks. And we're making our own kind of bubble now. Yesterday's hotel had free shampoo, conditioner, and a shower cap—"

"Not so, tonight," Wade interrupted, and they both rolled their eyes. "But you're right. To them, we're rich Americans. I've been hanging around with people with a lot more money at home, so there are two sides to things. Compared to people around here, we're like royalty. I wish I spoke Spanish better, with your accent." This conversation made him think about Jorge and Marita, but there was no way to tell Amelia that without telling her way too much.

"I've been working on it at Bard, with a guy from Costa Rica. I could teach you."

"Is he a boyfriend?"

"Dad, isn't that kind of a rude question? But no, I have no current boyfriend."

"*Si*. What's the Spanish word for *domani*?"

"Enough Italian—*mañana*."

"*Si, señorita Amelia, mañana.*"

"Dad, let's call it a night."

∞

Their toilet wouldn't flush. Wade lifted the lid and found neither water nor the parts to make it work. "Oh, well," he said to Amelia, "We only have to live with it for one night." As he closed the tank, he knocked the only roll of toilet paper into the bowl. "Damn!" He pulled it out and deposited it in the tin can under the sink, then went down to the lobby and brought up a roll of toilet paper and a bucket of water to flush the toilet.

They slept on narrow beds. He awoke at dawn, when Amelia was whispering, "Dad." She peeked out from behind the bathroom door. "I think I have the *tourista*."

"It's okay, honey, I'll go downstairs and get something for you. I looked up some words in your dictionary to get me by."

Thankfully, the room clerk was behind his desk. "*Farmacia*," Wade said. "*¿El mapa?*"

He pulled out a tourist map and opened it on the desk. "*Yo sé.*" He marked a place toward the center of town.

Wade pointed to his watch. "*¿Qué hora?*"

The clerk nodded. "Is okay. *Venga.*"

∞

Wade enjoyed exploring the early-morning streets of a place he never knew existed. The small town woke up around him as he walked. Perhaps the spring in his step was because he was on an errand of mercy for his Amelia. A large green cross identified the pharmacy— open indeed. Wade bought some Lomotil without a prescription. Walking back to the hotel, he experienced one of those moments where he felt completely alive. By the time he returned it was nine. Amelia had fallen back asleep. Wade left the medicine on the bedside table and went downstairs with a local newspaper, trying to discern what he could from the Spanish headlines.

When he went back upstairs, after ten, she was in the bathroom. "I'll be a while, Dad," she said. "Thanks for the medicine, and for cleaning up." She spoke weakly, sounding embarrassed. When she came out, she said she didn't think she could get back on the road again right away, but that she'd go with him to get some breakfast. "I'll just have tea."

At the outdoor café Amelia was much more subdued than the night before. She told him that the Lomotil was working—almost miraculously, she said—and apologized for the mess she'd made in the bathroom. "And I'm sorry about last night. Of course we can stop in Acapulco. This trip isn't just for me."

Wade was proud of his daughter. She was growing up. Less self-involved. When he thanked her, she talked about another guy at Bard, Jason. He wasn't the guy from Costa Rica, and she announced that he wasn't her boyfriend, either.

Wade considered probing a bit, but decided to talk about his own situation instead. "Diana and I are seeing less of each other now. I mean, I still want you to meet her daughter Beth, but Diana and I aren't quite the item we were when I first asked you. That may change, I hope."

Two policemen passed, cheerfully trailing behind a woman who swayed in front of them. Wade grimaced when he realized that her sensual walk reminded him of Marita.

Amelia asked, "Does she look like your new girlfriend?"

He shook his head. "Not really. Diana's more sophisticated. She's got it going on, too; she just doesn't flaunt it that way." After he said it, he worried he'd come close to crossing some line for what was appropriate for a dad and daughter to talk about.

"I'm just curious. I sure don't need another mom, but I want to see you happy, and you never seemed happier than when you talked about Diana and her horses. What have you told her about me? Does she know I am getting into horses in a big way, too?"

"Oh, I brag about you. You're my success story, and she always asks about Ahab. She likes Arabian horses, although she loves to jump Thoroughbreds. She says they jump like deer, so graceful and controlled. She's very natural with horses, the way she touches them and how they respond to her, everything. It's uncanny."

"She sounds like a winner, Dad," Amelia said. "So what's your hesitation?"

When Wade avoided her pointed question, Amelia changed the subject. "Let's push on to Acapulco. It is, after all, part of Mexico, and you deserve going where you like. Thanks for taking such good care of me. I'm almost myself again."

Walking back to the car, as they discussed the cities they'd been to, and where they were going, Amelia took her father's arm. The smallest happiness, like the hungry man in the necktie getting the bread he craved, can arrive as if from nowhere. Wade hoped it wouldn't vanish as quickly into the night.

15

Six weeks later, when Jorge and Wade were to meet at Buck's for lunch, Jorge called him at the last minute to say he was running late. Instead, he asked Wade to meet him at an Indian restaurant a block from the Enersystems office in Mountain View.

Jorge was sporting a new look—a black polo shirt with a blue blazer, and he wore wraparound sunglasses. As he approached the table, he turned them around, so the arms of the glasses went around his ears backward. "You'll like this place, good food," he said as he sat down.

"So should I start calling you Giorgio?" Wade asked. One of the walls was covered with red patterned cloth, and the storefront location was mitigated by white tablecloths.

Smiling, Jorge raised his sunglasses to his forehead and said, "You can call me Jorge, amigo. Hey, Wade, are you seeing Diana again?"

The fact was they had started seeing each other again, at least twice a week, but he shrugged. "Un poco, cabrón." Just then, their server, a young Indian woman with a red dot on her forehead, came into view. Jorge gave her a wave and said, "Hi, Chetana, you're lookin' good."

At their table, she tried to hide a smile and seemed to blush. "Hello, Jorge. The chef has very good lamb curry today."

"You know best, Chetana."

Wade nodded. "Sounds good."

"I will bring your naan."

She was back at their table quickly with hot bread on a plate and a green sauce.

"Chetana," asked Jorge, "How long have you been in America?"

"Almost three years."

"You must have studied hard—you speak English so well," Jorge said.

Lowering her eyes, she thanked him and turned away. "I will see if the curry is ready. As they watched her disappear around the corner, Jorge said, "That dot on her forehead's called a bindi—she told me."

Wade nodded, indicating he knew. "So how's Eva doing? Did those tests show anything?"

"She seems better. She still doesn't have her own room. We almost rented a bigger apartment, but Marita wants to save every penny for a down payment."

"You can afford to buy a house?"

"You're thinking the old SnyderSound way. Like you tried to tell me last fall, the Valley's *hot*. Half those stock options come due next spring. The stock's been going up fast, so if nothing changes it should be well over five hundred thousand dollars. Can you believe it? Marita wants us to buy a house in Palo Alto first thing."

As Jorge said this, Wade tore off a piece of naan and dipped it in the curry sauce, but was so surprised at this news that he dropped it. "It's ex-pen-sive."

"We know. Marita checks the real estate listings on the Internet at least twice a day, and drags me to open houses every Sunday now."

"Do the real estate people say you can afford it?"

"I sat down with a mortgage guy who said if I could come up with five hundred thousand dollars, maybe less, he could make it work. We have a few thousand salted away, so with the stock up, that should be no sweat, but we're scrimping anyway."

Wade had been wondering why Enersystems was paying Jorge so well. Snydersound didn't have stock options, partly because Ray and

Sherry owned it all, and this deal with Jorge sometimes made Wade jealous. "What, exactly, does Enersystems have you doing?"

Jorge dipped, too. "If I told you that, *compadre*, I'd have to shoot you."

"Come on. Let's start with the basics. Do you have to be at your desk nine to five?"

"*Eight* to five." Jorge laughed. "I can take all day for lunch, but they really want me to have my feet under the desk at eight. If I get in early, keep my mouth shut, and the presentations go without a hitch, I'm golden."

"What are the presentations like?"

"Don't ask. I really *could* lose my job, and I couldn't stand poverty again. I will say that the graphics are getting more and more elaborate. I set up surround-sound in some shabby office in Sacramento. It performs perfectly. I keep backups of everything they present in the Cloud now. The sales guys love me because I email updates to them the next day."

"You've always been able to set up anything."

Jorge took another piece of naan. "One thing I can talk about is how good-looking the young women are. There's eye candy everywhere. Boy, if I were only a bachelor."

It was a little hard to hear Jorge, the father of his goddaughter, talking this way, but at the same time he was happy for him. Wade remembered Jorge had been with him through his divorce and decided to just go with this banter. He thought about the woman who helped with travel at SnyderSound and laughed. "I'd have a hard time giving up Helen, the way she helps with our trips."

"The one who wore that brownish cardigan all winter? You'd give her up in a heartbeat if you saw this gal. Last Friday it was supposed to be very casual, so she wore a see-through blouse, brown-shadow nipples and all. The talk of the office. The office manager sent her home. He took his time doing it, but by eleven she was out of there."

Jorge's job didn't seem just different, it seemed like another world.

"She does the travel stuff too?"

"We have a separate travel department. That girl's a babe, too."

Wade sat back in his seat, looking his friend over. If something sounds too good to be true, it almost always *is* too good to be true. Was he just jealous? Wade was doing okay, but he'd never take home half a million dollars in a chunk like that. The energy Jorge exuded was palpable. Still Wade wanted to caution him. "I wonder about you and this job."

He shrugged. "Marita's never been happier and in some ways, and I'm having a blast. I'm headed to Houston next week; some muckety-muck insisted on approving these presentations and they don't want anything to go wrong. Another surround-sound deal, with tons of video. They booked a limo to take me to the airport, and one on the other end, too."

Wade raised his eyebrows. Although he was worried about Jorge long-term, it was good to see him feeling on top of things. "Living large, amigo."

Jorge sat back, smiling. "You betcha, gringo."

∞

While Diana and Wade had begun seeing each other again, they never mentioned their relationship. They just kept meeting, and he occasionally slept over. One Sunday, after he had spent the night, she invited him to church. Afterwards Wade sat reading the Sunday *Chronicle* in the sunny room next to Diana's kitchen while she baked a coffee cake. The noon sun filled the west-facing room with light. Seated across the counter from him, she asked, "So, what did you think of my church?"

Diana had taken Wade to a storied mid-Peninsula church with thousands of members. There were things he didn't like about it, but he wanted to be circumspect. He had noted a subtle "Holier than thou" tone in the service, but knew better than to bring that up. He decided to talk about the songs. "I miss the old hymns," he said, looking up from the paper.

"Ah, the new-music question. Young people like the new songs—they played similar ones back in Dallas, too, in a big church we used to go to out by the airport."

Wade put the newspaper down. The aroma of baking sugar wafted their way. "I'd heard *about* them, called '7-11' music; seven words repeated eleven times, but I had never actually heard them. Sometimes services seem to border on a rock concert."

"The youngsters like 'em," she said, "but I prefer the old hymns, too."

This evangelical world was something Wade had never paid much attention to, and Diana's comfort with it seemed so ingrained in her that he wondered if any reservation on his part might cause friction. Although he'd never thought of it that way, the church he went to was more mainstream Protestant. For now, he just responded, "Good." The kitchen timer still had fifteen minutes on it. He set a couple of place mats with silverware and braced himself to bring up the subject of her kids. Wade and Diana had taken them to a park with paddleboats the day before. It hadn't gone well. Beth had played the part of an overly polite southern girl, friendly but reserved. Robbie didn't even try. Wade asked, "By the way, have the kids said anything more about our outing yesterday?"

Diana didn't respond quickly. "It's going to take time," she finally said. "We always knew that. I'll have you to dinner with them in a week or two."

"Sounds like yesterday was hard on you, too," he said. "I lost sleep wondering if there was any way this could work with the kids and all."

"Oh, I'm sorry." Diana took his hand. "Worry seldom helps anything. Robbie adores his father, so I was surprised he came at all. He knows—they both know—that you're not just a riding partner." Maybe it was a good thing Amelia hadn't met Beth yet, Wade thought. Best to let things settle in a bit.

Wade went back to the paper. "Oh, in New York there's a memorial to Galway Kinnell."

"I know that name from somewhere," said Diana.

"Maybe from that poem I have on my refrigerator. He's one of my favorite poets. You know that poem, 'Oatmeal,' about an imaginary breakfast he had with John Keats. It's his." He handed her the newspaper.

"I chuckled at that poem when you read it to me." She looked at Galway Kinnell's photograph. "Was he really this handsome? I vaguely remember his name. Was he a big deal?"

"His poems were frequently in the *New Yorker*. He won a Pulitzer and started the Poetry Workshops at Squaw Valley. That's where I met him."

"Oh, it's coming back, what you told me about him. Didn't he write a poem about a bear—another one that you read? He's Irish, right?"

"*Galway*? Hmm, let me guess."

She laughed. "What was he like in his workshop—was he a decent man?"

Wade smiled as he slightly shook his head. "Only you would ask that. I can't judge whether he's a *decent man* or not, but I liked him, very much. He was an excellent teacher. I sometimes fantasized about following him out to Vermont and sitting at his feet. His voice is both strong and gentle. Here, I can pull up a *YouTube* segment of him on my laptop. He's reading 'The Bear.'"

They listened silently as Galway read all seven parts of the poem.

"Smart. He really was a good-looking guy," she said. "Nice voice, too."

If Wade was going to be jealous of Galway, he would have started long ago. "Galway's poetry was—is—sensual," he said. "He was exceptionally generous with his students. Sometimes one of us amateurs would feel so full of poetry we'd want to write it full time. 'Don't quit your day job,' he'd say. I guess Galway would say it more gracefully, he had a nice touch—but he didn't want us to do something rash. Once, during the worst time of my divorce, I attended one of his workshops. He asked me a few questions about my family, and I ended up writing a poem about Amelia."

"Oh, could I see it?"

Wade grabbed his laptop from his briefcase, pulled up the poem, and read it to her—

Japanese Graveyard on Kauai

One afternoon I drove Amelia past Kapaa,
deep into desolate cane-hauling roads.
We came upon an old graveyard on a hill near the ocean.
Before the tall cane it had overlooked the Pacific.

I got out, trying to convey my wonder to my young daughter.
Wooden markers, in Japanese with a little English,
marked the lives of turn-of-the-century fishing families.
I coaxed her out of the car and she walked

to one grave, then another, one with fresh flowers,
but most overgrown with weeds.
I told her about prosperous fishing fleets,
gone now. She stood silent . . .

"That's the first half of the poem. You can probably see where it's going."

Diana closed her eyes. "Divorce, so tough."

"Yes, the gift that keeps on giving. I wrote that poem so long ago it seems like an artifact. Maybe you see why I don't show my poems at work."

She waited a second and then nodded. "Yes, you do have to wear your game face at the office. I get it." She walked to the window overlooking Stanford. "But divorce, oh, divorce. Some days I wake up and would do anything to stop the inevitable process in its tracks. That's probably why I don't want to talk about it. Do you think kids get over it?"

"I'd like to think so, but I doubt it. It's not a happy subject. Here,
I'll read the last half of the poem—

> This is all that's left,
> I told her at one family's grave,
> after the tortuous trip from Japan,
> after building the fishing fleet
>
> after extracting an honest living from the sea,
> after constructing villages—
> they're tourist towns today, I said.
> No words from her as we returned to the car.
>
> I said I hoped we had more left than that
> even though I'd moved away from her mother.
> I watched her so silent,
> the rental car dwarfed by the tall sugar cane.
>
> I kept looking over at my small passenger,
> in a cotton skirt over her bathing suit,
> watching her father out at the edge of somewhere.
> Her eyes asked what can he teach me but chaos?

When he had finished, Diana said, "Oh, my. I think I'll put
some music on. You like Simon and Garfunkel, don't you?" When he
nodded, she put a CD in the player and turned back to Wade. "You
know what helps me understand divorce better? Your poem. And it
helps me understand you and why you write. There's no other way to
say some things, is there?"

"I've stopped thinking about why I write poems. It's something
I do, like eating. I'm looking forward to that coffee cake. But I see
it won't be done for another five minutes," Wade said. "Perhaps we
should dance."

Out the window, Wade noted the sparse houses in the hills over the red roofs on the Stanford campus. She stood, and Wade put his arms around her. As always, Diana felt light in his arms. He loved the way she followed him even when he messed up.

16

Diana had convinced the trainer Edward to give Wade jumping lessons, and he'd been taking them for a few weeks when, one Saturday, she took him on a long trail ride. Using trail keys she borrowed from someone in the hunt, Diana opened gates through which they were able to ride far off the Jasper Ridge Ranch, past nature preserves that smelled of redwood trees and grasses. From there they came to a busy road with traffic, Sand Hill Road, not far from Rob's law office, a major way people got from one freeway to the other. With cars whizzing by, it took patience and not a little courage to cross the busy street. Once he and Diana had crossed, he asked her where Rob and Billy lived. "Jorge went up there once and I'm curious. He said it's called Whileaway Circle. Could we ride past there?"

Diana hesitated, then said, "Of course I know where Rob lives, but it's out of our way. It would add an hour and a half to our trip."

"Neither of us has that kind of time." Wade was proud to have crossed such a busy road on horseback, enough to ask her a tough question. "Unfortunately, that reminds me of the one thing that keeps bothering me. I'm not sure about Billy. You know, with Marita and Jorge and all."

Diana shook her head. "Jorge was out of work. Jolene tells me he's going to make a ton of money—for him a ton of money anyway—in options. He's not a lawyer or an executive or anything. Not even middle management. Jorge has to be one of the luckiest guys in the world."

"You think Billy's actions here are on the up-and-up?"

Diana stood up in her stirrups and swung around on her horse. She had the same determined look she'd had that time she forced Gray Cloud to go over the bridge. "I've explained to you, very carefully. Billy is like family to me. Family. Everything is going so well for us now, Wade. Why spoil it?"

Wade thought of a few clever rejoinders revolving around Billy's character, but he held his tongue. They silently passed one elegant home with enormous manicured lawns and homes set back, others with circular driveways, and some set so far back they couldn't really be seen. The new Japanese-style estate of Larry Ellison had security signs posted everywhere, and two German shepherds barked ferociously from behind a barbed wire fence. Artemis, thankfully, didn't let the dogs scare her and was sure-footed even in traffic over the blacktop. Except for the conversation about Billy, which they never resolved, it was a perfect afternoon.

∞

In bed that night, they found themselves laughing at the fact they couldn't agree about anything. Diana challenged Wade to find *something*.

"Politics? I don't think so." Wade shook his head. "This can't be so hard." A few minutes later he said. "We're both Presbyterians?"

"There you go," Diana said, "although I suspect your Presbyterian church is a lot different from the ones I'm used to. Church, for me, is sacred."

"Presbyterian, nonetheless," Wade said. "And we like the old hymns. What else? Of course, horses."

"Bingo," she said. "It really helps that you like them, I'll admit that. I never imagined I could share that with a man."

"And at least now you can abide poetry."

"Yours and Galway Kinnell's poetry, for sure. That makes *four* things we agree on," Diana said with a laugh. "The Presbyterian church, hymns, horses, and Galway Kinnell." She put her hand on his thigh, and he covered her fingers, which felt warm. "You know," she continued, "from this angle, you're more handsome than Galway."

"You must mean with the lights out," Wade said.

She ran her fingers through his hair, which he imagined he could feel thinning on the spot. "Galway kept his hair into his eighties."

"I knew you wouldn't believe me," she said, as she moved over toward his side of the bed.

∞

Wade met Jorge for lunch roughly once a month that winter, almost always at the Indian restaurant with the red walls. The place seemed friendly to Wade, perhaps because he'd only been to this restaurant with Jorge, or perhaps because he enjoyed Chetana, their waitress, almost as much as his friend did. It wasn't as formal as Woodside restaurants. He and Jorge could relax there.

Jorge seemed subdued that morning, in a blue suit with a blue tie. He admitted to Wade, for the first time, that his job wasn't working out quite as well as it had in the beginning. "Enersystems is changing. Even before the stock took a dive, the company sucked, and it's worse now. People are worried it'll go even lower."

"But you're doing okay? The sales guys still love what you do, right?"

"Yeah, that hasn't changed. But no one would call me one of the in crowd. I seem to disappear into the woodwork."

"Well, the stock's still more than doubled from when you took the job. If I remember right, next month—poof—you'll get hundreds of thousands. Not bad."

He nodded, but even the prospect of an unbelievable payday didn't seem to cheer him up. Wade guessed Jorge mentally cashed that check months ago.

"I've worried about that company ever since I met Billy," Wade said. "But it's only recently that I'm starting to read negative articles about it."

"Even out here in Silicon Valley, they're just such *Texans*," Jorge said, shaking his head. "You wouldn't believe it, but the newly minted Harvard and Stanford *Business School* grads come into the Enersystems in cowboy boots! They seem so green."

Wade raised his eyebrows. "Hey, that's not all Texans, but I know what you mean. Is there stuff you can share with me?"

"No specifics, but I will say our guys call commissioners in Sacramento 'Sacra tomatoes' behind their backs. Then they shorten it to tomato. They say things like, 'What was it that tomato said about power spikes?' I'm expected to laugh with them. When I do, I don't sleep."

Wade tried to envision Jorge's work life. "So, you go to all these meetings with powerful people. Do you say anything?"

"Not a word. Sometimes I wonder if I'm their token techie or token Mexican."

"I'll buy you some thick black glasses and a serape. Go in as a dual threat."

"Not me, man," Jorge said. "I wear a dark suit and blend into the woodwork. It's the way to play the hand I've been dealt. To make it work for Marita and Eva."

"That's probably smart." Wade nodded. "All alone, huh . . . no friends at all?"

"They're MBA lawyer clones. They don't have friends, they have *con-nec-tions*. When a new server took their order, Jorge looked around. "I wonder where our favorite waitress is today."

"Maybe you scared her off, Lochinvar."

Jorge shrugged. "The guys who count are Texans. If Billy Tyler wants something, the only discussion is how fast it can get done. That's one thing I've learned. He seems to outrank everyone out here in California. I hear he talks to the Enersystems President several times a day."

"Billy's no energy expert. I mean, how much lawyering do they need? Does he really have that much clout?"

Jorge shook his head and looked around the restaurant, which, as their sandwiches came, was filling up quickly with the lunchtime crowd. "He does, but I give up. Let's not talk about Billy." He took a bite of his chicken sandwich. "Are you still riding horses?"

"I am. I've learned a lot about consistency from Artemis. She just goes out and does her job."

"I've been thinking about you and Diana. I like her. You two are finally doing it, right?" Jorge sat back."

Wade hesitated. "A gentleman's lips are sealed."

Jorge sat back. "I am sorry, man. I know I can sound crass. You seem really happy with this woman, that's all. Have you moved in with her?"

"No, that hasn't even come up. But we see each other a lot. Tonight we're taking a picnic up to Foothills Park."

"That's for Palo Alto residents only, isn't it? Speaking of Palo Alto, I told you Marita has her eye on a house near you, right?"

Wade nodded, but he hadn't known this. Right near *his* house? That couldn't be good, but Wade couldn't say that to Jorge. Instead, he said, "You'll need to pretend money doesn't mean anything."

"Well . . . with options, that almost seems true." He seemed to be trying to hide his grin.

Wade grimaced. "Yeah, I guess. That is how a lot of people are making money these days. Gates and Ellison are two of the richest people in the world. Can you imagine? As rich as kings and Arab oil sheiks. And now these guys from Facebook and Twitter and Tesla and who knows what else. Still, things can go wrong. A guy I met on a plane still owed taxes on his options, even though they're now worthless."

"What?" Jorge asked. "How could that be?"

"The stock was high when he exercised them, so he had to pay taxes on the profit. Then the stock cratered to under a dollar and he was left holding the bag. Make sure you set out money to pay the taxes the day you get the stock. Promise me that, okay?"

"Sure," he said, and then he shook his head. "I should be okay. The executives assure us business is great. Even when I hate the company, I smile knowing I'll get the big paycheck, and soon. How about if I ask around there for a job for you?"

"Hey, I'm just a kid from the Midwest," Wade said, "finally getting ahead of the game because my house value keeps going up. I'm putting Amelia through school and will still have a little money left. What an investment. One house down the street sold for twice what I paid. That's nothing like your fancy stock options, of course, where you make the money overnight. They somehow seem like magic."

Jorge flashed a satisfied smirk. "You should try it."

Wade smiled back. "I have so much else going on with Diana and horses and everything, I'd better keep the job a constant for now. Ray seems appreciative for what I do. But thanks."

Jorge leaned across the table. "Can I ask a question, and you'll answer truthfully?"

"Sure, Jorge, anything."

"Remember how Billy interviewed Marita alone? Have you ever heard of a *wife interview* before?"

Wade worried he could be implicated. He'd introduced Jorge to Billy and prodded him on. "Jorge," he said. "That kind of thinking could eat you alive. Can you just put it in the past?" As soon as he said it, Wade felt a pang of guilt.

"I'm not sure it's in the past. Marita disappeared for a few hours a couple of weeks ago. She started wearing this bracelet she says she's had for years, but I sure don't recall it." He looked directly at Wade. "I need your honest opinion. Before my mother died, she made me promise that I would forgive a wife anything. She said marriage is one long lesson in forgiveness."

Wade briefly thought of his relationship with his ex-wife, but decided to keep this discussion about Jorge. "You really think Billy gave Marita a bracelet? What kind?"

"You know, gold. Simple. She has a lot of jewelry I don't pay any attention to. Who knows? I get exhausted worrying."

"So stop. You could drive yourself nuts over this, Jorge." Wade wasn't comfortable after he said this. He pushed back from the table.

"Marita finally admitted last Saturday night that she was alone in her interview with Billy. That personnel specialist—Robin—should have been at that meeting. When I asked Marita if Billy gave that bracelet to her, she said she wouldn't honor the question with a reply. She made me sleep on the couch."

When Jorge said that, Wade knew that this was going to get a lot worse. What could he say to his friend? He stood up. Knowing he was asking the impossible, he said, "Jorge, you simply have to let it go."

Jorge stood, too, took a deep breath, and clapped Wade on the shoulder. "I know, I know. Let's get out of here."

17

On Saturday, a few weeks later, Wade fell off Artemis in his jumping lesson with Edward. He scraped up his forearm but didn't break or sprain anything. Still, falling off a horse isn't fun, and dinner at Diana's with her kids didn't go much better. Robbie was his usual rude self. With her kids there, Wade couldn't even give Diana a proper goodbye.

The next morning, Wade had a hard time getting started. Diana was taking her kids to Jolene and Billy's for the day. He wasn't comfortable calling her there and felt cut off. After he got up and retrieved the paper from the driveway, he broke his own rule—instead of getting dressed, still in his pajama top and boxer shorts, he tumbled back into bed.

Later that morning, almost noon, the doorbell rang. It was Marita, holding a newspaper. "Oh, hi. Let me get presentable," Wade said, opening the door and scooting back to his room.

When he returned in his robe, she was standing in the entryway dressed in a dark blue workout suit. "A house across and down the street is up for sale," she said, insisting on a quick, light hug. "I want to go to the open house, but I promised Jorge I'd be home around noon."

Wade was relieved to hear she couldn't stay long. "I haven't seen any signs up around here."

She turned around, re-opened the door and pointed at a house.

"It's almost identical to yours, I think."

Sure enough, a for-sale sign had sprouted up overnight on the front lawn of a house halfway down the block. "That's a different model, I'm pretty sure," Wade said. "It has a double fireplace between the living room and family room." As he looked at Marita, the covered-up conservatism of her stretchy athletic suit was lessened by the way she pulled the bottom of her jacket up to reveal an expanse of flesh above her hip-hugger pants.

"But yours is a three and two also, isn't it?" She paused. "They can't be that different. Would you mind if I just peeked around in here?"

Wade hesitated, but finally said, "Sure, of course. But the house is a mess. I'm not prepared for guests, sorry."

The second hug she gave him felt better than it should have, and he thought about it with a twinge of guilt. As he let her go, perhaps a second later than he should have, she said, "Oh, don't worry about picking up. Your house can't be worse than our apartment. I've been spending so much time house-hunting that I never get to the housework."

Wade offered to make coffee and moved into the kitchen as Marita surveyed the living room. She checked the view from each window. From behind the counter he said, "The houses around here are all pretty similar. We could be anywhere in suburbia."

"Oh, I like this neighborhood. You can walk to parks and shops. These houses may have started out alike, but with landscaping and remodeling, they look pretty distinctive."

"I haven't even made my bed," Wade said, working up the courage to ask about Billy. She was wearing an expensive-looking gold bracelet. Could this be what Jorge suspected had come from Billy?

She ignored what Wade said and entered the bedroom wing. She poked her head into Amelia's old room, which was now his study. "All these books!" she said. "I've never seen so many books in someone's home, and believe me I've been looking at a lot of homes lately. Have you read them all?"

"I wish."

"Is the master bedroom small, too?"

Rather than offering an opinion, he made the mistake of opening the door. At the center was the bed Liz and Wade had bought when they had a little extra money, a California King, unmade. A rumpled mess.

She walked alongside the bed. "This *is* roomy," she said, throwing her arms up. Laughing, she let herself fall backwards onto the bed. Any thought Wade had of asking her about Billy quickly receded. After a small bounce, she lay there, still with arms wide. "I feel like a kid in here." Her jacket bunched up around her breasts, extending her long torso. She made no move to cover up. "You know this is the fourth time I've knocked on your door, and only the first time you've been home."

His best friend's wife? Wade wondered what would happen if he dropped his robe and lay down next to her. *That would be just plain wrong.* But she held the promise of being so soft, so pliant. Wade's mind whirled. This was Jorge's wife, the mother of his goddaughter. And what about Diana? They still hadn't exchanged any committing endearments, Wade thought, rationalizing at warp speed.

Marita smiled as if she knew more about what Wade was thinking than he did, not completely unlike that first time he'd seen a strapless bra, when he was a child in Barrington, that mother who looked at him so knowingly. When she finally rolled to her side and stood upright she said, "Your bedroom's not small but somehow it's cozy. I feel relaxed here." She took a step toward him.

A familiar aroma wafting in from the kitchen snapped Wade out of his thoughts. "I think I smell coffee," he finally said, with some urgency, as if it might spoil. He turned and hurried off to the kitchen.

He cooled down by fiddling with coffee mugs while Marita stayed in the bedroom wing. When she came into the kitchen, she said, "I like these houses. This is about as high as we can go, pricewise. I think I'll work to convince Jorge to look very hard at that house down the street."

Wade handed her a hot mug. "How much do they want?"

"It's listed for just under two million, but I'm hoping we could get it for less. It seems like a suitable house for us, at the top of our price range. If it's got a good kitchen, it might be the one."

"Are you sure you want to pay that much? Even if someone would give you a mortgage, those payments could choke a horse."

"If we wait until the other half of the option money comes in, a house like that could be out of our reach. Houses around here are going up at least ten percent a year. We have to get in. I want Eva to grow up in Palo Alto."

"I can't believe the place is worth so much," Wade said.

Marita put on a fake pout. "You don't want me as a neighbor?"

"You know it's not that."

"It's important Eva starts in this school system right from first grade. Here, where she can ride her bike to school and be near her friends. Getting Eva into the Palo Alto school system," Marita said, "is what drives me these days. You know your goddaughter is a smart cookie, right?"

"These schools aren't for everyone. They're competitive, without the hand-holding of private schools. I know one girl who just transferred into them and isn't at all happy."

"I know that," Marita said. "It's that I worry about Jorge, too. He's not the risk taker you are. I don't know."

She murmured a meow and batted her hand like a cat playing with a mouse. "You're the one around here who understands me." She moved toward Wade in the kitchen.

He walked around her and opened the front door for her. "Maybe it's time to head home to the old Tom, pussycat." Wade's thin laugh sounded nervous.

She shook her head in disbelief, but she left. Wade wondered if all men felt an implied imperative when a woman offers herself. He knew he did, and having turned her down, told himself he had done the right thing.

∞

He couldn't clear the image of Marita from his mind with her bare midriff, laughing on the very same bed in which he slept. She could be right that Wade was the only one around there who understood her single-minded ambition for Eva. If he could understand the way she must have thought, sleeping with Billy wouldn't hurt her anywhere near as much as it would help Eva.

Beyond the chemistry he and Marita shared, he liked her. He didn't know her as well as he knew Jorge, but could see she had a strange kind of courage. It was not like Diana's horseback-riding courage. It was grittier. Wade admired the way Marita wanted to give her daughter the opportunities she and Jorge had been denied. She'd never said one thing to demean Jorge, and he liked that. She seemed to live by the dictum, "Never complain, never explain." Marita's ambition for Eva was palpable. She would do whatever she had to do, and there was no way Wade would fault her for it.

Wade saw the actress Drew Barrymore once stand on David Letterman's TV desk and flash her breasts—away from the audience, but toward Dave. The routine may have been rehearsed. Wade had suspicions that not much truly spontaneous happened even on live TV, but David seemed genuinely tongue-tied. "You don't understand, Drew," Letterman said after she buttoned up, "I'm from the Midwest. This is *work* for me—I come in to work." Wade, too, was from that part of the country where women—at least the women he knew—didn't engage in such explicit female display, especially to their husband's best friend. Marita hadn't exactly flashed him, but her intent was obvious.

Yet he had controlled his urge and turned on his heel. From an objective perspective, he'd done the right thing. He was involved with Diana, and he now felt responsible for his friend Jorge. It would have been *adultery*. So why was he so torn?

Taking out a pencil and writing pad, he wrote the beginning of a poem—

Offering

The opposite of someone who strays and feels guilty,
I have acted properly and feel blue.

My friend's wife offered herself,
attractively, unambiguously.
I pretended to ignore her,
retreated from bedroom to kitchen.

I've been down ever since I led her out the door.
Diana would be proud of me—

He stopped. The satisfaction of getting these words down on paper dimmed because he realized he probably couldn't ever show the words to Diana. Nor, as he thought about it, to anyone. Still, knowing the only way to finish his thoughts was to complete the poem, he went on, deciding to end the poem with a repetition—

but I don't always share her faith that
one only one of the two pulls in life is valid.
The inward-facing draw,
the one that will lead to heaven,
shouldn't be ignored,

but we must listen to the outward draw as well,
that hard-to-discuss pull,
the desire to open up to a stranger.

The opposite of someone who falls and feels guilty,
I have acted properly and feel blue.

When he finished, he tore the sheet from the pad, folded it in quarters and then eighths, and tucked it in the back of his nightstand drawer. He still replayed the scene with Marita. Hours later, in bed and tossing from side to side, Wade did some controlled breathing he'd learned years earlier from an Indian mystic so he could get some sleep.

∞

Wade's mind whirred with conflicting thoughts of Diana and Marita—Diana was so perfect, but Marita was so real. He was so anxious to get them off his mind that his weekly update for Ray on Monday felt refreshing. He had to make a dozen phone calls to bring his information up to date, a specific task. When he called the folks he'd visited in Chicago, they were evasive about their final decision, so Wade left them listed as a prospect rather than a customer.

At nine-thirty he got a call from Ray, asking if he could move their customary meeting to ten o'clock. When Wade arrived in Ray's office, he noted a little smirk on his boss's face. He asked, "So, what's going on in Chicago?"

"No decision yet," Wade replied.

Ray smiled. "I wanted to tell you this myself. They're going our way." He handed Wade an envelope. "For tax purposes, they want everything installed by the end of the year, so their business will put SnyderSound's year-end numbers over the top. Go ahead, open it up."

Inside the envelope were ten crisp one-hundred-dollar bills. Ray had never given Wade anything like this before.

"My favorite consultant gave me this book on sales management," he said. "It says I should do things like this. And Sherry and I would like to take you out to dinner soon. Maybe with this new gal you're dating."

"Diana," Wade interjected.

"Yes. There's a restaurant Sherry loves in San Francisco. Besides, this lets me write off an evening at her favorite place for dinner. She misses working with you."

Wade also missed Sherry. "That would be fun," he said. His mind jumped to Diana. If it hadn't been for the strange guilt he felt after his encounter with Marita the day before—he kept reminding himself that he hadn't done anything wrong—he would have been dying to tell Diana about this bonus. *Be here now.* "Shall we go over the other accounts?" Wade asked Ray.

"Ah, let the report slide this week. Why don't you get cracking on handing this Chicago deal over to the production guys? The book says I need to keep my salesmen selling."

"If Jorge were here, I could turn it over to him and never worry about it again."

"Let's not talk about the past, about what I've had to do. We're finally turning things around." He paused. "How's Jorge doing at Enersystems?"

"He's making a ton of dough," Wade said, nodding. "Thinking about buying a house near me."

"In Palo Alto? I understand nothing's under two million any more. *Jorge*? Did a rich relative die?"

"No, Jorge hasn't had any living relatives since his sister died a few years back. He made the bucks himself, through stock options."

"Wow." Ray, his eyes wide, didn't seem to be able to hide his shock. "Wish him my best," he said as he stood for Wade to leave.

After he left, he wondered if he'd said the right thing about Jorge. Wade still liked to think SnyderSound was the right place for him, but it would be hard to argue for that with Jorge's big paycheck coming.

∞

When Wade called Diana to tell her he had good news, she invited him over for lunch. But she didn't have her usual radiance when she met him at the elevator—none of her usual smiling cheerfulness.

"What's going on?" he asked.

"I had a bad dream, but we can talk about that later. You said you had some news?"

Wade told her about Ray's offer to take them out to dinner.

"Sounds like your sale put him over the top for the year," Diana said. "First time he's taken you out, huh? Congratulations."

Standing by the island of her tiled kitchen, he showed her the envelope of crisp hundreds.

She nodded and smiled. "Who could argue with that?"

But her sour mood remained. Was this too little money to show to someone with such wealth? Wade and Jorge had figured out that the law firm must be billing Enersystems at least a million dollars a month. He was suddenly embarrassed he'd shown her the envelope with the paltry hundreds. "Did I say something wrong?" he asked.

"No, it's nothing you've said. It's this dream I had. You were there with me, starting to make love, but you turned away from me. Suddenly you were a different man, someone I didn't know at all."

"Honey, it was a dream," Wade said, but shame from the day before tugged at him. He kept telling himself there was no way she could have known what had happened with Marita. And reminding himself that he'd behaved like a gentleman.

Diana had prepared tasty crab sandwiches, which they ate in strained silence. After lunch, she told him she'd set up more lessons for him with Edward. "He had a cancellation, so if it works with your schedule, you can take two lessons this week." She gave him the details, but something was missing. Perhaps it was that the episode with Marita that made Wade lose trust in himself. Not only could he not get Marita out of his mind, but something had changed in Diana as well—she didn't want Wade close to her.

∞

Even though Wade had several months of lessons with Edward, he still had Wade take Artemis through an agonizingly slow warm-up. Wade tried to mind his *p*s and *q*s since Diana was watching from a small grandstand.

"That's it," the wiry New Zealander said. "Sit on her like a sack of potatoes. Move *with the horse*." Edward watched intently. "Now kick her into a trot."

He tightened his legs around her wide body. Artemis kept walking.

"Don't massage her with your heel. Kick her, with authority. She doesn't know what you want."

As he dug his heels into Artemis's side, he remembered Diana telling him to just *do things*. He needed to do that. He gave his horse a kick with certainty this time. And the horse leapt into a trot. Wade concentrated on posting with each step—up down, up down.

"Come on 'round here," Edward commanded. Wade looked towards Diana, who was watching him on Artemis as closely as Edward was.

He brought Artemis around to where Edward was adjusting the jumps.

"You're continually giving your horse messages," the trainer said. "Make them the messages you want her to hear. Now, you've learned to ride rather later than some of the other chaps, but that's okay. Today we're going to see if you really can jump. Start with these poles." Edward pointed. "They're set for a trot."

Edward crossed two poles by raising them at opposite ends so that a horse could jump at the center of the 'X.' After Wade took Artemis over one of these jumps, the trainer asked, "Ever heard of a gymnastic?" He pointed to three jumps placed in a row so that a horse would jump them one after the other. "I've set the jumps pretty low. Take Artemis over to the rail and come back through the 'crossbars,' the X's."

Jumping the crossbars made Wade feel like he was on a roller coaster. After the first jump, Wade couldn't do much but balance with the horse as she hit the ground, feel her jump again, bounce off the ground again for the last 'X,' and it was over.

Edward walked up to him and talked quietly enough so that Diana couldn't hear. "Artemis almost stopped on you, you know."

"Before the first jump?"

"Exactly. Make sure Artemis has got her energy up *before* she approaches the gymnastic. Keep a leg on her."

Wade brought Artemis through the jumps again. This time he anticipated the staccato rhythm by tightening up on her to push her past her hesitancy.

Edward raised the jumps. "If they were higher, you'd have to slow the horse down in the middle, but you shouldn't have to worry about that." This time when Wade brought Artie into the first crossbar, he had been sure Artemis was about to jump, but she didn't. She ducked out at the last minute and threw him onto the X bars and over them to the ground. Except for his pride, Wade was unhurt. Diana stood up, slightly dazed, expressionless.

"Don't gawk over at the bleachers," Edward yelled. "Re-mount straight away. That's what I had to do in the goddamned Olympics— my horse quit. I flew into the jump. Seven years of hard work, gone in an instant. *Think!*" He grabbed Wade by his shirt and jerked him to his feet. "You looked down. Good dancers never look at their feet, and good horsemen don't either. Keep your head up, eyes on where you want the horse to go. Artemis was tiring. She saw that the crossbars were higher, and jumping three of them is a lot of work. She was looking for any excuse to stop. Your glance down was all she needed."

"She knows I looked down?"

"Of course. She knows everything you do when you're on her back. Now get up and try again." Wade wondered if Diana could intuit everything about him as well. It was getting toward the end of the hour, and Wade wanted to quit. "Leg, leg, leg," Edward said in rhythm with Artemis's steps as he approached the first jump. "Eyes up." She jumped like a dream—they sailed through one 'X' after another.

Edward raised the fences higher, to about three feet at the center of the crossbar, as high as Wade had ever jumped. "All right," he said. "This is about all she can handle without you having to slow her down between jumps. Let's go one last round to show you're a real jumper. Believe you can do it. Take her out to the rail and come 'round over these."

Wade concentrated on keeping his heels down. "Leg," Edward yelled again, "leg, leg." Wade clamped his legs as tight as he could around Artie's wide middle as he approached the gymnastic. Just as

Edward had taught him, Wade let the horse pivot his legs into jumping position. He felt her land and leap forward again and land, and finally one last leap and the final landing, where he turned Artemis back to Edward at a trot.

"I know people who've ridden all their lives who couldn't do that any better," he said proudly. "I'll tell you now what I couldn't say before. I was so unsure of you getting to this point, I almost didn't take you on as a student. Past a certain age, riders can be hard to teach. But you were together with her there for all three jumps. And I'm not just pissing in your pocket."

This time, when Wade looked up at Diana, who was smiling broadly, he knew he was being measured on how he could handle a horse as a measure of how he could handle her. She came down from the grandstand to shake Edward's hand and then kiss Wade. "Good work, both of you." Making upbeat small talk, she walked between them. When she dropped back and Edward and Wade walked together, Edward put his arm across Wade's shoulders. Here Wade was forty-four years old, and he could feel himself beaming like a cherished schoolboy.

18

After Jorge's options came through, he asked Wade to meet him at the house he and Marita were buying near Wade's.

Dee, the real estate agent who had sold Liz and Wade their house nine years earlier, a realtor he had encouraged Jorge and Marita to use, waited in her copper-colored hundred-thousand-dollar BMW as Jorge and Wade walked across the street. As they approached, Dee stepped out in a reddish-brown suit that matched her hair and her car and almost matched its saddle-colored leather interior.

As they moved up the walkway to look at the house Jorge was probably buying, Wade thought, *you see one Eichler, you've seen them all*—always large redwood beams, a flat roof, walls of windows, and openness throughout. Some were run down, but this one was in good shape.

"I just talked to Marita," Dee said. "She can't make it. Eva's got a little fever, so the three of us are on our own." She turned to Jorge. "You're lucky the first offer on this house fell through. I think you're getting a very good deal, Jorge. There were two bidding wars in our office this week, and a house on Middlefield went for three hundred thousand over the asking price. On *Middlefield.*" When she said that, Wade understood what she meant because Middlefield, the spine of Palo Alto, was a busy street. She fiddled with the lockbox, found the key, and threw open the door. "Come on in."

The house was the identical in age to Wade's, but it had new paint and floors. He followed Jorge back to the bedrooms. "That'll be Eva's," Jorge said to Dee proudly as they peeked into the second bedroom. At the third bedroom, he said, "Maybe I can set up the punching bag in there." The image of a punching bag got Wade wondering how angry Jorge might be underneath his cool composure. The first furnishing he mentioned was a punching bag?

After leaving the kitchen, which had swinging doors like in a cowboy movie, Jorge and Dee stepped down a steep cement step into the garage, with Wade following along behind. Except for a few avocado-green cabinets that looked like they'd been salvaged from a kitchen remodel, the garage was unfinished—two-by-four studs and black tarpaper. "There's something depressing about this garage, almost eerie," Jorge said. "You don't get much for almost two million, do you?"

As they came back into the kitchen, Dee answered in a professional, upbeat way. "Just put up some white wallboard, brighten it up. Midtown is very desirable. Young families want to live here. Almost half the homeowners in this town are Stanford grads. Maybe their parents help, or they've made money on options. A few just have big incomes. High tech execs, a few surgeons and the like." When Jorge didn't respond, Dee turned to Wade. "I hear you're dating a pretty horsewoman."

"Ah, guilty as charged, but where in the world did you learn that?" Wade asked.

"Palo Alto is still a small town sometimes," Dee said.

Realtors know everything, Wade thought.

Jorge beckoned Wade into the living room. "Dee says the disclosures show that the fireplace has a crack in it."

While Wade walked over and inspected the crack thoughtfully, Jorge turned to Dee, "The owner wants me to sign off on it. That's the situation, right?"

"I had a friend of mine check it out," Dee said. "He's a retired building inspector for the city. He says it's safe unless there's another big earthquake. He checked, and it draws well. People around here live with such cracks."

Jorge frowned and asked, "Wade, what do you think?"

"Sounds like Dee's done her homework. I like the double-sided fireplace." Wade touched the crack in the fireplace with his fingers. "Any chance the seller would knock something off the price for it?"

Dee shook her head. "They claim to have a backup offer. I know the realtor—it's probably true. Midtown properties are flying."

Wade shrugged. "I know the price is hard to get used to, Jorge, but Dee knows what she's talking about. I can vouch for that."

"Your wife knows it too," Dee said to him. "Marita was over here early this morning and she's convinced this is the best buy in the price range."

Jorge turned the water on and off at the kitchen sink. "Is there anything else I should worry about?"

"Everything else looks pretty standard. A decent-sized yard, and the hardwood floors are almost new. For a fifty-year old house, it's pretty solid. Should be a quick close."

"We want Eva to transfer schools as soon as possible," Jorge said.

Dee nodded. "The school district usually cooperates once you're in escrow. Marita signed these papers this morning, so she's on board."

If Jorge's going to buy something this expensive, Wade thought, this is probably as good as he could do. He trusted Dee. "The school's two blocks away," he said.

Jorge pursed his lips. "Let's do it."

When Dee set a thick pile of papers on the kitchen counter for Jorge to sign, Wade asked her, "There's a three-day grace period, right?"

Dee shook her head. "Even better. I've written the finance contingency so that Jorge can get out of the contract for nine days. All he has to do is say he hasn't found acceptable financing."

"What's your point, Wade?" Jorge asked.

"If you get cold feet, you can back out. It makes signing less risky."

Jorge took the pen Dee offered and started signing and initialing. As he turned page after page, Wade thought of some questions, but since Jorge had nine days to cancel the contract, he saved them for later.

∞

"For a guy who just bought a house in Palo Alto, you seem down," Wade said to Jorge as they finished lunch. "Are you okay?"

Jorge rested his head on one of his hands. "The job sucks more all the time, and the mortgage will eat up every other paycheck. If it weren't for Marita's wanting this so badly for Eva, I wouldn't have signed."

To hide Wade's own concerns about the finances and to cheer up his friend, he said, "Marita's right, it probably will be good for Eva. Palo Alto has a great school system, but I didn't want to encourage you guys getting in over your heads."

"Yes, Eva's schooling—that's what's driving this." He seemed relieved that Wade understood.

"You'll get a big tax deduction, and you're on the house-price escalator. Remember, Dee says it's a good deal." Jorge looked skeptical. "By the way, did you catch that huge Beamer she's driving? When she sold Liz and me our house, she was still teaching part-time, driving around in a beat-up VW wagon. Suddenly everybody's rich around here. Last year, this town had higher incomes than Beverly Hills. You sure wouldn't know it from the look of the houses, would you?"

Jorge ordered an after-lunch latte. "I'm not following you."

"She used to live like a schoolteacher and now she's driving a hundred-thousand-dollar car that matches her hair. Stuff like that's going on all over town."

Jorge shook his head. "You think there's something magic about Palo Alto, just being here? I should just count on everything working out?"

"Oh, no. Not at all. People go broke here, too. They forget to do things like you did—selling enough stock to pay the taxes you owed on your options." Wade saluted, touching his hand to his forehead. "Good move, there."

"Roger, my broker, recommended against it, but I followed your advice."

Wade waited a bit before he raised his eyebrows. "Roger wanted you to not sell one share, and borrow against it? Just run for luck?"

"I guess so," Jorge said. "What's wrong with that?"

"Assuming the stock goes up, that would be fine, but you could end up like that guy who got caught holding the bag. What if it keeps going down?"

The latte came, layered with milk on the bottom, then espresso, and the foam on top. Jorge added sugar and blended the layers together before he took a sip. "Everybody at Enersystems is holding on. They say, 'It was a good buy at $90 and it's an even better buy at $55.' Look at this report—everybody's still high on Enersystems." Jorge handed Wade a Wall Street brokerage report published the day before, declaring Enersystems undervalued.

"How much did you sell to cover the taxes?" Wade didn't mean to alarm him, but these were much bigger amounts of money than he was used to. Jorge must be even deeper in the woods.

"I sold almost a third of the shares. That covered what I paid for the shares and all the taxes. I paid for the stock and sent the IRS estimated taxes just like you said."

"Excellent," Wade said. "Let's just hope the stock doesn't keep slipping."

"Look, don't scare me now. Just because I don't necessarily like everybody at Enersystems doesn't mean they can't make money hand over fist. They've been doing it for years."

"What's your backup plan? You do have one, don't you?"

Jorge downed the rest of his latte. Frowning, he accused Wade of badgering him. "The stock shouldn't go much lower before it starts climbing again." He wiped some foam from his lip. "And you know Marita. No time to lose. Eva's about to start school. Marita thinks the backup offer on the house is real and may even be higher. Besides, I could borrow more in a pinch. I've come to grips with the decision, so you're the only one who seems worried. And even you say the house is a good investment."

"I didn't realize how many eggs you were putting into one basket. Until you told me otherwise, I assumed you were going to *sell* stock for the down payment."

He shrugged. "No. Just enough to cover taxes, like you said."

"I'm telling you, the ice you're skating on is this thin." Wade held his index finger and thumb a fraction of an inch apart.

"Wade, enough," Jorge said. "*Cut it out.*" He stood up.

Wade rose too, slapping him on the back and saying, "Okay. Just remember you can still get out of that contract."

It wasn't just financially that he didn't feel good about Jorge buying the house. It was also Marita moving in across the street from him. He didn't need that kind of trouble in his own back yard. As they parted, Wade said, "Take your time. It'll take a week for the financing to come through. You can back out without penalty until then." But Wade knew as he left him that Marita wanted that house, and she would get her way. He had to give her this much that if it worked out, it'd be good for his goddaughter. The school she'd go to, two blocks away, had an excellent reputation. Wade pictured Eva happily riding her bike down his street, and his face relaxed into a smile.

19

When the hunt season opening was a month away, Diana set everything up to go out with the hounds with Wade one Sunday. It was "hound training," a ride to prepare the hounds, horses, and riders for the upcoming season. The night before, Rob had a business dinner, and that meant he couldn't pick up the kids from Diana's until late, so Wade didn't come over until early the next morning. Diana met him at the door of her condominium, looking jaunty in her jodhpurs and a starched white shirt. Even in her crispness, there was a sensuality about her. She gave him a light kiss and led him down the hall. "Your clothes are in here," she said, opening a closet at the far end of her bedroom. It still felt strange to take off his clothes in front of her—they hadn't been intimate that many times and she had an innate modesty about her—so he ducked behind the closet door.

"I worried you might be influenced by your poet friends. I'm sure they'd get quite upset about the poor little fox," she said. "I thought you might cancel."

"No way. I've looked forward to this all week. Like you say, it's not *literally* foxhunting, since there aren't any foxes."

She nodded. "Right. And hound training is just an exercise."

After Wade put on breeches, knee socks, and a white collarless shirt, he sat down on the tile ledge of her Jacuzzi tub so that Diana could fix his stock tie.

"Time stands still out there. I get lost in all the tradition," she said as she jammed the pin through Wade's thick tie.

"Be careful with that thing," he said.

She concentrated until she fixed it to her satisfaction. "Here." She handed him two small safety pins. "These will keep the ends from flapping around. Pin 'em loose."

Diana then tied her own stock tie and said, "It's getting late. Let's stack the gear in the elevator and take everything down in one load."

They filled the elevator with hunting jackets, folding chairs, water jugs, buckets for the horses, and an iced picnic cooler. Downstairs they put all their gear into the SUV, and Diana drove them to the ranch and hooked up the trailer.

After they loaded up the horses, she pulled out her keys and handed them to Wade. "The ranch where we're going is two hours south, down past Gilroy. You've never driven with horses behind. It's different. But I was hoping you could drive down, and I could drive home. That way you could drink as much wine as you want socializing after the hunt. I know you enjoy that." She studied the keys before she handed them to him. "You will go super-slow around the corners, won't you?"

"Yes, dear," he said sarcastically, trying to lighten things up as he climbed into the driver's seat. To reassure her, he was careful making the tight turns to join the freeway, crawling along until he got on the ramp up to the freeway.

A few minutes later, as he made the turn onto 85, Diana leaned over and put her hand on Wade's knee. "You drive like an old pro. I shouldn't have worried."

It felt reassuring to have her hand on his knee. They hadn't been as intimate lately.

With her stock tie pinned perfectly so it bulged out a bit, Diana looked businesslike, a woman to be reckoned with. Part of her was tough, a toughness Wade felt ambivalent about—as the years would go by, he hoped her toughness might become less obvious. A warmth swept over him when he thought how it would feel to be an old married couple with Diana at his side.

Then Wade made the mistake of bringing Billy into the conversation, saying he worried Billy was taking advantage of Jorge.

She smiled. "Aw, Jorge's got it made. He's got a better job than he could ever get on his own, that seems obvious."

"He says he's miserable."

Diana cocked her head pensively, a bit surprised. "He does?"

"When Jorge worked for me, the way I'd keep him happy was to load him down with work. He thrives on it. This job requires very little of him. As for Billy, we don't really know—"

"Billy's done great things for that couple," Diana interrupted, and they didn't say another word for miles. "Why do you always infer otherwise?"

"Well, Diana, I'm pretty sure—" Wade started. But he knew that if he said what was on his mind, he'd ruin the morning, so he stopped. "I'm pretty sure that's one of the best sunrises I've ever seen," he managed to say instead.

∞

The freeway twisted east toward the morning sun, which rose through thin clouds over Mount Hamilton, the highest point near San Jose. "It makes me want to get up early like this every morning," Wade said.

Diana didn't seem to feel any of his nervousness. "Everything's new again at the beginning of hunt season, like spring training with baseball. The coyotes on this ranch haven't seen us for six months." She laughed. "I wonder if they've missed taunting us. Sometimes they seem to do that. They always get away."

Wade loved being out with Diana and these horse people who routinely enjoyed the kind of lifestyle he had previously seen only in movies. "We've been riding for almost a year now, but this is different. Do they catch coyotes?"

"Only one that's old or lame," she said. "Down in Texas, they might come across a *javalina*. The Portuguese brought them over to breed, but some got loose. There are a few pigs around here, too. An angry boar can rip fences and tear up pasture quicker than a tractor."

She took a deep breath. "I'm sure today will be like most days—we'll chase around and nothing will happen. Look at that sunrise—it's the pink next to the yellow that gives a girl hope," she said with a little laugh.

Nearing the ranch where they would hunt, the paved road turned to dirt. They arrived early and saw only three other rigs—two horse trailers and the hunt truck with its noisy hounds.

Diana and Wade unloaded the horses and groomed them for the hunt. The hunt master, whom Wade had met on previous outings, stopped by their trailer. He carried rounded crystal glasses of Bloody Marys, complete with celery sticks. Diana waved him off, but Wade snagged one. Peppery, he thought, after a sip.

∞

Within the hour, the master shouted, "Field, please." About forty riders decked out in black coats, with a few red coats on the most experienced, gathered around him. When he gave a nod, the huntsman released the hounds from the truck. They bounded over each other as they jumped out, excited in their freedom.

The master welcomed them. "Remember, today is to train the hounds. This is the first day in the field for some of them, so stay awake out there."

Wade took a minute to view the panorama, the acres and acres of meadows and glens just starting to get a little green amid the yellow of summer. Diana had told him that it takes an area the size of two thousand acres to hunt with hounds, and she was evidently correct. He took in a deep breath of the crisp fall air, cooler than it had been even a few weeks before. Winter, with bouts of rain, would be coming soon. You could almost smell it in the air.

The huntsman blew a long loud blast—"Away"—and they were off. The riders separated into three fields behind the hounds, moving quietly along the eastern edge of the ranch, trotting most of the way, walking only on steep down slopes, and cantering up a few hills. Artemis had her blood up ever since the hounds left their truck, and Wade had to hold her back.

In the middle of a large field with a few scrub oaks, the master nodded again and the huntsman cast the hounds. They spread out in larger and larger circles around him until they were covering an area bigger than a football field, searching for a particular scent in the tall grass. Wade concentrated on what he'd been taught, keeping his heels down in the stirrups.

∞

As the hounds went over a small rise to the right, one barked loudly. Quickly, a couple of other hounds fell in behind him, yelping. "They're on to something," Wade said, adding the language Diana had been teaching him: "They're giving tongue."

Wade took off behind the hounds at top speed, gripping his legs around his horse as tightly as he could. Diana yelled from behind, "No rules now, Wade. *Just go.*"

The hounds weren't imagining their quarry. Over the next hill, not forty yards ahead, Wade spotted a coyote, tan and lean, a little taller than the hounds. He relaxed, joining the horse's sprinting rhythm during all the excitement.

The hounds' cacophonous voices bellowed as they ran full out in front. Wade started to worry about the frightened animal ahead of him but then reminded himself that Diana had said a healthy coyote is almost never caught.

The hounds and their quarry were so closely matched in speed it seemed choreographed. The coyote, running for his life, stayed eight or ten yards ahead, followed by the hounds and the field riders who were in an all-out canter. Wade looked to both sides. Artie and he were alone in front of the other horses. She was breathing as heavily as he was, her nostrils flared, but they kept on. At top speed on this rolling land, her canter was surprisingly smooth. Wade had a moment of appreciation that felt spiritual. He was thankful for seeing Diana in her glory, for the riding experience over these hills, and for Artemis, who was giving her all to carry him.

At the edge of a wide field, they came toward a low stone wall with barbed wire strung above it. Just beyond the fence was a wooded glen. The coyote seemed to be tiring. For a moment the hounds gained on him, getting as close as a few horse-lengths. Then, perhaps sensing sanctuary, the coyote found a little extra speed and bounded over the wall, his scruffy tail flying just ahead of the nearest hound. The hound behind him, who had almost caught the wily animal, stopped, exhausted, at the wall. Moments later, a couple of hounds found their way over the wall, but most of them quieted as the coyote disappeared in the glen.

The master yelled, "Ware wire."

"Damn," Diana said, riding up to Wade. "The master wants to make sure nobody tries to jump that fence without seeing the wire. Ware is short for beware. Nobody could get a horse over that wall. We've built wooden coops all over this ranch to protect us from the barbed wire, but not here. The wire's almost invisible. No way."

Getting his breath back, Wade asked, "So the chase is over?"

She nodded. "Even full out, the nearest gate is five minutes down that fence, and the nearest jump is beyond that." She looked at him with a great big smile. "You rode like thunder."

"The closer we got to the coyote, the more I was rooting for him. I wanted him to get away."

"Most of us do," she said in a stage whisper. "It's bad form to talk about it, but it's the chase we love, not the kill."

"I never understood the thrill until now," Wade said. "What a rush."

The master yelled over to Diana and Wade, "That was a long run. We got a good view. That coyote's gone to ground. Let's cool the horses down. There's an outside chance he'll come back out."

Diana turned to Wade. "Sure," she mouthed skeptically.

∞

As the hounds searched diligently for a scent, Diana and Wade dropped back to second field, then third. "We had a great run, we can take it easy for the rest of the morning," she said. After all the excitement of chasing right behind the hounds, third field—hilltopping—now seemed tepid, a walk in the park after a drag race.

∞

They moved to a new vantage point. Diana called over to Wade, "Listen. The hounds are onto something." After a quick word to the master, "Permission to leave third field," she led Wade off at a canter. The hounds were making a loud racket past the second ridge. "Let's see what has them so riled up."

They rode toward the noise but still couldn't see what was going on. Diana's face glowed with anticipation.

When they cantered over the next ridge, they could make out a large animal surrounded by six or seven hounds barking furiously. It was a boar, squealing as he rushed in one direction and then another. He made a sharp turn and kicked one of the hounds, who dropped on the spot.

The huntsman rode up from the other side of the hill. As he slowed to a trot, he pulled a gun from a holster under his jacket. Wade had no idea he was carrying a weapon. The pig snorted loudly and ran straight for the approaching huntsman, scooting between his horse's legs. At least seven hounds chased him, a few so close they nipped at his back. As the boar frantically scurried away, the huntsman fired off a shot, but his horse bucked and the bullet missed. The boar headed toward Wade and Diana but veered off. As soon as there was no chance of hitting a hunter, the huntsman fired again. His second shot hit the boar in the head. It staggered two last steps and fell onto its side.

The hounds swarmed the pig, ripping into its flesh. The word "eviscerating" jumped into Wade's mind. As the boar lost all its defenses, rolling over in submission, Wade couldn't watch anymore. "I'll be over in that glen," he said, and guided Artemis away.

Diana followed at a distance.

With his back to the action, Wade asked her, "Is it as awful as I think?"

"Don't watch!"

But he shot one more glance. The hounds were crawling over the carcass, ripping into it savagely. The huntsman had dismounted and was in among them. What could he be doing?

As if hearing the question in Wade's mind, Diana said, "The Huntsman wants to make sure this is a kill and that all the hounds get some meat. Everyone says they'll make better hunters that way."

The huntsman remounted, then rode over and touched his thumb to Wade's forehead, leaving something behind. Blood? Wade tried to dig deep and stay out with these people—with the gore of evisceration, the hunters suddenly seemed like people with whom he had nothing in common. He couldn't stay out with them. He yelled over to Diana, "This is too much for me. I have got to get out of here. Let's go."

Diana looked embarrassed. "It's unusual to leave the hunt field like this, but okay, we'll go in." She shouted to the huntsman that they were leaving. They returned at a canter and came down to a trot when they approached the trailers.

∞

Once they'd loaded and closed up the trailer, Wade started toward the driver's door, but Diana had already scooted in front of him. "It's okay, I'll drive back."

They rode in silence until they neared San Jose. Diana said, "I'm seldom of two minds, but I am today. One side of me wants to apologize to you, and the other wants to ask if you always have to be so," she hesitated, "difficult?"

"The word you mean is *dumb*," Wade said. "I'm dumb. The reason you call it a hunt is because—da dah—it's a hunt."

Diana looked hurt. "Oh, Wade, don't be that way. It's many things. You're so new to it. What is this, your third time out? Some riders go out with us for years and never get that experience.'"

"Believe me, this is something I'll never forget. Oscar Wilde was right when he called this sport the unspeakable in pursuit of the inedible.'"

"All your quips and quotes." Her brow tightened so Wade could see lines he'd never seen before. After a few miles, she said, "You know I love that sensitive part of you. It's part of the reason I care. But out with the hounds, it's far from your clever poetry world. I know it's staged, but compared with our everyday lives, it's certainly gritty, with horses seizing up and riders coming off after low-hanging branches. Horses roll over their riders. Sometimes people get helicoptered out. Three years ago a rider had a heart attack and died. We take pride in how *real* it is, how close to the bone."

"It was real for that boar, I'll tell you," Wade said. "Quite a day for him. A bunch of people dressed in nineteenth century costumes appear out of nowhere with hounds and hidden firearms. How retro."

"What?" Diana said, shaking her head. "Is that really how you feel about it? Remember, this is a big part of my life."

They didn't talk for the longest time. Finally, Wade said, "You have the kids tonight, right?"

"Yes," she said as they neared Palo Alto. "It might be best if you didn't call me."

Wade nodded. Saddened, he said, "Yes, that might be best."

With her eyes on the road, she said, "We should step back, find some space to understand what we mean to each other. It's not just my religious thoughts, but sleeping together is so intimate. This is something I've been thinking about since that dream I had. I pray about it. I'm hoping we can be friends for a while, see what happens."

He suddenly thought, *Hey, she's cutting me off.* "Wait, Diana—"

"You're far more attentive that way than Rob ever was. I'll miss that. So you have to help me."

"How?" Wade asked.

"Restraint. I'm asking you not to approach me. The flesh is weak."

She laughed. "Mine, especially, it seems."

Wade shook his head, trying to show her how confused he felt. "I'm not sure I'm the right guy to help you rebuff me—something backward there."

"We'll see," she said. "It's not just about that dream I had. And it's certainly not just about what happened today. I'm starting to see the hunt through your eyes. Still, I'd looked forward to going to opening meet with you."

Wade wanted to say, "Of course we'll go to opening meet—it's next month, right?" He formed the words, but then he pictured that bloody flesh flying around the dying boar as he was being torn apart by hounds. Instead of speaking, he nodded.

When they got back to the ranch, they unloaded the trailer in silence and cleaned up the horses and their tack. Looking over at Diana as she polished her saddle, Wade was sure her mind was racing as quickly as his, trying to find a way to make sense of what was happening. But neither of them came up with another word to say. They parted with a long, sad hug.

20

Wade noticed that about the same time he was no longer dating Diana, she had begun to overcome her instinctual distrust of Marita. As Wade pieced it together from Jorge and Diana's remarks, a babysitter canceled on Marita at the last minute, and Marita called Diana. Wade figured she must have had her number from the party. At any rate Diana drove Beth to babysit Eva, and the two girls got along well. Considering the age difference—Eva was six and Beth thirteen—they formed quite a bond. That brought Diana closer to Marita.

Part of Wade was glad they were getting to know each other better through their daughters. But given his recent encounter with Marita, another part of him wasn't particularly keen that they were spending time with each other. His concern peaked when Diana called him saying Marita had invited them, Diana and Wade, over to dinner. "Her house is on the same street as yours, right?" Diana asked.

"Across the street and one house down," he said. "By the way, she still thinks we're a couple." As soon as he said it into the phone, Wade wished he could take the words back. She wouldn't want to hear that.

"People will think what they will," Diana replied, a phrase he'd heard her use before.

Wade broached the subject, and felt compelled to ask, "She's not right, is she, that we're a couple. I never know how to put things."

Diana didn't respond to his comment but asked, "Would it be best if we didn't go?"

He had no idea how an evening at Jorge and Marita's house would be—how Diana and Marita were getting on so well was beyond him. But he couldn't say no. "Do you want to go?"

"Beth sure wants me to," Diana said. "I don't know what it is about Eva, but Beth is crazy about her. She gave Eva a toy horse that I'd hoped she'd keep forever. It's a collector's piece, my big present to her a couple of Christmases ago." Wade felt sorry for Diana on that score—he knew she'd always tried to get Beth into horses, to no avail. Wade suspected Diana wanted more closeness with her daughter. Perhaps now, with Eva, that would be possible. It seemed like the three of them had more to share. Diana told Wade that when they watched the new *Les Misérables* movie, Beth said she loved Collette. Eva, Beth said, was 'just like Collette.'" Wade had to ask the question again, "Do you really want to have dinner at Marita's?"

"No, but Beth doesn't ask for much."

Then he asked, "Are you sure you want to see me?"

"Of course, that's not the problem." Diana said. "I'll set it up."

Wade had pretty much given up on pursuing a romantic relationship with Diana. Still, he'd be glad to see her again, even if it were to feel awkward in ways he still couldn't quite grasp.

∞

The evening of Marita's dinner party, Wade was late getting home from work, so when he drove into his driveway, he saw that Diana's SUV was already parked across the street.

Once inside his home, he changed into a denim shirt, splashed water on his face, and crossed the street. No matter what the evening held in store, he didn't like to be late. It would be strange to see Diana, especially at Jorge's new house. Wade had declined a couple of informal invitations to dinner there—one from Marita when Jorge wasn't home—he knew better than that—and one last-minute invitation from both of them, on a night he had other plans.

Marita, wearing a white apron over her outfit, opened the door. Wade was glad she greeted him with only a quick hug, before bringing him into the family room. Diana was sitting down, playing Monopoly with Beth, Robbie, and Eva. It seemed like a scene from a previous century. Jorge handed him a glass of wine, and they watched the Monopoly game. Robbie was winning big, with a thick stack of orange five hundred dollar bills. Like father, like son, he thought. When Eva's piece, a silver top hat she moved with meticulous care, landed on one of Robbie's four railroads, Wade couldn't watch any longer.

He pushed through the swinging door and joined Marita in the kitchen. Under her apron, she was wearing lime green pants and a dark blue V-necked sweater with yellow piping that contrasted with her tan. White bead bracelets danced as she chopped vegetables.

"What smells so good?" he asked. "What *is* all this?"

"Fish and salsa. Sautéed red snapper with cilantro butter sauce, from a recipe my mother gave me, and salsa from last week's *Chronicle*. Black bean, jicama and corn salsa." She waved her hands at each dish with an invisible wand.

Pots and bowls were strewn around the counters. "Looks like you're having fun."

"Tonight in my new kitchen, I get to cook for other people the way my mother did," Marita said. "And Diana is so much nicer than I remember her. Things are finally coming together."

Wade leaned over the salsa. "Smells kind of sweet and spicy, my favorite combination."

"Somehow I knew that," Marita said with a little laugh.

As she carried a full saucepan from one counter to another, Wade said, "I sometimes wonder about your interview with Billy."

Sauce spilled onto the floor. "What did he tell you?"

Wade grabbed a paper towel and stooped down. "I'm sorry, let me get that."

She motioned him off. When she leaned over with a sponge, she moved her other hand up to her V-necked sweater the way she'd done with her robe months ago.

"I'm concerned about Billy's . . ." Looking down at her, he searched for a phrase. "Office politics." He was digging in deep.

She stood, put a hand on her hip, and looked Wade in the eye. "Billy is a man of his word."

He raised his eyebrows.

She held a small piece of white fish with red sauce on a wooden cooking spoon close to her mouth. "Want to try the fish?" Wade had to lean in toward her to take a bite. It tasted as good as it smelled.

Diana pushed through the swinging door holding two empty wine glasses. She looked at Wade and then at Marita as they moved apart. Diana, not smiling, said, "Jorge and I need some refills."

Marita ran her hands along her sides. "I'll get another bottle." She opened the refrigerator.

As Wade searched in a drawer for the wine opener, he noticed Diana's shoulders relax as she offered a kind remark to Marita. "Eva's so well behaved."

Marita handed Wade a chilled bottle. "She loves that horse Beth gave her."

"We'll have to get Eva up on a real horse," Diana said to Marita. "The trainer who taught Wade to jump doesn't normally teach kids, but he might do it as a favor."

Marita pulled a huge wooden salad bowl out of the refrigerator. "I imagine Beth's terrific on horseback."

Diana pressed her lips together in a half smile. "Unfortunately, she never took to it."

Wade filled two glasses and handed them to Diana, who pushed back out to the living room through the swinging door. Once they were alone together, Wade avoided Marita's eyes, but stayed back long enough to ask, "Anything I can do?"

She laughed derisively. "I can't believe you asked me about Billy. It's nobody's business. *Nobody's*. Go on, now, get out there with your fancy girlfriend," she said, shooing him away with her hands. "What I do to make things work around here is between me, . . . and . . . me."

In the living room, the Monopoly game had ended. Robbie was reading a comic book while Beth and Eva played with Lincoln Logs. They'd made a barn from the logs, seemingly not bothered that the horse was bigger than the barn.

"Can we call him Star for that mark?" Eva asked Beth, pointing to a white spot on the horse's forehead.

"Star. Sure, he'll whinny when you go to see him. That's how horses say hi," Beth explained. She imitated the sound. "I'm sure he'll always whinny when he sees you."

"I hope so," Eva laughed.

Wade smiled at Eva's response, realizing he was rooting for her to like horses.

Marita asked Jorge to help her serve. They took their places around the dining room table.

"Sorry about the small table." Marita laughed nervously. "We haven't had time to buy new furniture right away."

"I like it," Diana said. "It's cozy."

He smiled at the way Diana, no matter what was going on inside her, always tried to make people around her feel good about themselves. He was sorry she seemed distant toward him, though. *Let's face it*, Wade thought, *I miss seeing her more than she does me.*

∞

After dinner, Diana, Beth, and Robbie were the first to leave. As Diana helped the kids with their seat belts, she turned to Wade, saying, "Nice evening. Good to see you again," in a matter-of-fact, friends-only way. She turned to Jorge and Marita and thanked them effusively.

As Jorge and Wade watched the taillights of her SUV, Wade turned to him. "Guess I'd better be getting home, too."

Jorge looked disappointed. "Aw, let's go downtown for a nightcap."

Wade looked to Marita for her recommendation.

"Yes. Why don't you two go out?" she said. "I'll tuck Eva into bed."

Wade drove Jorge to a college bar with pool tables in downtown Palo Alto. He asked for a beer and was surprised when Jorge ordered a double bourbon. When he asked Jorge if he wanted to play some pool, Jorge picked up a stick and started racking the balls into the wooden triangle. "Sure. Eight ball," Jorge said. "Call your shot. By the way, I could tell you and Diana were cooler to each other tonight than I remember. Is everything okay?"

"You're very perceptive," he said. "Things could be better."

Jorge broke the rack, with balls scattering wildly but none going in. "Things could be better for me, too. I'm having more financial problems than I let on to Marita. I haven't been completely straightforward with you about it, either."

Wade took a shot and sank a striped ball. That meant Jorge would shoot the solids. After he missed his second shot, he said, "I've been watching the papers, Jorge. Enersystems stock has been dropping steadily. House prices aren't rising the way they were in early spring, either."

Wade missed a long shot to the corner, and Jorge sank three solids. "I'm in trouble, my friend. And I have a business proposition, sort of," Jorge said. He missed his next shot, looking over at him to take his turn. "I may have to ask your help."

He knew that Jorge was going to ask him for money, something he'd never done before. He closed his eyes and took a deep breath, so he could concentrate on his shot. He finally sank one, the striped ball seeming to change colors as it spun. Jorge signaled to the bartender with two fingers. Another double. *That's a lot of liquor*, Wade thought.

Jorge got up and retrieved the drink from the bar as Wade sank another one.

When Wade missed, he said to Jorge, "You can always sell stock."

Jorge put his cue stick on the table and sat down in an empty booth, abandoning the game. "There's not much stock left. They sold stock out from under me three times last week. You know, margin calls. If the stock keeps going down, they could sell the last of the stock and I'd still owe the brokerage. If we get to that, Roger—you know, my broker—worries that the brokerage could demand payment. He thinks I may have to sell the house we only bought months ago."

Wade grimaced. He had no idea that push was coming to shove so soon. "I'll have to think this through, buddy. If I weren't putting Amelia through college, I'd help you in a heartbeat." After he said it, he wondered if that sounded too generous, but, hell, he's the godfather here. Wade would have to come through. "I sure don't want you to lose your house, Jorge, or Eva to lose her new school. The three of you seem so *at home* there. There's no sense in my doing anything until we understand the situation better. I hear what you've said, Jorge. I'm not sure I can help, but I'll do some figuring."

Jorge took a large gulp from his drink and sighed. He nodded as he chugged his drink and got up from the table.

"Let's call it a night," Wade said, and drove across town to drop Jorge off and then fall into bed at home. The evening had been exhausting.

∞

After the dinner at Jorge and Marita's, Wade kept seeing Diana but less often and without the intimacies they'd shared earlier. One Sunday night it had all seemed a little unreal. Rob had flown Beth and Robbie to Dallas for his mother's birthday, so the kids weren't there. So why was Diana standoffish? She'd rented a movie, *The Queen*, starring Helen Mirren. Both Princess Diana and Queen Elizabeth II, antagonists in real life, were portrayed so sympathetically that he and Diana were both moved. At the end of the story, she sniffled and dabbed at her wet eyes with a tissue.

He had put his arm around her. While she didn't withdraw, she didn't move toward him, either. "If we're going to ride in the morning, you'd best get going," she said, and he quietly pulled back. When they headed toward the door, they shared a light embrace and then, poof, the evening was over, leaving him feeling terribly alone.

Although Wade no longer rode to hounds, occasionally he'd go on trail rides with Diana. A couple of weeks after the pool game with Jorge, when he stopped by Diana's on a Saturday to take her riding, she invited him in for coffee. He followed her into the kitchen. As Diana measured coffee grounds into the machine, Wade's cell phone rang and displayed a name. "It's Jorge," he told her.

"Go ahead, answer it," Diana replied. He moved into the dining room to take the call.

This was the first Wade had heard from Jorge since they'd had that drink downtown. "Sor to bother ya," Jorge said. "Roger says if Enersystems doesn't go up on Monday . . ." Jorge slurred his words as if drunk. "I need to talk to ya," he finished. Until he played pool with him, Wade hadn't thought Jorge was much of a drinker, so what had happened to him?

With Diana in the next room, Wade didn't want to prolong this conversation. He wasn't at all sure he could help him and was only partially convinced he should. But he thought of Eva. "How about we meet before church?" he asked Jorge. "Tomorrow morning? Coffee? Seven thirty at the Palo Alto Café?"

Jorge agreed, his voice relieved. The fact they had a plan to see each other the next day didn't assuage Wade's apprehension. But he was glad he'd have more time to think about how far to go in bailing Jorge out—he could sleep on it.

∞

The horseback ride Wade and Diana had scheduled for that Saturday was short-lived. Diana didn't seem her usual cheery self, and then she said, shortly after mounting up, "Gray Cloud is off a little on his right foreleg. I doubt it's serious, but I'd better take him back in. You should ride, though."

Wade thought Diana might have felt slightly injured somehow, not just Gray Cloud. What was going on?

"How about if I go out to the jumping ring and set out a few crossbars for you?" she asked.

Diana set up four jumps that were about as high as Edward made them but farther apart. Wade had to concentrate to keep Artemis on course, especially with Diana standing next to a critical jump. After he rode through the course three times, she asked, "Got one more in you, maybe a little higher?" She raised the jumps to three feet. Wade took Artie through one last time. Artemis hit a rail with her back leg on the second jump, but it didn't come down and she didn't let it faze her. Although Wade started to lose his balance, he managed to keep one leg on each side of the horse's broad body and get balanced again.

At the barn, after he gave Artemis one last hug, Diana asked him if he would go to church with her the next morning, something he didn't really want to do. One good thing, he thought, is that they shared the same faith, more or less, and he wished he could just say yes in a heartbeat. But it wasn't as simple as that. He hesitated because they didn't share the same *brand* of faith. Wade thought of different brands of soap, of Ivory and Evangelical. And Diana took it all far more seriously than he did. And the fact that they weren't dating confused him further. He couldn't give her an answer either way. "Diana, I'm not sure what you want from me."

"I'm still working on that, but I've figured one thing out. You're getting to be a much stronger horseman."

"I miss being close to you."

"I know what you mean," Diana said. "I do, too, a lot of the time. How about we have brunch after church and we go from there?"

Wade thought about the song, a cowboy lyric where the guy gets jacked around by his girlfriend, "Every Which Way but Loose." Still, he said, "Sure, sounds great."

∞

At home Wade had a voicemail from Amelia, saying everything was fine, but she had "some stuff going on." She said not to bother calling her and that she'd call again soon. That got Wade's attention for sure.

Even though he hadn't talked to Liz for over a year, Wade called his ex-wife to see if she could shed some light on the situation. He and Liz carefully limited their conversations to only one subject—Amelia. Unfortunately, she didn't know anything more than Wade knew about what was going on with Amelia. "Her teacher recommended she apply to Yale for next year and said he'd help any way he could. I wouldn't worry about her. She's doing fine. You've been a good father to her."

Wade couldn't remember Liz ever saying that before. "Thank you. Trying to figure out what should be next for Amelia has been rough, hasn't it, Liz? The conclusion I always reach is that Amelia has to take the lead. She's not sixteen anymore."

"Yes, whatever we've taught her will either carry her through or it won't. I agree, all we can do now is support her decisions," Liz said, as she hung up.

21

That evening Wade sacrificed most of the bacon in his deli-bought BLT to Keats. When Keats realized he'd get no more people food, he settled for some kibble Wade left out for him and then brought in an old towel to play tug-of-war. Right-handed, Wade always won. Left-handed, though, try as he might, Wade couldn't pull the towel out of Keats's clamped mouth.

Later Wade worked on a poem, then settled in for the ten o'clock news. When he heard a knock at the door, he got up and peered through the peephole. Marita! The evening was warm for late September, so why was she wearing a fitted jacket snapped down the front over a short skirt and heels?

She looked endearing, but seeing her evoked competing emotions—warmth, lust, and fear—all bundled into one. It reminded him of the time a few months back when she was looking at the house down the street and came in to get a feel for the neighborhood. She'd been hard to resist. Should he invite her in? He couldn't leave her standing on his porch. "What's up? Come on in. Where's Jorge?" Wade asked.

"He tied one on and is sleeping it off. I need company. Don't worry, I'm not here to talk about our financial problems. I know you'll help Jorge as much as you can. You always have. You've never given him money before, but you sure helped him at SnyderSound. Hell, if it weren't for you, we could still be spending our evenings in bars around UTEP the way we were doing when we met you. Tonight, all I ask for is your company. I'm all alone, Wade."

"Yes, I've been worrying about Jorge. Can I take your coat?"

"No, I'm fine," she said. "How about a glass of wine, though?"

Wade had a bottle of Chardonnay open in the fridge and poured her a glass. He poured one for himself, too, as he tried to figure out why she was wearing the jacket. She must be looking for some kind of effect, he thought.

"I talked to Jorge this afternoon," Wade said. "He was upset. He told me he needs money. We're meeting in the morning."

She shook her head. "He's not acting like himself. He's had so much to drink. I mean, he almost blacked out tonight. He thinks we're going to lose the best thing that's ever happened to us—the new house. Eva's asthma or whatever it was—the doctors never made up their minds—disappeared when we moved in. And for the first time Jorge felt equal to you gringos." She attempted a laugh as she fidgeted with her wine glass. When Wade didn't laugh, her mood shifted. "I guess Jorge's right. Everything's probably gone."

"Jorge still has his job," he reassured her. "He'll pull through this."

Marita shook her head. "I don't know, Wade. The stock's gone down so much, he's sure we'll lose the house. He told me you warned him not to finance on stock options, which depressed him even more. When I got home today from Eva's school, he was drinking, which is strange enough in itself. But he was watching daytime TV, a rerun of the old Jerry Springer Show. He said, 'We're just like those guys on the show. I mean we don't hit each other, but it's almost the same.' That isn't like Jorge, not at all," Marita said.

"No, it isn't." Wade touched her arm.

"Jorge never understood why you couldn't save his old job at SnyderSound. But that anger has cooled. Once again, you're the big brother he never had. He has no family, you know." She slumped on the stool. "Ever since my family had to leave Cuba, I've been waiting for things to get good again. And they did pick up for a while. I know you don't like Billy, but to his credit he did what he promised he'd do. Not many young couples get to buy in Palo Alto, and Billy made that possible for us. These schools are so good for Eva." She took a deep breath. "And now, this problem with the stock options. Who would have figured mighty Enersystems would come crashing down?"

"I'm sorry, Marita."

"Something like that wouldn't happen to you, Wade. For a sensitive poet type you do quite well in everyday life. In your own way, you take charge." She took a deep breath, seeming to relax. "This wine tastes good. Can I have a few drops more?"

Wade was surprised Marita thought of him as someone in charge of his life when he felt the opposite. "Sure," he said. "While I'm up, I'll put Keats in the garage so he doesn't bother us."

When Wade returned and he filled her glass, she looked at him from out of the corner of her eye, her other hand on her jacket's lowest snap. "Have you been wondering what I'm wearing under the coat?"

The coat was familiar. She stood across the counter from him. "I'd been afraid to ask," he said.

"I wore it especially for you." Starting at the bottom, snap by snap, she pulled her jacket open. "It's what I wore at the first party. I could tell how much you liked it."

The evening came back in a rush. "Yes, of course. The outfit that so enchanted Billy," Wade said as she removed the jacket, revealing the same gauzy blouse, almost transparent over her red bra.

"Billy's interest is what everybody else noticed. You were the one I was watching that night. When you didn't think anyone would see you, you'd look over at . . ." She moved her hand across her breasts, pausing before she finished the sentence. "Me."

Wade tried not to stare at the red of her bra and what it concealed above her tanned midriff.

"It's okay, drink it in. Tonight, you can look to your heart's content," she said, lowering her voice. "You can get a real eyeful. Isn't that what you guys say, an eyeful?"

Wade looked away. It was no use, he still saw the image of her. He couldn't do this to Jorge and Diana, although they were technically still broken up. Still, he looked back at her again.

"Come over here, silly," she said. "Relax."

Wade walked around the counter.

Smiling, she put her fingers inside his shirt pocket and pulled him toward her. "You're nervous. How am I going to get you to relax?" She moved toward him, inviting a kiss.

He should have resisted, as he'd done in the bedroom weeks earlier. All he could think later is that he hesitated, at least. He didn't really kiss her, but he didn't pull away either. "It's not you, you're wonderful. It's Jorge," Wade said. "I couldn't live with myself."

"Jorge will be okay. You've done so much for him. And it's not me that's wonderful, it's you."

As he said, "I just can't," she leaned over. Maybe just one kiss, he thought.

Her lips, and the tip of her tongue, when she pressed it between his lips, tasted a little of the wine. Soft. Insistent. "Let's go into the other room." She took his hand and led him. Once inside the bedroom, she closed the door. "I've thought about this moment since you came home with Jorge that first night years ago in El Paso. And, be honest with yourself, Wade. This is what you've been wanting, isn't it?"

She unbuttoned her blouse. When Wade removed it, she lifted her bra and offered herself, he suckled. When he pulled away, she had loosened his belt and unbuttoned his pants. "Lie back on the bed." His trousers came off in such a rush that, pulling them, she fell back against the wall, but she recovered with a laugh.

Wade had the presence of mind to use a condom, which he pulled from the nightstand before he reached for her. They took from each other, thieves at a treasure chest, shifting positions as their passion grew. Toward the end she was on top of him, his hands cupped beneath her bottom. He wanted a third arm, and a fourth, so he could fondle her all over. The tip of her tongue crept out between her lips in her concentration. The front fringe of her hair showed a few gleaming droplets and smelled of rain. "God," Wade gasped. "I love this." His gratefulness almost had him saying, instead of "this," "you."

∞

After they made love, they lay on their sides facing one another, his arm beneath her neck. When she fell asleep, he pulled away and drew the sheet over her. Wade thought of Diana, but Marita turned over then, throwing off much of the sheet that had been covering her. How unexpected she was.

He sat up on the edge of the bed, his head in his hands. He'd have to sort the Diana question out later. Wade had long thought the adjective for a perfect female lover was *generous*—a woman who could forgive a man's pressing nature. But Marita went beyond generosity. She demanded her own pleasure, using his body as a means to that end. She didn't look past his lust, she shared it. She placated a loneliness he hadn't even known he possessed.

∞

Later—how much later, Wade couldn't tell—a phone's ringing woke him from his sleep. Wade integrated it into his dream, something about a fire alarm. He woke up as he realized he was reaching across a naked body to pick up the phone. Sleeping Marita!

He heard raspy breathing and then a mumbling voice. "Jorge?" Wade guessed.

Marita's eyes snapped open, and she slid off the bed to gather up her clothes. "Is this Jorge?" he asked into the phone. "Are you drunk?"

Wade watched Marita as he waited for Jorge's response. She worked to refasten her bra strap behind her back. She did this quickly, and threw on her blouse in seconds. She had a hard time with her skirt. The blouse stuck out of her zipper like a long delicate handkerchief.

Jorge managed to string some words together. "Marita's gone. Do you think she's with Billy?"

Wade tried to make his voice as soothing as possible. "You need to rest." He paused and then said, even more quietly, "Look, buddy, I'll be seeing you at the café in just a few hours. Get some sleep."

As he hung up, Marita took charge. "I've got to get back across the street before he even thinks about coming here." She had given up on the skirt zipper and thrown on her jacket and snapped it up. She turned toward the front door.

"Keep the jacket on," Wade said. "He'll remember that outfit. Fix your skirt, where your blouse shows." When she nodded, he asked, "Could you answer one thing?"

"Sure."

"We both know Jorge needs money. Did you do this so I would help him?"

"No, of course not. I wonder if you understand me at all. I've wanted to be with you since our eyes met way back in El Paso. I know it was Jorge who asked you to be Eva's godfather, but didn't you ever realize that the idea was mine? I thought it would keep you close by. And it has."

Wade *had* wondered. "Will you be okay?"

"Don't worry, I can handle Jorge."

Before he opened the front door, he kissed her.

As she walked out of the front door into the darkness, she said, "I'll call you in the morning, as soon as I'm alone."

∞

Wade brought Keats in from the garage and crawled into bed but couldn't sleep. Maybe it was just guilt, growing by the minute, but Wade thought he heard violent noises across the street. Still, there was no way Wade could go over there or even phone without alerting Jorge. All he could do was wait for the sun to come up and see what the new day brought. Later, he thought he heard a different sound. Forget it. Things can look so much better in a new day's light. Wade would meet with Jorge over coffee and then go on to church with Diana. Could he look her in the eye?

The money question with Jorge still bounced around in his head. What could he do for him? He had only six hundred dollars in his checking account—that wouldn't help. What was Wade's obligation to Eva? He had a never-used thirty-thousand-dollar line of credit that he could write a check on but had promised himself he'd never do that. "Good as cash," the banker had told him when he signed the mortgage papers. How stupid would that be, to go into debt? Still, thinking of all three of them, Jorge, Marita and Eva, Wade couldn't stand by and let them lose their home. Wade would probably let Jorge talk him into writing a check. He'd have to draw the line somewhere— maybe five thousand. That should get Jorge through, shouldn't it? Thinking he had found a possible solution helped calm Wade down. He took a deep breath.

His mind jumped ahead. No matter what arrangement Wade made with Jorge, he'd meet Diana at her church. Church. He tried to tell himself that God was big enough to forgive even this, but he shook his head. No way. After he'd betrayed the man who thought of him as a brother—the same way Wade thought of Jorge. No, God would not forgive him, nor could he forgive himself. No one would. Would he be able to even stand next to Diana in church?

He thought of that poem he'd written and put away because he could never show it to Diana. He turned on his light, pulled it from the back of his nightstand drawer, and unfolded it. "I have acted properly and I feel blue," he read aloud. Well, now he felt the opposite; he had acted improperly and felt, along with the guilt, strange twinges of happiness. His mind shuttled back and forth, acknowledging how irresistible Marita had been. Still, the guilt was inescapable. He hadn't been true to anyone, including himself.

Diana—where did that dream she had come from, after he'd sent Marita packing that day? Do women really have some sixth sense? And how did this sex with Marita fit in with Diana? He was in some kind of start/stop process of falling in love with Diana. Was it easier to be so physical with Marita because there were none of the complexities of an extended relationship? Was sex easier when he knew he'd never share grocery lists or parent children together?

In the long term, though, wasn't what he and Diana shared the more genuine article, the real deal?

His thoughts about Marita were confusing, too. Some men dismiss a woman after they've slept with her. "Been there, done that," they must think. But that wasn't the case for Wade, certainly not concerning Marita. Would he get to see her again? How soon? Knowing he'd betrayed Diana, wanting to change what he'd done, realizing he couldn't, admitting he might even do it again, he finally fell asleep.

22

Wade was dreaming of Marita when the phone rang. Could it be her? She had said she'd call as soon as she could. But the images he'd been conjuring up faded when the caller identified himself as Sergeant Ames from the Palo Alto Police Department.

Police?

"Mr. Middleton?" he said in a monotone, professional voice. "We'd like you to come down to the station."

Wade got up on an elbow. "What's going on?"

"Something I can't discuss over the phone. It involves your neighbors, the Calderons. It's best we talk about it down here."

"Are they okay?" Pause. No response. "Can't you tell me *anything*?"

"Check in at the front desk. Bring your driver's license for identification. Ask for me, Sergeant Ames. I'll be waiting for you."

Keats came into his bedroom wanting some early morning attention. As Wade petted his dog and scratched behind his ears, a feeling of foreboding rolled over him. Before Marita had walked across the street, she had told Wade she could handle Jorge. But she had also told Wade that Jorge was different last night—a different guy than she'd ever seen before.

He hurriedly dressed and headed up Middlefield to the police station.

∞

When he showed his license at the front desk, Sergeant Ames, a middle-aged officer with a kind demeanor and a trimmed moustache, came out from behind a locked door and led Wade to a bare beige room inside. He indicated a chair, then offered coffee. When Wade shook his head, he sat down. In soft tones, the officer asked, "You're a neighbor of Jorge Calderon's, correct?"

"Yes, he's my friend. I used to work with him. Actually, he's probably my best friend, like a brother."

"I'm sorry to have to tell you that Mr. Calderon is in a coma at Stanford Hospital."

"What?"

He nodded and proceeded calmly. "They've put him in a special oxygen chamber for carbon monoxide poisoning. The medical report also lists head trauma and abrasions to his right arm."

Wade's stomach tightened. "Carbon monoxide?" He had to clutch his hands together to keep them from trembling. And possibly a stroke, he thought, what could have caused that? Stress of job loss, home loss, and then Marita—yes. Excessive alcohol? Hard to picture Jorge surrounded by machines and tubes. He'd always seemed so vital. Then Wade's mind moved toward watching Marita walk toward her house, where Jorge waited. "What happened?" he asked the officer.

The sergeant leaned back in his chair. "Sure I can't get you that cup of coffee?"

Wade nodded and looked around at the gray table in the middle of the room with the sergeant across from him. No windows. No two-way mirror like you see in the movies, just a beige wall with a picture of four flagpoles flying American flags.

The sergeant rose and stuck his head out the door to ask someone to bring coffee before he turned back to him. "It appears Mr. Calderon attempted suicide by running his engine in a closed garage. He was found collapsed on the floor close to the exhaust pipe."

Tears formed in his eyes. "I was going to meet him this morning for coffee."

The sergeant raised his bushy black eyebrows. "Do you visit him often? Do you have a key to his house?"

He shook his head so hard that he feared he was showing impatience, or guilt. "No, I don't have a key to his house. Why would I? But tell me what's going on. Is Marita okay—his wife?" Wade asked. "And his daughter? Is Eva okay? She's my goddaughter."

An aide entered the room and gave the sergeant a Styrofoam cup of coffee, which he handed to Wade. While he took a sip, the sergeant said, like a kind uncle, "Mr. Middleton, your goddaughter's okay— Eva's the one who called 9-1-1, which is why Mr. Calderon is still alive. His wife, though, was not so lucky. She had massive head injuries in the garage. They may have combined with the carbon monoxide."

Wade dropped the cup, spilling coffee on his trousers. He burned his thigh, but didn't move. *This couldn't be true—no way. Was he saying Marita is dead?* His coffee cup bounced on the floor, contents splashing. *What have I done?* Wade asked, almost aloud.

Sergeant Ames nodded before he motioned toward a box of tissues on the table. "Yes. Their six-year-old daughter called at 4:27 this morning. When we got there, the poor kid appeared to be in shock. She took us to her parents in the garage. The car was still running. She has said very little since."

"Eva. My God!" How slowly Eva would move her Monopoly piece—she chose the silver top hat—from one real estate property to another. The other day Wade had run into Jorge at the neighborhood park, and he had tossed a softball underhand back and forth with Eva. How could a six-year-old possibly get through losing her mother? And maybe her father too?

"She's with a case worker from Child Protective Services down the hall," the officer said. "She mentioned your name, and she asked Diana and for Beth. Is that your daughter?"

Wade put his head in his hands and told the officer, "Beth is Diana's daughter. Diana's my friend."

"Well, you and Beth and Diana were the only people Eva

mentioned," Sergeant Ames said. "That's why I asked you to come in, Mr. Middleton. Our detective has already given us his assessment as to what happened. What he described is much more common than first-degree murder. Someone shoves, someone else falls and hits their head. We won't know until the tests come back, but alcohol often plays a role and I suspect this is no exception."

Wade rubbed his eyes. "But it was an accident, right?"

"It looks that way but we don't know for sure," the sergeant said, almost apologetically. "We're looking into that right now."

"Give me a minute." Wade stood up and had to sit back down. Marita was in Wade's bed not ten hours earlier, he thought. Now her life was ended. Marita, gone! Jorge nearly dead, to boot! Oh, my God, oh, my God—that was all his brain could repeat. He broke into a sweat and clenched his hands again to keep them from trembling. *And it's my fault.* When Wade stood up again, he asked the officer, "Would it be okay if I called Diana?"

"I was going to ask you to do exactly that. Ask her to bring her daughter Beth in, too, if she's the one Eva asked for. Your cellphone won't work in here. You can use that phone over there," he said, pointing. "Can I tell the case worker you'll meet with Eva? Mrs. Spencer is anxious for the girl to see people she knows."

"Of course."

"Make your phone call. I'll be right back."

Wade punched in Diana's number.

"Hi, I'm just leaving for church," she said. "Robbie is with his father, but Beth is coming with us."

"There's been an accident, Diana. Jorge and Marita," Wade started. It was strange to say their names. "Jorge's in the hospital on life support and Marita is . . . she's dead."

He heard Diana gasp. "What happened?"

"I'm at the Palo Alto police station. Can you come here so I can fill you in? Eva's here."

"Is she okay?"

"She's unharmed, at least physically. Can you come down?"

"Oh, Wade. I was just leaving for church. Could I possibly handle this later?"

Wade was surprised and disappointed Diana wasn't willing to come in right away. "Eva wants to see Beth," he said. He wanted to yell at her to come in, but managed to use persuasion instead. "The police asked me to call you. Honey, I know this is awful, but Eva needs help. She found her mother dead this morning and must have seen her father being carted off in an ambulance. Imagine the state she's in."

"Beth is still a child. I'm not sure about getting her involved. I just don't know."

Wade couldn't mince words any longer. "Diana, Eva is six years old. I'm not asking for myself. Please."

"Wait. I need to talk to Beth." She must have covered the mouthpiece because Wade couldn't make out what she was saying. Then she asked, "The police station on Hamilton?"

"Yes."

Again Wade heard muffled words. Then Diana got back on. "Okay, we're on our way."

∞

Sergeant Ames led Wade to the small yellow room where Eva sat on an examining table. As soon as he saw her, he moved to hug her, but the woman next to Eva shook her head. Eva, her head lowered, was still in her pajamas and robe. She was wearing felt slippers with bunny heads sticking up on top of the toes. They looked so incongruous that Wade almost lost it again. What had he done? The sergeant introduced him to the caseworker and left. Miss Spencer, dressed in a crisp blue blouse and blazer, seemed pleasant and earnest. But his eyes quickly moved back to Eva, who was motionless, frozen.

"Hi, sweetie," Wade said.

She didn't look up.

Miss Spencer said, "We've been concentrating on her breathing.

She drank a whole cup of water. She's a very good girl. You can go over to her now."

Wade told Eva, "Beth is coming," hoping to get her to smile, but she continued to stare at the floor. When he got to her side, Wade said, "She should be here soon." Again, no reaction.

A doctor came in with a stethoscope draped across her shoulders. "Could you give me a moment?" she asked, and Miss Spencer and Wade slipped into the hallway.

"I need to make a phone call about next-of-kin," she said. "You don't know of any nearby relatives, do you, Mr. Middleton?"

"No. In fact, I'm quite sure there aren't any."

She ducked into an empty office, leaving him alone in the hall.

Wade worked to grasp what had happened. Marita had been so alive, so passionate. Now she was gone. And it was his fault. He wanted to mourn her, but Jorge kept entering Wade's thoughts. Jorge could gain consciousness at any time. What did he know? What would he say?

The sergeant came up the hall toward him, with Diana and Beth close behind. Mother and daughter looked chic in summer dresses, ready for church. Diana and Wade came together for a short hug, from which she quickly drew back.

Diana took a deep breath. "Sometimes I think I'm in one of those movies you only watch when you can't sleep. How's Eva doing?"

"Yes, how's Eva doing?" asked Beth.

"She asked for you—I'm so glad you came. Thank you so much, both of you. We can see her as soon as Miss Spencer comes back."

Beth smiled and turned to get a drink from one of those fountains with a huge clear bottle on top. A bubble rose in the bottle as she filled a small cup.

Wade whispered to Diana what the sergeant had told him. Repeating the story only heightened his guilt.

When Miss Spencer joined them, Wade introduced Diana and Beth. As Beth turned around from the fountain, he noted that Miss

Spencer treated her like an adult—and Beth did look very grown-up, especially wearing heels, which made her slightly taller than her mother, who wore flats.

Miss Spencer took them into the small room where the doctor was saying goodbye to Eva, who was now lying on an exam table on her back, still in her slippers. Her eyes were closed; she seemed almost passed out. Wade guessed the doctor had given her a sedative.

Beth walked over to her. Eva opened her eyes and looked up at her. "Mommy was all bloody," she said flatly. She seemed half-asleep, almost talking in a dream. "She was wearing her party bra."

Beth and Diana gasped in unison. Diana shook her head and whispered to Wade, "Oh, this is just so sad. I'm lost."

Wade turned to Eva. "Your mommy loved you very much."

"Where *is* Mommy?" she asked, her eyes barely open.

"It might be hard to see her today," Miss Spencer said. "But don't worry, you're safe."

Beth, fighting back tears, took Eva's hand.

Diana stood on the other side of the room. Was she, too, close to crying? Wade walked over to comfort her.

"Things like this aren't supposed to happen on Sunday mornings," Diana said. "This is God's time." She took a deep breath, staring at Eva. "That poor child."

Wade reminded himself that one of the things that drew him to Diana was the warm heart that she hid behind her stoic exterior.

Apparently soothed by Beth, Eva shut her eyes. Wade was glad she had Beth to comfort her. How grown up Diana's daughter seemed.

"Can I stay with Beth?" Eva said.

Miss Spencer wrapped her in a blanket and pushed the back of a chair next to the table to keep Eva from falling off. "Beth, will you be okay alone?" she asked.

Beth nodded yes.

Motioning toward the door, Miss Spencer invited Wade and Diana into her office. "Let's go where we can talk."

With the sergeant, Wade and Diana crowded around Miss Spencer's cluttered desk. "We need to release Eva, but we haven't been able to locate a place for her," she said, rummaging through papers. "The closest relative seems to be her mother's mother, a widow in El Paso, Texas. But she's in a nursing home. Mr. Calderon 's parents have both passed away, and we haven't identified any aunts or uncles. Unless we can come up with a plan with people she knows—she keeps asking for Beth, someone like that—we'll have to line up foster parents, which can be dicey on short notice, or the emergency shelter. Or send Eva to Valley Medical, you know, the county hospital." She looked at us. "Someone she knows would be so much better."

"I could take her for the night," Wade said. "I'm her godfather."

"Sorry, Mr. Middleton, but the county doesn't place children with opposite-sex single people in situations like this, even blood relatives. And you seem to love her, but you're not a blood relative."

The way she said it, Wade knew not to push Miss Spencer any harder. He gave Diana a pleading look. "Could you possibly?"

Diana quickly said, "Sorry. I couldn't. I mean we're not equipped in any way."

Beth said, "Mom, you're always talking about our Christian duty. We do have the guest room."

Diana hesitated before she spoke. "We wouldn't know how to handle things that might come up, Beth." She shook her head. "Eva needs someone who's trained in these situations."

"Couldn't we at least bring her home for a few days?" Beth asked. "The guest bedroom's just sitting there."

Diana turned to Miss Spencer. "It would be a great responsibility, even temporarily. What would the long-term solution be?"

The caseworker looked down at her papers on the desk. "We can usually find a relative who can take in a child like this. Even if her father pulls through, he could face charges. I understand we can't expect him home anytime soon. If she were to go with you, Mrs. Buchanan, it would require a temporary order from a judge. Do you have a lawyer who could work with the judge?"

Sometimes Wade thought he might be the only person in Diana's life who wasn't a lawyer. But she wasn't smiling, and he hated to see her backed into a corner.

"Diana, maybe you and I should talk alone."

Wade and Diana rose and went into the hallway, leaving Beth behind, her wide brown eyes pleading.

After they were outside of everyone's earshot, Diana said, "I've been working to keep everything stable so Beth can have a great sophomore year. I would have no idea how to care for a traumatized child."

Wade reached out to her, but she didn't move. "If she stays with you," he said, "I will help in any way I can."

Diana didn't respond to Wade's offer. She slowly said, "If I *did* take her in it would have to be for a short time. There'd have to be an end to it. An exit strategy, as they say."

Wade touched her hand. "I know. But imagine her going to the county hospital, not knowing anyone, or with foster parents she's never met."

She looked pensive. "I wish Robbie were here so he could weigh in—it's his house, too. And I try to never make long-term commitments on the spur of the moment."

"I agree with that, too, in general," Wade said. "But Beth's awfully good with Eva. It might be good for both of them."

"Beth and Eva have seen a lot of each other in the last month. I agree that perhaps their friendship could help them both." Diana stood with her hands apart as if she were surrendering. "Faith is empty without deeds, I believe that. And Beth is right, the guest room's just sitting there." She hesitated for so long he wondered if she was changing her mind. Finally, she said, "Okay, Eva can stay with us, at least tonight. Maybe even a few nights. I'll call the law firm to work out the details with the judge and come up with something to sign."

∞

When Beth learned that Eva would be coming home with them, she beamed. She and Wade hugged.

Even Diana seemed relieved. When Wade asked her if she wanted to tell Eva, she pointed to Miss Spencer, who was smiling as well. He asked her, "Why don't you bring Beth down to Eva to tell her the news?"

He took Diana's arm as they walked down the corridor to Sergeant Ames. He was still in the beige room where he'd first talked to Wade. "Diana and I are about to leave, if that's okay."

But the officer motioned them to come in and sit down. "Two things have come up. One is that the judge says, under the circumstances, that Eva can go home with Mrs. Buchanan while we finish the paperwork. But the second thing is what I need to talk to you about."

The sergeant closed the door behind them. "The phone company's pretty responsive in a case like this, with the possibility of murder," he said. "They just e-mailed us their records, which show only one completed phone call from Jorge Calderon's house last night, at 11:37 PM." He stared at Wade. "It was to your home, Mr. Middleton. What was that about? Why did he call you?"

Diana's eyes opened wide.

"He was upset, drunk and upset," Wade replied quickly. "Marita and he had quarreled. She had come over earlier." *Why did he even mention Marita?* Too much was happening, too fast. He wasn't acting smart.

Diana looked like she wanted to flee the small room but remained seated.

Wade looked at each of them as innocently as he could, but when he felt his face flush, he feared he was acting guilty as hell. He said, "She went right home, as soon as he called."

Sergeant Ames said, "Thank you. Why was Mrs. Calderon at your residence at 11:37? Does that have a bearing on the fight Mr. Calderon had with her? Do you have any insights, Mr. Middleton?"

"He thought they were going to lose their home because of his risky business decisions."

"Let's be real here, sir. Economic stress can be a contributing factor, but what set him off? I'd imagine there was more to it than that." He looked from Wade to Diana and then back again. "Was it Mrs. Calderon's habit to visit you?"

Wade said, "No," and watched Diana twist her hands. Wade doubted she'd ever seen the inside of a police station before. He hoped she didn't think too much about the phone call to his house, but he couldn't worry about her. He had to worry about himself.

"And the phone call to you," the officer said. "That was pretty late. We don't have a motive. The DA will hone in on a motive."

Wade was nauseated. On TV, they always find the villain's DNA on the murder victim. And Diana will eventually be concerned. This wasn't good.

The officer interrupted his thoughts. "What did Jorge say on the phone?"

Wade started, "He was drunk, concerned—"

Wade stopped speaking when there was a knock on the door. "Come in," the sergeant said.

Miss Spencer entered with her phone in hand. "I've got Stanford Hospital on the line. The judge has ordered twenty-four-hour security for Mr. Calderon. Here, I'll put this on speaker. It's the charge nurse, Belinda McIntosh, who wants to compile a visitor list."

They all listened as Belinda asked, "Does anyone know if Mr. Calderon has a pastor or a priest?"

Eyes turned toward Wade. "No, not that I know of," he said, leaning in toward the phone. "They're both Catholic, but I don't know anything else. I'd like to see Jorge as soon as possible, if I may."

From the phone, Belinda said, "Come down any time. Even if charges are filed, he has a right to visitors."

"Add Wade Middleton to your visitor list," the sergeant said. "Mrs. Buchanan?"

Everyone looked at Diana.

"No, I'd have no reason to see him." She closed her eyes and took a deep breath.

"We still haven't found any relatives," Miss Spencer said, both into the phone and to the others. "What about other friends?"

When there was no response, Sergeant Ames thanked Miss Spencer, and she left.

"Thank you for helping with Eva," the Sergeant said to Diana. "It's so lucky that she knew you and Beth or CPS would never let her go with you. I'll sleep better tonight knowing she's with someone she knows."

He stood up and turned to Wade. "I hope you don't have any trips scheduled."

Wade considered trying to explain more to the officer, as a fellow human being. But Wade knew he wasn't as adept at lying as he'd need to be—he'd have to think it all out, or they'd catch him in a lie. So he simply shook his head and said, "No. I don't have any trips scheduled."

"Good." The sergeant looked directly at him. "If you travel, call me beforehand. I have to be able to contact you." As they prepared to leave, Wade wondered if Diana's face wasn't showing new suspicions.

∞

Diana told Wade she didn't want him to follow her home from the police station. She said she needed time. She said it was in order to help Eva settle in, but Wade suspected she'd had her fill of this entire situation. He didn't want to be away from her. That would make it hard to measure how suspicious she was. But he also wanted to be close to Eva. Wade begged Diana to let him bring some lunch over later. Diana relented, but not happily. They said their cool goodbyes in the flat, fluorescent-lit halls of the police station.

Diana walked out ahead of Wade to her car across the street. From the sidewalk, he watched her carefully belt Eva into the back seat. Beth buckled up next to her. Diana glanced at Wade but looked away quickly, pretending not to see him.

23

Wade drove the long way home from the police station, past Jorge and Marita's house. In his hurry that morning he'd driven in the other direction, so this was the first time he saw the yellow caution tape across the driveway. He shook his head and looked away. He pulled into his driveway without looking back.

As soon as he got inside his house, he took his first deep breath since Sergeant Ames had awakened him. Wade had left Ray Snyderman a voicemail telling him he'd be in and out of work the next day for personal reasons, an obfuscation he'd never used before. A day at the office would seem like a vacation compared to this. Wade also told him that Jorge was in the hospital. "He's involved in a real mess, Ray. I'll fill you in later."

Now that Wade was alone, he was no longer anxious to bring lunch to Diana. He wished he hadn't been so insistent but remembered he needed to track her suspicions. He'd just pick up some sandwiches.

Wade's thoughts returned to Jorge. He wanted him to live, of course, but part of him was hoping he wouldn't wake up. Now that Wade was part of something that left a child virtually an orphan, he felt hypocritical for giving Diana such a hard time about the wild boar, as if participating in a generally-respected sport with her friends could anywhere near rise to his part in his friends' deaths. With the possibility of an autopsy coming up on Marita, he was thankful he'd used a condom, but that didn't keep him from worrying.

∞

Around noon, toting a shopping bag, Wade buzzed Diana from outside her condominium elevator. Working to lighten things up, Wade said, "Hey, it's your sandwich guy."

When he left the elevator, his eyes jumped to the bench next to her front door, where they'd shared their first kiss. Less than a year had passed, but it seemed like ages ago. When Diana came out to join him, he reached for her, but she stepped back.

"Beth wants to eat in the bedroom with Eva," she said. "Let me take those." She stepped into the kitchen and put the sandwiches on plates. "Here, why don't you take a seat while I deliver these." Micah scampered down the hallway with Diana, not to return.

Wade sat on Diana's balcony overlooking the red roofs of Stanford and the foothills, which were turning brown between patches of green. It was a typical seventy-degree Northern California clear-sky day, but the day didn't feel the slightest bit typical now. He and Diana made small talk for a while, but as they were finishing lunch, she said, "I can't get my mind off that midnight phone call from Jorge's house to yours. What happened there?" Her tone was friendly, but Wade had the intuition that she'd rehearsed the question. Thoughts of Jorge and Marita crept back.

"Like I said, Marita came to see me, and Jorge called. She needed a friend."

Diana stared, her eyes sharp. "A friend, huh? What did she want to see you about? *Oh, don't tell me.*" As she ran her hands through her hair, the red highlights appeared and disappeared around her fingers. "Really, Wade, don't say another word. I don't want to know."

"She was concerned they'd lose their house—and even more worried about Jorge," Wade said.

Diana folded her arms. "After what I went through with Rob, this is absolutely the last thing I need." She stood up. "Have you thought about a funeral for Marita?"

He hadn't. "I don't know. She has no relatives here."

"It's needed. Eva needs it," Diana said. "Well, they're a member of a church. I'll try that."

"You shouldn't have to do it," Wade said, wondering who else might.

"No, I'll do it for Eva. Wade, if you thought, because Jolene gave Billy a wide berth, that all my ethics are situational, you don't understand me at all. I have standards in my own life. Oh, never mind, it might be best if you leave now." She stood and removed their plates.

"Diana," Wade said, "I mean, I just got here." But when she didn't react, he stood and started toward the door.

"This is the best thing," she said, as she walked with him to the door. "Eva seems pretty calm, at least for the moment. Beth has been a marvel. Maybe this wasn't a bad thing for her after all. Robbie seems to be taking it in stride. But everything's too raw. It really would be best for you to leave."

"I feel pretty alone, right now," Wade said.

"Believe me," she said, "That's not the slightest bit unfamiliar. This has been a Sunday I'll never forget. I was looking forward to church with you, and then . . ." She pushed the elevator button. The door opened immediately, and Wade leaned over to kiss her, but she turned away. She left without a touch, much less a kiss.

∞

Later that afternoon back at home, Keats wanted to roughhouse. Wade welcomed this moment of levity and, once he had had enough, he scratched his dog's tummy and stood up. But Keats went over and looked at the leash hanging by the front door. He wanted more. Giving in, Wade took Keats for a long walk through South Palo Alto. At the park, the same place he'd thrown a softball back and forth with Eva a week earlier, Wade started an elegy to Marita in his head. He wanted to describe how she had opened him up the night before and how the world had shut down today. When Wade got home, he managed to jot down a few lines, but when he looked them over, the lines read like sentimental doggerel. He stored the page in a file he had for poems that didn't work and turned on the TV.

Wade boiled ravioli in a pot, heated up spaghetti sauce, slathered it on them, and ate. Dinner felt more solitary than ever that night. Just after dark, seven thirty or so, he called Diana. "There must be something I can do for Eva. There's a park I could take her to one morning, or we could go out to a movie? Or I could play catch with Robbie now that he's taken up baseball?"

When Diana told him, "Not really, Wade. It's too soon," he said a quick goodbye. Wade was bone tired. He fed Keats, closed the blinds in his bedroom, and climbed into bed. It had been less than twenty-four hours since Marita had knocked on his door with her jacket snapped up, a scene that now felt like it was from a different life.

∞

The phone rang in the middle of Monday morning—a phone number Wade didn't recognize. He thought, *Bad news always comes in threes.* First, it was Jorge's call, then the sergeant's, now what? This could not be good.

But it was only Jorge's nurse, Belinda, saying that Jorge's vital signs had improved. She was a great believer in visitors, and she thought Wade might want to come in to see him.

It would be hard to see Jorge as a virtual prisoner in the hospital where they had a policeman outside his room, but Wade threw some clothes on, put one foot in front of the other, and took care to not make any wrong turns. He drove across the Stanford campus, with its usual construction delays, arriving at the hospital shortly after eleven.

Wade followed the signs to Intensive Care, noting that they did a good job of keeping the hospital clean. There wasn't even any of that cover-up disinfectant smell, at least where Wade went that morning. He could have been in a pristine office building, for all he knew.

When he took the escalator up and checked in at the nursing

station, an aide summoned Belinda, who turned out to be a tall woman with an assured manner. Young, under thirty, Belinda was a take-charge kind of person. She had him sit in the area's small lobby and took a seat next to him. "You're his first visitor, Mr. Middleton. I'd better prepare you before you go in. We finally have him off the IV, but the effects of his stroke are quite evident."

"Can he talk?" Wade held his breath.

"He's mouthed a few words, but I wouldn't categorize him as conversational."

Wade's face fell at this news, but she continued, "But don't let that bother you. Studies have shown that even unresponsive people still process information, and he still is responding."

"Has he said anything?"

"He asked for water early this morning, but not much else. Follow me. He's down this way."

When she opened the doors to the unit, he got his first whiff of hospital—half disinfectant and half worse.

A tall police officer stood with one hand behind his back outside a room at the end of the hall. With his free hand, he checked Wade's ID. "Thank you, Mr. Middleton," he said as he returned the license.

Belinda and Wade stepped inside the room, which was larger and emptier than Wade had expected. "I thought he was in an oxygen tent." The policeman followed them and stood behind Jorge's bed.

"That was just the first few hours, to counteract the carbon monoxide." Belinda walked over to the patient and checked the wires that were monitoring him.

Wade couldn't believe how small Jorge appeared in his hospital gown with his one of those needle setups so he could get an IV at any time. The look on his friend's face was somewhere between scared and belligerent, simply out-of-it. How much damage could Jorge do? Wade was terrified.

The policeman stood behind Jorge, arms behind him in a military stance.

"Here, I'll sit him up," Belinda said, pressing a button that raised the bed to a sitting position.

Wade nervously walked over to him. He seemed so pale compared to the Jorge he'd remembered. "Can you hear me, buddy?"

"He moved. Did you see it?" Wade asked Belinda as he looked at Jorge's eyes.

The nurse nodded before she turned toward the door. "I have some things I need to finish up. That monitor shows his vitals. The needles just moved, so you're right, he knows we're here. Don't say anything that will stress him. There's always the possibility of another stroke. There's a repeater at my desk, so if he gets too excited, I'll know." She walked over to the bed and took Jorge's hand in her gloved hands. "I'm going to leave the room," she whispered into his ear. "Your friend Wade is here to visit you."

The left side of Jorge's face sagged. Wade walked closer to him, and leaned in to whisper in his ear. "Don't worry about Eva. She's doing well. She's with Diana and her daughter, Beth. Eva's living like a princess."

Jorge's head moved up and down, almost imperceptibly. A nod?

"Are you comfortable?" Wade asked.

Slowly his lips moved—was he trying to talk? He raised a finger. A sound came out of his mouth. "Wa—" Did he want water? Then something that sounded like "te." Wait?

No, he was looking right at him. He was saying his name.

The monitor rose again. "Calm down, Jorge," Wade said. "We have all day." The officer stood behind him, stiff as a Buckingham Palace guard.

"Marita's dead, isn't she?" he whispered, amazingly lucid. The needle on the machine jumped farther into the red.

Belinda rushed in, sucking the contents of a vial into a hypodermic needle's cylinder. "I shouldn't have left the room."

Wade concentrated on Jorge. "Yes, many things have happened, but Eva's fine."

"Sk-kirt zi-zipper," Jorge said, as the needle jumped again.

Jorge seemed to stare right through him. "I th-thought you w-were a good guy, W-wade." Then his mouth sagged, and he closed his eyes. The cop remained expressionless.

As Belinda gave Jorge the shot, he mumbled again.

"Bastard." The word was unmistakable and hit the mark.

Belinda gave Wade a quizzical look. "That should sedate him," she said. "It's only medium strength—we don't want him slipping into a coma. Did he just say 'bastard'?"

"He must be having an awful dream," Wade said.

"Yes, and something about a skirt zipper," Belinda said. She tried to look Wade in the eye, but he avoided her gaze.

"We'd better let him rest," she finally said. "It might be best you head home, get some sleep yourself."

The policeman maintained his poker face. Wade wanted to respond to Jorge, but his friend had gone limp.

∞

The visit with Jorge filled him not only with guilt, but fear. What if Jorge had been able to befriend one of the policemen outside his room and then blabbed to him?

Back in his home, Wade could hardly function, in a state an English friend of his called "sixes and sevens." He kept losing things—keys, wallets, tickets, lists—so he spent a lot of time searching for what he'd misplaced. All the time he thought about Jorge, both his tragedy and his potential to reveal Wade's night with Marita. If he got a call from Sergeant Ames, would he come clean or try to be coy? Should he get a lawyer? Wade played out one scenario after another in his mind, and his memories would jump to Jorge's life as he'd known him—the firing, getting the money to move to Palo Alto, so many scenes. And that waitress—what was her name? Chetana, yes. Wade thought most people wouldn't bother with this Chetana detail, but she and Jorge liked each other, so he should stop by that restaurant and tell her something. But what could he say with Jorge's situation still unclear?

How hard it was to avoid thinking of something—to *not think* of Jorge. Wade needed to find something new to concentrate on. Diana? No, she, too conjured discomfort. Artemis would be better to think about. Wade had been riding her at the ranch almost every day after work. He'd mouth long soliloquies into her ear, sometimes about Jorge and how sorry he was, and sometimes he'd whisper about Diana and how wrong she was to judge him. Wade didn't take Artemis over jumps, except for hopping over an occasional small log. Every time he'd do that, inside his head he'd hear Diana saying, "Sometimes, even when you're not planning to jump, a log just gets in your way." In the hunt field, they called that 'larking', and it was strongly discouraged.

For fear of falling off Artemis with no one around, Wade saved the real jumps for Saturday afternoons during his lessons with Edward. The trainer had slowly raised Wade's jumps six inches or more. In one area of his life, at least, Wade was making progress.

His mind jumped to Jorge. What happened to Marita, technically, wasn't murder. But Marita died as the result of his anger, no doubt about that. Still, Wade hoped Jorge would live and somehow be absolved. No matter how the courts handled it, Eva needed a father.

∞

Belinda called Wade to tell him Jorge had dropped into a coma. "But he's very much alive. I'd recommend you come in to see him, Mr. Middleton."

But Wade just couldn't go back to see Jorge, at least that week as he continued to sort things out. Instead he worried about him dying. And about him waking up.

∞

For the eight years Wade had Keats in his life, the dog had never been allowed on the bed. There was one exception when Wade had the flu, but that was it. Never at night, even then.

But after he got into bed that evening, he clapped his hand against the bedspread and urged Keats to join him on the bed. The beagle didn't jump—he'd learned the rules. Finally, though, Wade got up, went to the kitchen cupboard and got him a treat to coax him up. From that night on, Keats slept on the bed by Wade's feet. Wade had to be careful whenever he turned over to not knock him off. He would pull one leg up and then the other, hoping that Keats would sleep through it, which he usually did.

24

Wade observed a curious fact since Eva had moved to Diana's condominium—it seemed to improve Beth's satisfaction with California, and even Diana's relationship with her daughter. Diana's deep commitment to her family and by a blessed extension, to nurturing Eva, had made her even more attractive to Wade. Yet he worried that he had likely blown the possibility of a long-term romantic relationship with Diana.

Wade's days went by in a blur. In addition to worrying about Eva, or whether there was anything left between himself and Diana, he had to screen his phone calls. "Police Investigating Possible Murder-Suicide," had appeared on page three of the paper. Wade's name wasn't in the article, thank God. Like one of those politicians gone wrong, he became determined not to answer the phone for a reporter, no matter what.

Wade would have loved to take Eva to the park, but Diana had stopped returning his phone calls.

The last time he'd seen Diana was at Marita's funeral. There's something depressing about a priest doing a service for someone he hardly knows, and, try as this middle-aged bearded fellow might, his words had come out a bit off key. "I'm sure, when she sees God, she'll recognize Him," the man had said unconvincingly. Even Diana, who was there with Beth and Eva, had grimaced.

The ceremony for Marita that followed, in the church multipurpose room, drew no more than thirty. The mourners included some women who concentrated on their rosaries. Wade inquired and was told they were from the Altar and Rosary Society and attend such events regularly. Most of the others were young mothers who had children in day care with Eva. There was no burial service. Instead Marita's ashes were mailed to Florida, where, he overheard, her remains would be buried between her mother and father. He formed a mental image of Marita the time she had come over to his place before she'd bought her house, lying on Wade's bed. He shook his head, remembering the time he'd turned her down and written a poem about it. And the time he hadn't turned her down.

∞

One day the following week, Ray took off for a finance meeting in Reno, so Wade was able to go into the office privately, lie low, and stay in touch with customers. This was a welcome respite from all he had been going through. The Chicago installation was running into cost overruns. To keep that problem in check, Wade made some phone calls and persuaded subcontractors to bring the cost down by about half of the overrun.

That evening, he looked to poetry for consolation and wisdom, but modern poems didn't speak to him. He was drawn, instead, to John Keats's odes. The poet had died young—at twenty-six. Wade marked "Ode to a Nightingale," hoping one day he would be able to read the lines to Diana, but instead, tried to read them to the dog—

> My heart aches, and a drowsy numbness pains
> My sense, as though of hemlock I had drunk . . .

Keats the beagle, though, couldn't help him now. In the evening, when he brought Wade the rope toy in his mouth, Wade just couldn't muster the energy to play. Sometimes he put Keats in the garage until bedtime and listened to his whimpers through the door.

Late one night, Diana finally returned one of his phone calls. She quietly described how things were going with Eva. Sleeping alone in the guest room scared the little girl, so she had moved her into Beth's room. Eva had asked to see Wade, Diana told him, so Diana invited him to dinner. "Robbie will be with his father, so it'll just be you and me and Beth and Eva." Diana ended the conversation with three crystal-clear words, said almost like a schoolteacher, which wasn't Diana's style, "Only for dinner."

Well, he thought, *I've wanted to see her, so, despite her reluctance, I'll make the best of it.* He was doing a lot of that then, just putting one foot in front of the other, taking only steps that seemed required of him.

∞

Wade didn't want to show up at Diana's empty-handed and thought of the perfect gift—the horse Eva loved so much because Beth had given it to her. The problem was that the horse was at Jorge and Marita's now-cordoned-off house. He called the police, who, on his third phone call, finally agreed to escort him into the house.

Wade found the horse easily but, despite the deputy sheriff's desire to cut the visit short, had to go into the garage where Marita had died. He stared at the three cement steps down into the garage, understanding how she could have died.

"Come on, we don't have all day," the policeman said, interrupting Wade's grief.

"This horse is their daughter's favorite toy, and I'd like to bring it to her," Wade said.

"This is still a crime scene. Nothing can be removed."

"She's my goddaughter. I need to help her," he said.

The deputy looked at the horse, then at Wade. "Are we leaving now?" he asked.

Understanding the offer, he tucked the horse under his arm and said, "Yes, we're on our way out the door."

∞

When Wade arrived at Diana's with the plastic horse, Diana, Beth, and Eva met him at the door. Eva's eyes lit up at the sight of the horse. The child looked more like her mother, especially about her jaw and chin, than he had remembered. But Eva had a look of sorrow that she couldn't hide now, a scared look. He had never once seen Marita scared. *Don't think about Marita now.*

Eva, either forgetting or not fully understanding that the horse had come from Beth, shyly showed the horse to Diana and Beth.

Wade said to her, "It's good to see you smile."

"Thank you, Uncle Wade." Eva asked Beth if she could take the horse back to the bedroom. Beth took her hand as they walked down the hall.

Diana led Wade into the family room. "Dinner's almost ready."

They made awkward small talk, in which each of them used the word *fine* so many times that they finally laughed about it. "Jolene's fine?"

"Yes, Billy's fine, too," Diana said, laughing.

After they both stopped laughing, they each took a deep breath. As they seated themselves in the family room, Wade took the risk of sharing the Keats poem with her. He had hopes that the poetry that had comforted him would comfort Diana, too. "I hope you'll like it—some of the best poetry in the English language." As he pulled the poem from his pocket, though, Diana looked down at her hands. She didn't want him to read. Still, Wade stuck to his plan and began the last three longish stanzas of "Ode to a Nightingale"—

> Thou wast not born for death, immortal bird!
> No hungry generations tread thee down
> The voice I hear this passing night was heard
> In ancient days by emperor and clown
> Perhaps the self-same song that found a path
> Through the sad heart of Ruth, when, sick for home,
> She stood in tears among the alien corn—

"Please stop, Wade," she interrupted.

Wade folded the poem and, perhaps with more ceremony than was appropriate, returned it to his pocket.

"I don't want to hear some guy from two hundred years ago," Diana said. "What's going on with *you*? Don't talk about what happened to Jorge, or anything about that night or Marita. None of that. How about the rest of your life—how about Wade Middleton? What's going on with that sales guy who writes poetry?" The soft tone Diana used as she asked this comforted him. Perhaps she really did care for him.

What could he tell her but the truth? "I'm not sure I even know who Wade is, Diana. I've been spending a lot of time thinking about Marita and Jorge—wondering if there was anything I could do. I saw him yesterday at the hospital. He even said a few words."

"Billy thinks if Jorge recovers, he'll go right to jail."

"Even with that hanging over his head, I sure hope he lives," Wade said. "It was a terrible accident." As soon as he said the word, he realized how appallingly he'd been lying to himself. Accident was way too forgiving a word.

Diana nodded. "I've spent a lot of my last two weeks in prayer—I even went to church two mornings last week. And in prayer, something came to me, quite clearly, Wade. That Eva must have been put into my life for a reason. God doesn't just let things happen. And she really has been a blessing. That little girl has certainly brought me closer to my own daughter."

Wade nodded passively, but his mind raced. He knew there was a God, but wasn't as sure as Diana that humans could understand his doings. If she was right, what was God's plan for Jorge or for him? He needed to face his part in Marita's death head-on, but couldn't. The last thing he wanted was an elaborate investigation. And Wade knew if he told Diana, she'd truly write him off.

"They're even helping at the law firm. Billy's sorting through the legalities," Diana said. "If he dies, assuming it's before a trial or anything, he'll get something like eighty thousand in insurance from Enersystems, so that will at least get a good start on Eva's education expenses. A lot depends on whether Jorge makes it through." Diana looked up at Wade. "Billy's working the insurance angle. He's pretty effective."

"I believe that," Wade said.

Diana raised an eyebrow. After looking away, she continued, "So, anyway, I'm doing all I can to keep myself going. I try not to think about that night."

"I'm sorry, Diana. Will you let me explain?"

"Maybe someday. Now all I want to do is get through the day and take care of myself and my kids. And Eva. That takes up all there is of me."

But Wade could not let it go. "How about next week? I have to deal with this. What if I took you to dinner next week?"

"I don't think so. What would be the purpose?"

"Diana, you're taking responsibility for Eva in a way that no one would have expected. I've done some things wrong that I want to explain to you. How about the Village Pub? You know, in Woodside, where you took me for my birthday. It wouldn't be a date, I promise."

Diana laughed. "I see, you'd take me to our favorite restaurant, and it wouldn't be a date."

"It's killing me, holding everything inside. Please."

"Tell you what, Wade. I won't say yes, but I won't say no either. I'll give it prayerful consideration." She smiled. Wade took her comment as an effort at self-mockery after all the time she was spending in church.

Wade laughed lightly along with her. Even if they weren't intimate as they'd once been, they were still communicating. He exhaled with relief.

∞

Diana finally agreed to go to dinner with him, and Wade agonized over what to tell her about Marita, going over one imaginary conversation after another. He finally decided to simply trust his instincts in the moment when he would be talking with her.

When he picked her up, Diana wore a French blue summer dress and white sweater that brought out the red in her hair. She looked carefree and sexy. He missed being with her. As they drove up to rural Woodside, she said, "You didn't need to take me someplace so fancy," but she seemed happy to be with him.

"I remember your treat on my birthday fondly," Wade said.

She smiled. "There was no need, but I appreciate it."

When they'd ordered, and both had glasses of wine in front of them, Wade said, "I want to apologize about that day with the boar."

"That's okay. I've had some discussions with the Hunt Committee. They're old school, but the idea of changing procedures is at least being considered. If nothing else, I made them aware of my concerns."

Wade reached across the table and touched her hand. He was honored that she'd listened to his concerns about the hunt. Maybe this night was going to go fine. A few moments later, he said, "I want to clear the air about that night with Jorge and Marita."

"Why go over that?" She frowned as she slowly twirled her wineglass. "You have to look forward now. We both do." She put down her glass. "But there is something I need to say to you," she continued. "You've lost some of that old spring in your step. Don't let this tragedy rule your life, Wade. Put that night behind you. I'm not saying you should lean on the Bible, but you know that's how I get through things."

Lean on the Bible. Wade took a sip of wine as he tried to figure out what that meant. "There are some weird passages in the Bible, Diana. Sometimes I wonder if they were slipped in as it was being copied. Or lost in translation."

She shook her head dismissively. "God wouldn't give us a book people couldn't trust. He loves us."

Wade was constantly astounded by her simple faith. The Bible was something you had to pick and choose from—didn't everybody think that? But who could argue with whatever it was that had brought her to take Eva in and treat her like her own?

Still, Wade couldn't imagine having confidence in every word of the Bible. Nor was he sure he wanted to. "Do I need such a faith to have a place in your life?" he asked.

"Your beliefs have to be your own. I wanted to show you how I get through times like you're going through. God is real to me." She got a faraway look in her eye. "I think of a bird taking flight and soaring." With her free hand, she gestured upward.

Should Wade ask her to make this clearer? This reminded him of other conversations with people of faith, of their sureness. He had always asked for more explanation, but people wouldn't explain much. They would stop, like Diana had. If faith were explainable, Wade mused, it wouldn't be faith. Unfortunately, her faith didn't bring him any closer to her. He wished it had.

Wade still wasn't sure where he stood with Diana. Throughout dinner he argued with himself about whether he should bring up Jorge and Marita again. He couldn't think of any other way to put this behind him. He was sure Diana would ask if he had previously thought Jorge was capable of such violence or if Wade had ever been in love with Marita. He'd prepared answers for either of those questions.

After they ordered dessert, he blurted out, "Diana, the main reason I wanted to take you to dinner was to clear the air about that night. I am sure you have questions. Don't you?"

The waiter rolled a cart next to their table and started serving cream puffs filled with ice cream—profiteroles. He placed them on two plates and ladled hot chocolate sauce over them. The cold of the ice cream pleased Wade as it met the warm chocolate on his first bite.

Diana took a spoonful. "Delicious." She paused. "Okay, if you insist, I'll ask the obvious question. That night, did you sleep with Marita? All the way?"

Her question was more straightforward than anything Wade had imagined her asking. He'd rehearsed for softer questions, but this one threw him. Wade repeated her question aloud to give him time to think. He thought of the time Marita tried to seduce him, when she was looking at real estate in his neighborhood, and started to say, "It wasn't the first time," but, realizing this could be misinterpreted, he stopped himself and finished off his wine.

He thought of saying that Marita had come to his house, worried about Jorge, asking Wade to help them financially, but he knew Diana would ferret that out as a half-truth. He didn't say anything. Almost imperceptibly, he felt his head going up and down. His nodding head was admission that he had slept with Marita.

Diana shook her head. "So, it's no wonder you've been acting so guilty." She poked at the cream puffs with her fork until she pushed the plate away. She looked as if she might cry. Then she stiffened. "That changes just about everything."

"What went on between me and Marita wasn't about you in any way. I was weak. I can't tell you how much I regret what I did. You and I hadn't been intimate for a couple of months."

She searched his face. "More like six weeks. At any rate, it was wrong. Were you in love with her?"

"No, if I'm in love with anyone, and I think I am, it's with you. It was a weak moment. Do you think I did wrong by her because I wasn't in love with her?" he asked.

Diana looked away and then directly at him. "I can't comment on Marita. But, Jorge."

Wade couldn't defend himself there. "You always told me I worried too much about him."

"He trusted you, Wade. Anyone could see that. And . . ." she drew a deep breath, "you were his *friend*." She looked away. "I never thought I'd feel sorry for him, but I do."

"I probably think of him a hundred times a day." Wade agonized.

She put her fork down. "Wade, as much as I care for you, I can't be romantically involved with you anymore." She wiped tears from her eyes, "To think I was about to invite you to the master's dinner next week, with all the folks you like."

She gathered herself together and continued. "I do hope, though, that you'll keep seeing Eva. It's not just that you're her godfather. She needs a male influence in her life. But you and I cannot date. Oh, why did you take me to this nice dinner to tell me what you'd done? I like you, I do. I might even love you. But I specifically told you I didn't want to know."

"Yes, I screwed up. I couldn't go on without telling you." Feeling his eyes water, he grabbed her hand. "I don't want to lose you."

She pulled back. "This is about trust, Wade. I always thought I could trust you."

Wade remembered he wanted to trust his instincts, but this certainly wasn't the outcome he was looking for. He'd blown it again.

After driving Diana home in silence, Wade went up in the elevator with her, but she maintained her distance. At her front door, they said their goodbyes without touching. "Isn't there anything I can do to try to fix this?" Wade asked.

Diana shook her head and looked down as she shut the door behind her.

∞

It was still light out when he left Diana's—the end of a long summer day. Diana had been right—Jorge had trusted him, and he had abused that trust. He suddenly needed to see Jorge, desperately. Even if he was in a coma, perhaps he could hear Wade's apology. The nurse, Belinda, despite the upset last time, had encouraged him to come in. She thought Wade might bring Jorge out of it.

Wade pushed himself away from the wheel and started the car. As he drove, he tried to translate *Mea culpa—Mea maxima culpa*—into words that would resonate with Jorge. He would promise him that he would take care of Eva as if she were his own child, something he had already promised to God, and something that, through Diana, he felt he was doing. But it was Jorge to whom he had to confess.

When Wade got to the nursing station at the hospital, he asked the tall woman behind the desk for Belinda.

"She's still in L.A." She looked at him as if he'd ask another question, but Wade reminded himself it was easier to gain forgiveness than permission. "Okay, I'll go on back."

The whiff of unclean smells and cleaners that he encountered when he opened the door to Intensive Care seemed muted and so familiar that they were almost pleasant. The area was much quieter than the previous time, almost deserted. He looked down the hall to the police desk. No one was there. Except for a custodian mopping the floor, the hallway was empty. Wade rehearsed the words of his apology as he headed toward Jorge's room. No matter how Jorge would respond, Wade reminded himself, he'd be glad to have gotten it off his chest.

When he stepped into Jorge's room, it was empty, the mattress folded over. He turned and walked up to the young man with the mop. He pointed to Jorge's room. "Where is he?"

"*No sé.*" He shrugged.

Wade headed back to the nursing station. When the tall nurse looked up, he asked, "Could you tell me where Jorge Calderon has been transferred?" He gave her Jorge's room number.

The nurse asked him if he was a family member. After a slight hesitation, he nodded yes.

"Yes?" she asked.

"I'm his uncle," Wade said, not feeling very convincing.

"I'm sorry to inform you that your nephew passed away at 2:26 this afternoon. It appears he had a massive stroke. If you have any questions regarding the disposition of Mr. Calderon's body, please contact the business office."

Wade, stunned, found his way to a chair across the way and sank down into it. His left hand started shaking on its own, the way it had done in the police station a few weeks earlier. Life had handed him more than he could bear. The only other time Wade had felt that way was when Liz left him, but this was worse. He wanted to run out of the hospital, get in his car and drive—just keep driving. Even then, he wouldn't be free, just another guilty guy with no home. He held himself together enough to walk back to the desk and say, "Thank you very much."

Gathering what strength he could, he wandered back down to Jorge's room. The place where the policeman had sat seemed like an abandoned military post from a battle long lost.

Inside the room, near the bed, Jorge's last place on earth, images of a vibrant Jorge flashed before him—the way his friend had been jealous of the Mexican gardeners outside of Steve Job's house after he was fired; how happy Jorge had been to get the job with Billy and his talk about Sacratomatoes; how proud he was to buy the house. Wade would never be able to look him in the eye, never get a chance to apologize, much less make up for the harm he'd done. Wade had tried to help Jorge and failed. He betrayed him by going to bed with his wife, and she died as a result. Now, Jorge was gone, too.

∞

At home, Wade turned to a two-hundred-year-old poem by William Blake, "The Sick Rose," one of the best-known poems in the English language, one Wade had almost memorized, and read it again.

> O Rose thou art sick.
> The invisible worm,
> That flies in the night
> In the howling storm:
>
> Has found out thy bed
> Of crimson joy:
> And his dark secret love
> Does thy life destroy.

The poem stood the test of time, and Wade wondered if it was because of its bleakness, or despite it.

∞

The next night was the only time Wade considered suicide—the guilt-ridden messes that suicides left behind—did suicidal people target their loved ones?—were usually enough to keep Wade away from such thoughts. He had played a role in Marita's death and now Jorge's, too—the man who had thought of him as a brother. Wade asked himself if he had thought of Jorge as a brother in return. Perhaps, because Jorge was his subordinate at work, Wade had considered him a much younger brother at best.

In the back of his medicine cabinet, Wade found twenty or thirty Valium tablets left from when he had muscle spasms in his back.

If he were to swallow the pills, how would his body be found? What would he wear? Pajamas? No. A suit didn't sound right either. Wade suspected most guys would want to be dressed formally, perhaps in a tie. Would a button down shirt and khakis be perfect for a guy in the middle?

How would news of his death affect Amelia? Or Eva? After the loss of Marita and Jorge, how could Eva cope? And what would happen to Keats? Would Diana take him in? Probably not, she didn't care for Keats as much as Wade did. It would be wrong to ask her after all she had done for Eva. Diana had been incredible with that little girl, literally a lifesaver.

In the crass brightness of his bathroom, he held the plastic vial of tranquilizers. But he couldn't empty them into his hand, much less into his mouth. Picturing the impact his suicide would have on Amelia and Eva, Wade returned the bottle to the cabinet.

With suicidal thoughts behind him, he re-read Blake's poem. Blake was a man of faith, a Christian, but not in an orthodox fashion. His beliefs, as revealed in his poems such as "The Lamb," and "The Tiger," were complex, even contradictory. In "The Sick Rose," Blake seemed to ignore the sacred qualities of forgiveness and grace. Wade had long-ago realized the absolute bleakness of the poem was part and parcel of its strength. Wade's faith had always argued with the poem, this bleak Blake.

Could he reconstruct the poem, using Blake's rhythms? He put together two short verses:

The Well Rose

O Rose thou art well.
The invisible worm,
Who flew in the night
In that howling storm

Has grown to forgive
Your crimson joy:
And his higher powers
Did he thus employ.

Wade printed the poem and held it, realizing it was something he could never show anyone . . . imagine, Wade Middleton re-writing William Blake. Such arrogance. He reached to the back of his nightstand drawer and re-read "Offering," with its notion of acting properly and feeling blue, the poem he'd written when Marita first approached him. New pockets of grief opened within him. Wade folded the new poem inside "Offering," pinched the two pages tightly together, and returned them to the back of the nightstand drawer.

Part III

The Thaw

Over the land half-freckled with snow half-thawed
The speculating rooks at their nests cawed,
And saw from elm-tops, delicate as a flower of grass,
What we below could not see, Winter pass.
—Edward Thomas

25

Even in the months after Wade staved off suicide, he continued to be hemmed in by his dreams. One dream happened in the darkness just before dawn. *Marita enters the garage through a side door and unzips her jacket. She can't hear Wade or see him. he's not physically in the dream but experiences the garage as if he is right there. Jorge opens the door from the kitchen and stands on a cement step. He's in his pajamas, carrying a baseball bat. "I thought it was a burglar," he says.*

Marita pointedly ignores him. She casually hangs up her jacket.

"Why is your skirt half-zipped, with your shirt sticking out?" Jorge asks.

She moves toward him.

When Jorge raises his bat, she crouches in unexpected fear. As she steps back, her foot falls off the top step. She falls, bashing her head on the cement with a bang that could be heard down the street. Jorge gets down on the garage floor and holds her as her life fades away.

Wade woke up sweating. He hugged Keats, took a bath as the sun came up, then went back to bed. When he got up again hours later, he did another thing he'd never done before—he called in sick when he wasn't. In and out of bed, by noon he was still under the covers. Jorge's guilt in the dream was, like Wade's own, unpardonable. What was Jorge thinking? What had Wade been thinking? He may not have been thinking about suicide any longer, but he was still barely functioning.

∞

He only saw Diana Saturday mornings when he picked up Eva. He'd take his goddaughter out for ice cream or to see the horses at Jasper Ridge Ranch. A couple of times they went to children's readings at the library on Middlefield Road. Wade felt like a twice-divorced dad, but the regularity of his visits with Eva buoyed him. At first his time with her had their awkward moments, but eventually they relaxed and got on well. These visits with Eva were somehow more gratifying than his memory of similar jaunts with Amelia years earlier. Perhaps it was because there was no doubt Eva needed him. That was one appointment to which he was never late. On Saturday mornings, he'd set two alarms.

When he would bring Eva back to Diana's, Wade often watched Diana, wondering if there was any way to rekindle their relationship. A new formality had set in, and it was one he couldn't ignore. He had to conform to it. Seeing Robbie was particularly difficult as Wade felt in some ways that the boy's father had won—that is, Diana was, once again, not dating. Not a word passed between him and Robbie.

One Saturday Eva asked him if he would come to her back-to-school night. He ducked her question, but later, when he was alone with Diana, he asked if he could go along.

"It's okay. I've got it covered," she said, but Wade asked twice again. In the end they both went, though in separate cars.

The soft-spoken young teacher, who seemed to have been born with the unlimited patience required to teach first grade, had the adults sit at the children's small desks. She talked them through a typical classroom day as they fidgeted in the tiny chairs. After her talk, she came around and discussed each student privately. When she got to Diana and Wade, she showed them Eva's penmanship and artwork, which looked a little sloppy. One of Eva's printing assignments seemed to have ended prematurely—it was half-done. Wade looked around the room at the assignments on other desks, which all looked finished.

When they had time with the teacher, Diana introduced Wade and then asked, "Is Eva able to keep up with the class?"

"Her mind wanders," the teacher said. "Sometimes Eva's in her own world. All kids are, at this age, but it's harder to bring Eva back. I understand she's seeing a psychiatrist."

Diana nodded. "Yes, the school nurse put me in touch with her."

The teacher nodded. "It sounds like you're doing all the right things. Underneath Eva's shyness, I think she's quite bright. She's still suffering, but there's been a definite improvement."

Neither Diana nor Wade said much after that. They listened and thanked the teacher, and before long he walked Diana to her car. "Tough session," he said.

"I'm not sure what could have been worse. It was so hard to see her sloppy work." Her face was drawn tight as they approached her car. "That was hard."

"I don't know," Wade said. "Remember, Eva's world was destroyed. We can't expect her to just snap out of it. But what you have done for her is so wonderful. I didn't even know you had arranged for her to see a psychiatrist—you've been amazing."

She pressed a button on her car key that turned on her lights and unlocked her SUV.

Wade opened the door for Diana. "Can I buy you a goodnight hot chocolate or something?"

"I'd better get home and relieve Beth so she can get to her homework. I'd love to but I really should get back."

"When I went to buy Artemis some treats, I ran into Jack in the feed store. He's a master through and through," Wade said. "I hear you guys had fun at opening meet."

"Yes. People asked about you."

He wanted to keep the conversation going, but Diana's tense expression didn't invite further inquiry.

∞

When Wade got home, he made himself a stiff drink before going to bed, which didn't keep the nightmares away.

In his dream that night, *when Jorge appears, he calls Marita a*

Jezebel. He tells her he'd thought Wade was better than that, better than Billy, that she was a slut and a whore. Jorge moves toward her, and she falls off the top step again, with the same loud sound, like a giant tree falling.

The dream woke him up. It was still the middle of the night. Unable to fall asleep again, Wade started a poem about drinking at night. At the start, Jorge and Marita were in the poem but as Wade went on writing, they weren't. If they'd stayed in the poem, he knew they'd confuse the core of the poem, which was about guilt and drinking. He came up with a first line:

"You are not good enough, the voice says."

Once Wade had written that line, he went back to bed with Keats at his feet. Thankfully, no nightmares followed for the rest of that night.

∞

Over the next few months, the economy fell into a spiral of no-confidence. Nearly everyone in the Bay Area had to work harder to make ends meet, and higher prices, as well as increased traffic, became a frequent subject of conversation. SnyderSound's sales dropped, leaving only some residuals from deals Wade had made in the spring. After one of his weekly sales updates in his office, Ray told him he was being forced into another layoff, this one even deeper. "And tomorrow morning I'll be announcing that Lydia will manage all customer interactions. She thinks she can do the job with fewer people—that's the order of savings we need."

To make matters worse, Ray berated Wade about cost overruns in Chicago—a double whammy. "We might actually lose money on that deal." His eyes probed Wade's.

"Don't give up on me yet," Wade said, trying to convince his boss. "It's been a challenge to manage a project from two thousand miles away. The subcontractors really—"

"This is a small company," Ray interjected. "We absolutely must make our margins."

"I know. I spent three hours on the phone to Chicago last Saturday. I even got the customer to call some of the subcontractors—they don't like to see us jacked around, either."

Ray nodded but didn't smile. He was wearing his game face. "In the report you just gave me, I didn't see you pulling in one dollar of new business."

"I didn't want to be a Pollyanna. Nobody's spending a dime right now."

"That's pretty negative. It doesn't sound like you. As bad as things are, Lydia stays upbeat. You need to make some sales and soon." Ray let his words hang in the air as he opened the door for Wade to leave his office. Wade's concerns moved from having to report to Lydia to losing his job entirely.

∞

Wade's nightmares continued. One night the dream starts the same, *but Jorge violently bashes Marita's head with the bat. As usual, he is a helpless observer, invisible and impotent. Why hadn't he seen that Jorge was a violent person? Once again he watches her die in Jorge's arms. Jorge cries, mumbling through his tears that he didn't mean to kill her.* He sat up in bed, wide-awake, sweating and crying.

∞

No longer dating Diana, with Jorge and Marita gone, and with his job at risk, Wade had a hard time making it through the day. He knew no one would buy anything from a dour salesperson, so he did his best to put a good face on things. He compiled lists of sales prospects. He called the customers he knew first off, but no luck. The Andersons, who had gotten Jorge fired, had moved to Cabo San Lucas in Baja and didn't return his calls.

Wade intended to phone every name on the list, but once he'd started, it was tough. Some of the people he talked to mentioned they were worried about their own jobs. Asking their organizations to spend money frightened them. After a hundred rejections, his mind would flash back to the garage—*Jorge raises his bat, Marita falls, he holds her while she dies.* Wade finally crossed some names off without phoning them. Work, which had been a respite from his personal trauma, now made the days long. Fear made the nights longer.

As the fall ground on, Wade's duress must have shown in his face or body language because people he knew casually and his friends at work came up to him and asked if he was taking care of himself. He'd lost some weight, but no more than ten or twelve pounds, so how did they know?

∞

Early in December Amelia called. "It looks like I'll be coming out sometime over Christmas vacation after all. I can't stay long, but I have some things I want to talk over with you."

"That'd be great," Wade said. "I feel so far away from you. Your mom said your professor wants you to go on for a master's degree next year."

"At Yale, no less, but I want to discuss all that with you, Dad. I'll fly out to Palo Alto from Mom's after Christmas. A girlfriend invited me to some big family get-together in Boston on New Year's, so I'll only be out a few days. But I want to see you."

"I'm not going anywhere," Wade said. "I'll fix up your room."

"One last thing, Dad. Remember in sixth grade when I had that awful fight with MeDee, the tall girl with the red braids?"

He searched his memory and came up empty. "Just barely," he said.

"You didn't seem very interested," her voice pouted.

He started to interrupt but she broke in, "This time I really need you."

"Okay, got it, I'm there," Wade said. He kept her conversation in his mind as a reminder of what he needed to do, right up with his resolve to pay attention to his godparenting. *Listen, really listen, to Amelia.*

∞

One Saturday when Wade brought Eva back to Diana's, they talked in her kitchen. With every progressing Saturday, Wade had noticed that Diana had seemed less angry. This time he decided to push his luck. "Any chance you can stick around for Christmas?" Wade asked. "Amelia's coming out. She wants to discuss ideas about what to do after graduation."

"I haven't made plans yet." Diana dipped pieces of chicken in flour and placed them in a casserole dish. "By the way, I hear you went out with the hounds on Thanksgiving."

"Yes, I knew you'd be away, so I called Jolene, who encouraged me to ride Artemis. When I showed an interest, she had Jack invite me. We went out on that big ranch down near Gilroy. It was good to see the old gang." Wade sat at the counter while she cooked. He resisted the urge to move closer to her. "There were only a handful of riders, plus the huntsman and a whip. Jack led us. We got a few views. I rode with Cliff, often at a full canter—I barely stayed on, but I came back in one piece." Wade had learned that a canter is like a gallop only slower with a slightly different rhythm. As he learned the nuance, he preferred the canter.

"I'm glad you got out with them."

"Thanks. But now, about Christmas, do you think Amelia and Beth might hit it off? I thought it might help Beth to talk with someone who's made it through Paly."

Diana took a while before answering. "My parents want me in Dallas, and Billy says I have custody now so I can legally take Eva out of state, but maybe this is the year to stay in California. It would be my first Christmas away from home."

"Think about it," Wade said. "It would be good for Eva to stay here, where she's familiar, too."

"Possibly," she said, and then she nodded. "Yes, possibly that could work."

∞

Since Wade never heard any more about Christmas from Diana, he assumed he would be as alone as the previous year. He decided to do the same things he'd done the year before—attend his old church on Christmas Eve, then on to San Francisco for breakfast the next morning, and then a rent-a-horse-by-the-ocean stint.

Diana called four days before Christmas and threw Wade's plans up in the air—she'd decided to stay home for Christmas after all.

"Great. Will it work for me to take Eva horseback riding in Half Moon Bay on Christmas Day?"

"Sure," she said. "Perhaps we could go to church together Christmas Eve."

"That would be great. Can I pick you up?" Wade asked.

"Um, no, I'll be coming right from a party. I'll have to meet you there. In fact, maybe you can hold a place for me in that line by the side door?"

"Sure. Can we do something after?"

"Sorry, but one of Beth's friends is having a party and her mom asked me to help, so I have to get right back."

Wade worked to concentrate. He was glad Diana was staying home for Christmas but wondered if he was setting his expectations too high about the chance of any quality time together. "So we'll meet up there and only see each other in line and the pew?" He'd had a memorable Christmas the previous year and if Diana's comments meant they would barely see each other, he would prefer to repeat all the same things that made his last Christmas memorable. When Diana didn't respond, he said, "We'd hardly see each other. I'd better stick with my own church then, if that's okay."

"Sure," she said softly. "I'd better get off the phone now."

∞

Wade had a bad moment in the church service on Christmas Eve. The minister lamented about the children put to death as part of King Herod's edict, calling them the first Christian martyrs. She had a knack for bringing the Gospel alive, making these children's deaths seem so real that it made Wade think of Jorge and Marita. Would they ever leave him alone?

But moments later, his pastor cheered him up. Like the year before, she had everyone shout "Merry Christmas!" at the end of the service. She announced this from the back of the church so she could greet people on their way out. When Wade saw her, he kidded her about it. "Not a very Presbyterian ending there," he said in mock seriousness. "Aren't you supposed to end with 'A King is Born' or at least 'Alleluia'?"

She laughed as he passed by, saying, "You sound like all the male teachers I had in seminary. How are you, Wade? I heard you had a rough year. We even tried to reach out to you, but you didn't respond. Good to see you smiling again."

∞

The next morning, Wade went to Union Square in San Francisco and again took himself out for breakfast at Sears Fine Foods. He managed to snag the same window table across from the costumed doorman, the table he had enjoyed the year before. He wondered what Diana was doing—should he have worked around her scheduling problems and been with her instead of being here alone? On his computer he looked up the fragment he'd written the year before about the stranger with the shopping cart and read it over, wondering whether it could be part of a longer poem. He thought of putting Jorge into the poem but couldn't see how to do it.

He was starting to look past Jorge's death and think about the man's life, how difficult it had been—and short, of course—but with blessings as well. Wade would never forgive himself for that night, but before then he'd been a pretty good friend to Jorge. Wade immediately thought of the tired quip, "Except for the shooting, Mrs. Lincoln, how was the play?"

On Christmas day, Wade let Eva ride the trustworthy Appaloosa he had ridden the year before while he rode an ancient nag behind her, nose-to-tail all the way to the ocean. He kept a close watch on them, but Eva and the Appaloosa never faltered. She later said stepping into the ocean on a horse was the best part of her Christmas. It was a good afternoon for him, too. After he dropped Eva off, he realized that his mind hadn't wandered to Jorge or Marita or the baseball bat since he'd picked Eva up.

26

Amelia arrived three days later on a cold, crisp Tuesday. When Wade picked her up at the airport, she lingered a bit as she hugged him and said, "It's good to see you, Dad," a sentiment he echoed. He wasn't sure why she was there, but it was like old times to see her—they'd been close while she was in high school, but that was four years ago.

After he left the airport parking garage and pulled into traffic, he asked, "So what's up? Everything okay in school?"

"I'm putting together a wall of thirty or forty photos for senior project. It's a lot of work, but fun."

"You said you wanted to talk about something, and it's not school. Let me guess," he said with a smile. "A guy?"

"Sort of. Listen, Dad, let's save any talk about Jason until we get home. I'm sure in the long run I'll end up telling you more than you want to know about him."

Wade filled the rest of the ride home with small talk, asking her one trivial question after another. Her answers were far more thoughtful than his questions. When he asked her remembrance of Palo Alto High School, she rambled on about how she'd had to get used to heavy competition early, and how the suicide of a guy in her AP History class had affected her sleep for months. Wade tried to remember the suicide, but couldn't. He wished he'd been more attentive to his daughter back then. He wondered why she had decided to spend time with him now but tried to just concentrate on how fortunate he was to have her with him.

∞

Amelia took more time than he would have expected looking around the house. She didn't say anything, but the lines in her usually-unclouded forehead showed concern. He wondered if she was worried about his clutter, which through her eyes, must have seemed everywhere. If a person lives alone and knows their things will remain undisturbed, it's so easy to leave an open book here, a bill that's not due immediately there. After a while Wade made some tea and they sat in the living room. "So tell me about this guy," he said.

"He's a teaching assistant, you know, a TA. He's helping me select and arrange my photos for my senior project."

"So, tell me about him," he said.

Amelia took a sip of tea. "Sure, I will. But listen, Dad, before we get into all that, let me say how tough it must be for you to lose your friends, Jorge and Marita. I've been thinking about them a lot. You said they'd moved nearby, and I could tell you really cared for them."

He gave her an expurgated version of what happened. Even sanitized, it was a hard tale to tell.

"That's truly tragic," she said. "We somehow don't expect things to get so close to the bone, do we?"

Wade took a deep breath. He was impressed at his daughter's care and maturity. He told her about plans he'd made with Diana to go to the ranch the next day. "Your return flight is Thursday, right? That means tomorrow is the only day for you to meet Beth and Eva."

Amelia nodded. "So, you and Diana are still dating—"

"Not the way we were, no," Wade interrupted. "But I want to hear all about Jason."

"He's a nature artist, Dad."

"Nature artist? That's a new one on me."

"You know, using natural materials—leaves and trees and found objects."

Wade nodded, imagining twisted leaf and bark creations drying on the walls.

Amelia added, "He's intense about the environment and finds ways to integrate it into art. Except for that passion, Jason is laid back. You'd like him, I think."

Wade raised his eyebrows. "Hard to argue with his vision. I'll bet he's great. So you've been dating him awhile?"

"I started seeing him before we went to Mexico, but I didn't mention it because it was so new."

"You've been with him almost a year. That's a decent time to get to know someone. Is he good to you?"

"Until recently, very good. I thought we were in love. Then last month, that time I called you, I thought I was pregnant."

Wade's teacup shook in his saucer. Amelia had never admitted she was sexually active before. He'd assumed so, but this was a first. "So, this was no accident. You knew about birth control. Liz has assured me, several times, that she went through that with you."

"Jason can be a little unconnected. I thought a child would ground him."

"What?" Wade began to sweat, but he knew he had better keep his cool. "Amelia, raising a child, even as committed parents—"

"Dad," Amelia interrupted. "You're not listening. I assumed that we'd *be* committed parents."

"You were planning to get married?"

She shook her head. "No, no. I mean when I told him, I mentioned marriage as casually as I could, but he pushed for an abortion. I couldn't abort a baby . . . then, as it turns out, it didn't matter. A week later, I had what the doctor called a spontaneous miscarriage."

"Amelia, honey, I'm so sorry you went through that." Wade started to say that Jason sounded like an ass, but instead said, "So now you've broken up?" He hoped he could hide the relief in his voice.

"Yes," she said slowly as her eyes welled up.

"You want to tell me about it?"

"Maybe later, Dad?"

"Sure. We have time."

"Let's go shopping together and make dinner here." She looked around the room and he noticed her eyes resting on stacks of papers, books, magazines splayed on the coffee table. "I see lots that needs doing."

Looking at the clutter and mounds of dirty laundry through Amelia's eyes, Wade hopped into gear, relieving table surfaces of junk mail and old receipts and straightening furniture. Later, they talked casually as they prepared pasta, and after dinner, they took their wine glasses into the living room. Wade turned to her on the sofa and took her hands. "Amelia, honey, it could be best that you didn't have that baby. We'll never know."

She took a deep breath. "You're right. I'll get over Jason, I will. It's just taking longer than I thought."

"Don't be hard on yourself. He must be an impressive guy to have attracted you in the first place."

"He's a charmer is what he is, cute in a shirt-ad sort of way. Next time I'll try to fall for an ugly guy." She laughed. "I just have to move on. I'm thinking about a lot of things, Dad. The East Coast is fine, but I'm not sure I'm ready for graduate school, even if I got in. Yale has a great photography program, but I can't imagine me there, can you? The art scene here seems more exploratory—vibrant is how they describe it." One way or another, I feel less constrained in California."

"I thought all the action was back East you used to say—that's why you went to Bard."

"Yes, but now I miss the energy here at home. I need some time before I go to grad school, if I go at all. Mom's farm is remote, but there are plenty of colleges here. I'm starting to think the Bay Area is the right place for me now. Here." She hesitated. "With you, Dad."

Wade hadn't expected this. Once Amelia had gone back to Bard, he'd figured she'd stay out East, especially with Liz being in Massachusetts. "Have you mentioned this to your mother?"

"I talked to her right before I got on the plane in Boston—she came up to see me off."

"What did she say?"

"She was pretty cool about it. Mom has nothing but good things to say about you, by the way."

"This house isn't exactly a castle," Wade said. "Are you sure you want to stay here? Your room's intact, frozen in time," he sheepishly added. "From when you were still in grade school, almost."

"We'd have to paint over the purple walls and change the rug, but what's that, an afternoon's work? No biggie."

She'd at least thought that much through. "I'm pleased you'd want to live with your old dad," he said. "I'd love it, actually."

"Are you sure I won't cramp your style with Diana?"

"I wouldn't worry about that. We aren't as close as we were before. If it weren't for Eva, I'm not sure Diana would see me at all." Wade was sad when he said that, but it was true. "But that's coming from her side—I still like her a lot. I'll be interested to see what you think of her."

Amelia soaked in this news. "Well, as you say, I'll meet her tomorrow, right? But Dad, I'm pretty psyched about moving here."

Wade smiled. "I'm pleased." He leaned toward her and she reached over and gave him a light hug. This whole idea of having another person at home might take some adjusting to. But he loved her and he already began imagining breakfasts together, walks in the park, long talks about her studies, about life. Maybe even riding together.

∞

Diana, Beth, and Eva met Wade and Amelia at Jasper Ridge Ranch the next morning, a brisk day under sunny skies. Between nervous introductions and tacking up the horses, the morning took forever to start, but eventually Eva rode Gray Cloud with Diana. Eva sat half on the front edge of the saddle and half in Diana's lap. It looked uncomfortable for both of them, but they seemed to make do.

Once things were going well with Gray Cloud, Beth and Amelia shared a ride on Artemis, who ambled alongside Gray Cloud. Wade walked between the two horses so he could grab a bridle at the slightest sign of a problem.

Diana, after whispering to Wade that she really liked Amelia, surprised him by inviting them to lunch afterward. Rather than concentrating on problems, they each made a point to relax and enjoy each other's company. It was one of those days that keeps people going. Artemis and Gray Cloud, each docile and patient with the kids in their own way, were a big part of the morning's success. Even if they'd never be a couple again, Wade realized he would always be grateful for Diana.

And Amelia liked Diana, too. Amelia didn't oooh and aaah over her—his daughter wasn't one to do that—but as she turned in for her last night at her father's before heading back East, she told him she liked Diana. "It'd be great if things work out for you two. But things will be okay if it doesn't, too. I'm looking forward to coming back out here to be with you, Dad."

∞

After he dropped Amelia off at the airport, knowing she'd be back within the next six months to stay, Wade knew he had to get his act together. Seeing himself through her eyes, more than anything, helped move his focus outward. As hard as it would be to move forward, he had no choice. Putting his life back together, which had been a distant wish, became an immediate imperative. Children, Wade thought, can make you grow up yourself.

∞

In January, as he walked down Santa Cruz Avenue, the main street of Menlo Park, he thought he saw Diana. She was on the other side of the street, walking toward El Camino. He turned around, followed her down the block and broke into a run until he caught up. As he approached, the woman he was chasing, obviously concerned, turned and stared at him. She wasn't Diana. Once he got over the shock of the episode, Wade realized he'd had similar things happen at the ends of other relationships, so he thought he might have the start of a poem. He dropped into Ann's Coffee Shop, found a booth, pulled out a notecard, and jotted down a few lines.

> Perhaps one love is like another when it ends:
>   only the one who wanted it to last
>   understands what was at stake.
>
> At least once you must have lived in that lovesick daze
>   and glanced up to see someone who looked
>   almost exactly like the lover who had scorned you,
>
> and didn't you jump up from your table just to make sure,
>   and run full-tilt wherever this phantom took you,
>   driven by adrenaline, driven by hope?

It felt good to start a poem that wasn't about Jorge, Marita, or drinking. The poem wasn't upbeat, but it wasn't morose either. Things picked up at work, too. When he called a prospect he'd worked closely with in the past, Wade got an invitation to meet with him in Sacramento the following week. "We thought we'd sold the theaters, but a deal fell through, so we've decided to refurbish them before we try again. We like your sound systems, Wade. If you can get us a good price, I think I can make it worth your trip."

Finally, a break.

That Wednesday, Wade drove to Sacramento to close the deal. After another pre-planned phone call to Ray, he came home with an order to re-wire three theaters and possibly five more in the spring. The sale wouldn't have meant much a year earlier, but it just may have saved his job. He knew it helped with Ray. It didn't come any too early, either. At the next meeting, just as Ray was announcing layoffs in Lydia's group, he said, "Wade Middleton will now report directly to me." He could see Lydia grimacing.

Wade continued to see Eva every Saturday morning, throwing himself into the world of a six-year-old. If it wasn't raining, they would ride bikes. He discovered a safe-if-circuitous way to get from Diana's house to his own on bicycle, but he wouldn't let her ride alone yet. Often they'd ride to the park. Every week, by car if it was raining, they would drop by his house and play with Keats. Feeding the beagle and walking him on Saturday mornings became Eva's job, which she took seriously.

Some Saturdays, after the bike ride, he drove Eva up to Jasper Ridge Ranch. He began by putting her up on Artemis and walking alongside. As she gained riding skills, he'd let her circle around in a ring at a walk without him holding on to the bridle. That went perfectly too. Artemis knew to be gentle—she never made one false move with Eva on her back.

∞

One evening, for the first time in months, Wade decided to go back to the poetry group he used to attend, Waverley Writers. The poets had been meeting the growing hard times with agonized humor. Wade learned at the break that several of them had lost their jobs; it was good to get back to them and their wry sensibilities. Their lives were moving on—the woman who'd written the frog-licking poem was so sick she couldn't get up to read, so she read from her chair. A young couple who'd met at Waverley Writers announced their engagement. When he came home that night, he wrote two more stanzas of the poem he'd started—

> And when, panting, you overtook this stranger,
>   what did you do then? Were you apologetic,
>   did you say, "Sorry, I mistook you . . ."
>
> or did you find the righteous power of the jilted lover
>   and set things straight right then and there,
>   describing the monstrous treatment you'd received

He didn't know where to go with the poem from there, so he printed out what he'd written and went to bed with Keats nestled in at his feet. The poem needed a last push, something unexpected but inevitable. He thought of Diana's soaring image of God—the poem had to take wing. In the morning, Wade woke up with an ending he felt might work, which he quickly typed up—

> you, who could have made it all work! Did you seize the moment
>   and tell the tale in that wonderful, out-of-control,
>   desperate way that we only get to perform a few times
>
> in real life, standing squarely at center stage for once,
>   stating, of all the people on this planet,
>   you are one of the handful driven by love?

Wade had reservations about his new poem. In college, when he had taken a psychological test to determine what kind of work he was most suited for, he answered every question honestly, but somehow those answers tripped a wire saying he was lying. He had the sinking feeling that's how this poem would be read—by trying to tell the full truth, he came off as a liar. One way or another, he called it "One of the Handful."

∞

Wade was invited to Eva's birthday party at Diana's the same way he had been invited to Parent's Night at her school—Eva asked him about it, and Wade dropped hints to Diana until she finally relented.

Once at the party, Wade stayed in the background soaking up the energy of seven-year-olds. He'd forgotten how much noise kids make. Eva seemed so relaxed that, if he hadn't known, he wouldn't have had any idea what she'd been through. There was only an instant when she got a distant look on her face, and another time when she whispered to Wade that she "missed Mommy and Daddy," but for the rest of the party she played the perfectly happy birthday girl.

After the children went home, and Beth and Eva went back to

their bedrooms, Diana turned to Wade. "Thanks for being so great with Eva," she said cheerily. She invited him into the room overlooking Stanford. "It's obvious that you're getting through things. You seem changed."

Wade gazed across the Stanford campus from Diana's balcony. "I don't know about that," he said to Diana. "I just keep doing what needs to be done."

She raised her eyebrows. "You're tougher than I thought, Wade Middleton, and more gentle at the same time. And, I have to admit it, I've been missing you. In many ways. We didn't quite make it to opening hunt, but I'd like for you to accompany me to closing hunt, if you are open to it. It's only three weeks away. Would you come with me?"

He noticed how nervous Diana seemed when she asked him, looking at him and then looking away. He wanted to put her at ease. "Sure," he said. "I'd forgotten hunt season ends so early."

She took a deep breath. "It's tradition. We hunt from November to May. It wouldn't be sporting to chase a pregnant fox, now would it?"

"Of course I want to go with you," he said. It was good to be back in her good graces. Driving home, he wondered if he'd accepted her invitation too quickly. But a guy who thinks of himself as uniquely driven by love probably wears his heart right where Wade wore his, out in the open, right on his sleeve.

27

The morning of closing hunt, long before sunrise, Diana met Wade at her door in her jodhpurs and a starched white shirt. He had learned to see through Diana's stiff exterior to the soft heart that she worked so hard to protect. As they moved gear into the elevator, her fast walk and crisp demeanor put out a message: *Don't talk about anything personal.*

What could he say to thaw the ice? "If we get on a boar," he said, "I'll kill it with my bare hands or have Artie stomp it to death. Whatever seems right at the time." She laughed, shaking her head.

They headed out the door. Sitting in the passenger seat of Diana's SUV felt like old times, but so much had changed.

After they'd driven about an hour south, she said, "It's hard to ignore your persistence, Wade. I didn't think you'd go riding on Thanksgiving without me. I used to think that if it weren't for me, you wouldn't ride. You keep surprising me."

"You led this horse to water, and I drank. Despite my reservations about that poor boar, I like these people and this nostalgic world they inhabit. And . . . I like you, of course," he said, leaning over and pecking her on the cheek.

She moved toward him, which warmed him. "You've been great with Eva, Wade—such consistency. It's made me miss you, terribly sometimes."

As he rested his left hand on her knee, she put her hand over his.

∞

Once mounted, Wade concentrated on keeping his heels down and his gloved hands keeping almost no pressure on Artie's mouth. The hunt went predictably—the hounds gave tongue a few times but never got on a coyote, much less a boar. But their ride was not without incident. As they rode through one of the most remote parts of the ranch, Diana yelled over to Wade, "Your saddle's leaning to one side. Keep your weight off your downhill leg." They were moving at a fast trot with the others in second field, working to catch up to first field. "You have to tighten that girth. Can you cinch it up while you ride, or do we have to stop?"

"Let's catch up to the hounds. I'll get it later," Wade said.

They trotted down a narrow path cut into a steep hill. Diana yelled over, "Keep your weight level along here."

Artemis picked along the slope confidently. Fearful of the precipice below, Wade didn't stay balanced and the saddle slipped to the left. After a few more steps, it slipped again, further this time. Wade quickly leaned uphill, but it was too late. He was falling. He reached to grab a fistful of Artie's mane but failed. She gave out a whimper, which scared him even more. Before he knew it, Wade was face-up on the ground, half under a still-moving horse. He held one hand as high as he could, trying to cling to the reins, but then let them go. He tried to roll away but ended up directly underneath Artemis.

Her back left hoof came toward his chest like a sledgehammer. Her weight could kill him instantly. He instinctively moved his gloved hands toward her leg and wrapped them around her hoof and drew his breath in sharply for the blow.

The hoof landed on his chest, but the blow never came. As soon as her horseshoe touched his jacket, Wade felt Artemis's leg rise in his hands. He quickly rolled over, trying to get out from under her without rolling down the precipice.

Diana jumped off her horse, dropping to her knees. "Can you breathe?"

He touched his chest and took a deep breath. "Yes, I don't believe it, but I can."

Diana prodded Wade's shoulders and his chest, as thorough as a doctor. Then she put her arms around him. "Artie found a way to move her weight to her other hooves."

Wade caught his breath. He looked up at her, stunned. As he realized he wasn't seriously hurt, and that Diana was holding him, he was almost giddy with relief.

"Look," she said as Artemis nuzzled over toward them. The horse had circled back, her saddle hanging upside-down around her broad middle.

"Artemis, get back," Diana said, shooing her.

Adrenaline rushed through Wade, but he lay still. "For a moment I thought I was going to die." He sighed.

"You could have." She touched his face. "Can you stand up?"

"I'd better sit first."

When Wade carefully rose to his feet on the steep slope, he lightly shook his arms and legs. "I'm a little lightheaded. Let me stand here a minute. I'll be fine."

"I'll help you mount up when you're ready," Diana said, fixing Artie's saddle and tightening her girth. "See that rock up there? When you're steady enough, stand on it and I'll bring her to you."

After his breathing settled, Wade climbed the rock. With his heart pounding and adrenaline pumping, he mounted once again.

Diana got up on Gray Cloud and looked toward where the others had cantered off. She took a deep breath. "Let's head back in. If we go this way, I'm fairly sure there's a gate." She led Artie and Wade at a careful walk while their pulses slowed.

They met the others on the trail where first and second fields had joined together and were hacking back. Only when Wade rejoined the group and dropped behind them did he think of Jorge and Marita. Until that moment, the mishap had cleared them from his mind for the first time in weeks. The colors on the trail looked brighter and the air smelled cleaner as the memory of Diana's arms around him moments earlier coursed through him.

He'd never felt so alive. The word *joy* popped into his head.

∞

Safely back at the trailer, Wade took off his black hunting jacket and examined the hoof print. The mark was so clear you could see a few nail holes outlined in dirt against the black of the jacket.

After he quietly told the others what had happened, he hung his jacket on the trailer's tack door. When the master came by and examined Wade's jacket, he shook his head. "Wow, hard to believe. That *was* close."

Cliff offered an explanation. "She relaxed her fetlock."

Diana came from the other side of the trailer, nodding in agreement.

"Here," said Cliff, running his hand down Artemis's leg. He pointed to where her hoof jutted forward from the rest of the leg, far below her knee. "This is the fetlock. She can relax it in a split second and take all the weight—a hundred percent—off the hoof."

"Still, it's a miracle," Diana said.

"Good horses don't like to step on humans," Cliff said. "I once saw a Quarter Horse throw its body around in the middle of a jump and take a bad spill rather than step on its rider. It was nasty."

Wade ran his hand along Artie's leg. He couldn't tell if he was still light-headed from the shock of the accident or from Diana's tenderness.

∞

When Wade drove the SUV toward home, Diana left a button undone on her hunting blouse, showing cleavage. He kept glancing her way. She talked nonstop, as if she'd been storing up things to say. She mentioned Eva's school and Beth's plans for the summer and how Robbie was spending a lot more time with his dad. She said Billy was working with the social agencies so Diana could keep Eva. She said she didn't understand it, but Billy talked about guardianship.

"Oh, that's wonderful," Wade said. "Billy gets things done."

She laughed. "Okay, he's not perfect, but, yes, we both agree he's not a guy to be on the wrong side of."

As the miles went by, Wade suspected Diana wanted to say something but was hesitant. She would be about to speak and then stop. As they neared the freeway exit to the Jasper Ridge barn, she said, "Speaking of Billy, I was talking to Jolene the other day. They're starting a series of dancing lessons on Friday nights at her club. Ballroom, you know, swoops and droops. Would you be interested in going together?"

Wade was so thrilled that Diana wanted to start seeing him again that he had to remind himself he was driving a rig he wasn't used to. Soon they were at the ranch, where he was forced to concentrate on the horses as he pondered how to respond to Diana's question. The horses, seeming to sense they were at their own barns, unloaded easily. Diana took Gray Cloud to his barn while Wade took Artemis to a wash rack that had hot water as well as cold. He adjusted the knobs for a moderate temperature.

He soaped Artie down carefully with a sponge, then ran the warm water along her back to rinse the soap away. He streamed the water from angles that would clean every square inch of her. Then, using a sweat scraper, he dried her flanks off as best he could. He took a towel to Artemis's face, taking care to make sure she was clean behind the ears and all around the bridle where sweat builds up. Being gentle with Artemis reminded him of how gentle Diana had been with him when he'd fallen.

Diana had mixed a bran mash, the traditional reward meal for horses after a hunt. Wade hosed warm water over the bran until it became the consistency of oatmeal. As he led Artemis to her barn, he worked to keep her away from the mash.

Once Artemis was in her stall, though, Wade held the bucket up to the horse's mouth so she didn't have to bend down to eat. He knew she couldn't connect his care with the fact that she'd spared his life, so at some level his action made no sense. Still, he held the bucket up for her until she'd eaten every mouthful.

When Diana finished at Gray Cloud's barn and came over, she touched Wade's shoulder and they turned to one another and hugged each other tightly—a lingering embrace after the long day and his accident.

She kissed his cheek. "You and your poetry, I can't believe how it's growing on me," Diana said. "I found a Shakespeare quote that helps explain our last few months together. The bard netted it out by saying, 'The course of true love never did run smooth'."

"No, certainly not smooth," Wade said. "But, well, here we are, together again."

"I'm beginning to understand you, I think, and I like you a lot. Eva seems to have settled Beth in, and you've been a big part of everything coming together."

"Thank you," Wade said.

"Yes, I don't think we should get ahead of ourselves, but, like Shakespeare said, while sometimes things are not smooth, we've seemed to be able to get through. I've been thinking long-term. I didn't tell you, but Billy's looking into what it would take for me to adopt Eva, to make this new family more official."

Wade hugged her again. "That sounds like a good idea." He could feel his chest heave.

"We may have to promote you from godfather to father. But for now," she said, "let's just take it one step at a time."

His mind raced. She considered him as a potential father. *What else did that mean? Husband?* There would be time to work all that out. "Yes, I was thinking about your plans for dancing," he said, "Swoops and droops, huh? Sounds like fun. What else would you like?"

She smiled over at him as he rinsed out the feed bucket. "You may find my demands are endless."

He smiled back, full of promise and hope. "Trust me, the ride will be good."

Epilogue

When Eva turned nine, Diana and Wade arranged for her to start jumping lessons with Edward. The night before her first lesson, they wrote her a letter and left it on her night stand.

Dearest Eva,

Now that you're thinking about jumping, we want to tell you a few little lessons we've learned. A rider can't jump a fence, only the horse can do that. If you try to help the horse by raising your body, you'll throw your horse off.

The key is to let the horse know what you expect. Set the pace and direct the horse to the fence. She must know she's taking the jump—period. Sink as low into the stirrups as possible, so you stretch your Achilles. If you grip her with your legs like a clothespin, as you approach the jump, you'll pivot into place automatically and be joined to her as you clear the fence.

At the top of the jump look in the direction you want the horse to go next. Step into the stirrup and open the reins that way.

Once a master told Wade that to jump in the hunt he'd have to throw his heart over the fence. Over time, Wade understood that's exactly what he needed to do. And it is what you need to do, Eva. As you approach the fence you must throw your heart clear to the other side. You'll need confidence in both yourself and your horse. The horse will sense your determination and do all it can to not let you down. Don't think about the possibility of falling and you will learn to trust the sureness of horses.

Love,
Wade & Diana

Appreciations

I am overwhelmed by the generosity of the gifted writers who helped with this novel.

Award-winning novelist Antoinette May guided me from conception to completion.

As I worked for my Master of Fine Arts at San Jose State, Persis Karim, Al Young, John Engell, Kristen Iversen, Nils Peterson, Erica Goss, Chris Fink, and Alan Soldofsky helped me create an early draft.

Thanks also go to the Squaw Valley Community of Writers, especially Louis B. Jones, Brenda Hillman, Richard Ford, Robert Hass, and Al Young (again), as well as the late Galway Kinnell and Alan Cheuse.

Galway Kinnell encouraged us to write as if teaching someone from another planet what it is like here on Earth, which helped me grow world-building techniques to describe the burgeoning Silicon Valley, its fox hunt, and Wade's narrow poetry world.

I thank the late Ray Carver, with whom I was lucky enough to spend a week at *Centrum*. He discussed a novel, *The World According to Garp*, written by a friend of his, and he told us that every novel should have those words as an imagined subtitle—mine should be *The World According to Kevin*. This encouragement helped me concentrate on my known worlds of poetry, human relationships, and horses. An article about my week with him, "Raymond Carver Remembered," is available at USRepresented.com.

From the Yale Writer's Conference, I thank Julia Glass, Jennifer Maritza McCauley, and Terence Hawkins. One year the writers in Julie's novel workshop, who had read the entire manuscript, called me up short. When I told them that I was not inclined to write a romance, they told me if it didn't work as a romance, it would not work as a novel.

Thanks to Eric Stephenson, the editor of USRepresented.com, who published an earlier version of the novel online. And thanks to the English Department at Pikes Peak Community College, as well to the Gold Rush Writers and Waverley Writers.

Several novelists from the Kenyon Review novel workshop, including Greg Michaelson, Geeta Kothari and Nancy Zafris, convinced me to change the story from first person to third person limited, which is the literary equivalent of open-heart surgery.

From Stanford Continuing Studies, great gratitude extends to the late poet Denise Levertov and novelist Sara Houghteling. Thanks also to Genanne Walsh from Black Lawrence Press. From my writing group, warm thanks to Andrew Grose, Sally Lindsay Honey, Del Coates, Patricia Ryan, Rob Swigart, and Jan St. Peter. From the Portola Valley Arts Council, thanks go to Carolyn Rogers and Holly Eger.

I am tremendously indebted to those at Manzanita Writers Press, especially Monika Rose, Sally Kaplan, and Suzanne Murphy, whose editorial skills polished the final copy.

Each of these has given generously of themselves, for which I am truly grateful.

"One of the Handful" was originally published on USRepresented as "Driven by Love."

"If—" is a poem by English Nobel laureate Rudyard Kipling, written circa 1895 as a tribute to Leander Starr Jameson. The poem, first published in Rewards and Fairies (1910), is written in the form of paternal advice to the poet's son, John. The poem is in the public domain.

Kevin at Bard College in Annandale-on-Hudson, NY
Photograph by Scotty Arnold

About the Author:

A graduate of the University of Wisconsin and having served in the US Navy, Kevin Arnold has published fifty stories and poems in literary journals and a book, *Nineteen Poems around a Divorce*. He earned a Master of Fine Arts degree from San Jose State University in 2007, the same year he helped found the *Gold Rush Writers Conference* in the California Mother Lode. He has ridden to hounds since 1999, earning his colors with the Los Altos Hounds. He served as President of *Poetry Center San Jose* for twelve years. Besides being a member of the Academy of American Poets, and being a longtime friend of the Squaw Valley Community of Writers, Kevin is an Elder in the Presbyterian Church. The San Francisco/Peninsula California Writer's Club recently named him Writer of the Year.

CPSIA information can be obtained
at www.ICGtesting.com
Printed in the USA
FSHW022120240319
56639FS